I felt too uneasy to go to my own room to lie down. I decided to have cake and coffee in the kitchen to revive my spirits . . .

"It's a lot more pleasant in the dining room," Mrs. Babbage said, noting how I made myself comfortable at her table.

"Yes, but I'd be alone. I don't like being alone in a storm."

Mrs. Babbage almost smiled at me. "Neither do I," she confessed, "though no one else thinks the way I do." She glared pointedly. "There is no telling what horrible things could happen when you're like this, trapped on top of a mountain."

"Good afternoon, Lydia," Mrs. Reynolds said as she entered the kitchen. She wagged a finger at her friend. "A small storm and a grown woman like you takes fright."

Mrs. Babbage crossed her arms. "Wait till this 'small' storm is over. It will be spring before they dig us out." She nodded at her own words.

"A day or two at the most," Mrs. Reynolds said to me.

"A day or two of endless howling winds, the house groaning like some soul in hell . . ."

A HAVEN IN WINTER

ANNE KRISKE

JOVE BOOKS, NEW YORK

A HAVEN IN WINTER

A Jove Book / published by arrangement with
the author

PRINTING HISTORY
Jove edition / December 1991

ISBN: 0-515-10819-7

Jove Books are published by The Berkley Publishing Group,
200 Madison Avenue, New York, New York 10016.
The name "JOVE" and the "J" logo
are trademarks belonging to Jove Publications, Inc.

PRINTED IN THE UNITED STATES OF AMERICA

10 9 8 7 6 5 4 3 2 1

To my husband,
John Benson

All places that the eye of heaven visits
Are to a wise man ports and happy havens.
Teach thy necessity to reason thus;
There is no virtue like necessity.

William Shakespeare
Richard II, act I, scene iii

❧ 1

Tuesday, February 21, 1888

I HAD MY FIRST GLIMPSE of Bradford when the carriage crested the hill, and since this was to be my home for the next six months, I studied the village with curiosity. There was not much to see: a large redbrick mill with a clock tower, a white steepled church, slate-colored dormitories for unmarried mill employees, several rows of two- and four-family houses, and on the edge of town, where the more prosperous lived, neat cottages. The single main street was almost deserted. I couldn't see any stores or public establishments of the sort that would draw people from their homes on a wet winter's day. Bradford looked like a dismal, lonely town. Perhaps it was the barren trees marching solemnly down the rolling hills of northeastern Connecticut, or the knowledge that only a narrow ribbon of road connected Bradford to other towns, that gave me this feeling. Having left Providence, Rhode Island, for the first time in my life, I keenly felt the loss of family, friends, and familiar surroundings.

I pulled the collar of my borrowed coat higher to shield myself from the dampness as the carriage crossed a sturdy wooden bridge spanning a small river and started to climb the steep slope. The trees again closed above us. There was a melancholy isolation about this road that the two farmhouses with their plumes of gray smoke could not erase. As I stared at the squat stone walls that divided the rocky land into a patchwork quilt for the farmers to work as best they could, I reminded myself that I could not expect to hear the constant sound of carriages as they rattled over the roads, or the chatter of smartly dressed ladies as they gazed into one shop window after another. This was the country, where the wind rustling the branches of the trees would not be overwhelmed by the furious roar of the train. It seemed to me that I had never heard the subtle sounds of nature before, and my ears rebelled at being deprived of the layer upon layer of accustomed noise. I found myself listening intently to the steady beat of the horses' hooves as they traversed the deeply rutted road.

My apprehension mounted steadily. Why would the Eldridge family choose to live here, so far from the pleasures of the wealthy? Surely, I reasoned, it would be better for Mrs. Eldridge to recuperate in a more congenial environment. Of course, this wasn't my home; what I regarded as desolate, she might find peaceful. It wasn't as if she were suffering from some serious malady. She was only weak and prone to minor illnesses after the birth of her child some four months ago. She needed someone to read to her when she became fatigued and supply assistance in the daily concerns that were temporarily beyond her capacity. For these reasons I had been engaged as her companion.

Reminding myself that such a fortuitous position was not easily obtained for one only nineteen years old and without any exceptional qualifications, I endeavored to be as dignified as possible. I must have made a very good impression on Mr. David Veazey for him to recommend me to his brother-in-law, and I would do my best in return for such confidence. I would be attentive and prompt and cheerful and whatever else was expected of me. How could I be otherwise when so much depended upon this position?

"The house," the driver, Mr. Reynolds, called to me.

I leaned out the window. "Oh, my!"

The Eldridge mansion fully met my expectations. It was built of gray stone, three stories high with a tower rising even higher above the many-gabled roof, reminding me of a miniature Tudor palace. A large stable and various outbuildings stood farther away. Even in winter the grounds with their discreetly placed shrubs and trees bespoke wealth and order. In my mind, I could see the smooth expanse of green summer lawn, the ornamental flowers perfuming the air, the ladies and gentlemen of the house playing games of tennis and croquet. And from the tower, a man who must be Mr. Eldridge gazed down upon the town and the mill and the church as if this house were a medieval castle and all around lay the fiefs of the prince.

The horse stopped obediently under the porte cochere, which merged with a porch that wrapped halfway around the house. "Here we are, Miss Hall," Mr. Reynolds said pleasantly as he opened the carriage door. He was a thin man with a short gray moustache and a gentle, quiet manner that had quickly endeared him to me. "Hope the ride wasn't too bumpy."

"Not at all," I lied, accepting his outstretched hand and alighting from the carriage.

At the same moment the front door opened, and a stout, middle-aged woman with faded coarse hair and a stern expression walked halfway down the stairs to greet me. "How do you do, Miss Hall? I'm Mrs. Reynolds, the housekeeper."

I looked at the immaculate white apron and cap, the black dress with the lace collar covering all of her throat, and instantly felt insignificant. "Hello."

"We were expecting you yesterday," she said as stiffly as the starch in her cap.

My stomach fluttered. "Yesterday? There must have been a mistake. I was told to be at the Putnam train station today."

"I see," she replied in a tone that conveyed the opposite. "We were concerned when you did not arrive, but assumed you had been delayed by a day because of all the trouble caused by that fire in Providence." She turned to her husband. "Mr. Reynolds, please bring Miss Hall's trunks to her bedroom."

He nodded curtly in reply.

"This way, please," Mrs. Reynolds said to me. "I will show you to your room and then take you to Mr. Eldridge. He wishes to speak to you."

These were not the circumstances under which I would have preferred to meet my employer. I hoped he wouldn't hold this confusion against me. Mr. Veazey told me to be here today. I knew it was most unlikely that I should be dismissed from my position because of a misunderstanding, but I could not help fearing I would be sent home.

For the last two years, ever since my father died, my family had been facing utter destitution. My mother sewed from dawn to dusk, as did my youngest sisters, Caroline and Louise. My other sister, Eugenia, worked in a millinery store. I had secured employment in a dress shop two years earlier, but then my own health began to fail. Even with all our income combined, it was barely sufficient to pay the rent on the two-room tenement and keep us in food and clothing. I simply could not go back and be an additional burden. If I were dismissed, I should never find another position paying twenty dollars a month plus room and board, and the happy plans I had made for a comfortable future secured with my good references would evaporate.

"Mr. Veazey told me to be here today," I repeated, barely containing the agitation in my voice.

"Well, it can't be helped then," she replied in the nasal tones bred into the people of this part of New England. She pushed open the large oak door.

I had no idea what Jonathan Eldridge was like, but his home gave me the impression of gloom. The entrance hall had a deep red carpet so large that only the edges of the white marble floor showed. The walls and ceiling were painted red, relieved slightly by a border of black and white fleurs de lis. Because the window was of blue and red glass like some cathedral rose window, the only light was somber. The one bright note was a huge yellow vase that I fancied was Chinese. Before me, a wide ornate staircase rose, and a woman of about my age was polishing the banister.

"Miss Hall," Mrs. Reynolds said, "this is Julianne." The young woman curtsied in my direction. "Put the towels and a pitcher of water in Miss Hall's room and see that the fire is laid."

"Yes, ma'am," she replied and turned quickly, but not before I had seen the appraising look she gave me.

She could not have failed to notice the old coat or my dated hat and worn muff, just as I was aware of her glossy black hair laboriously pinned into place, the large gray eyes, oval face, and the way her black dress accentuated her slender figure. She had an élan that I could never hope to match, and she knew it.

"Julianne is the chambermaid and will take care of your needs. If there is anything she cannot do or that you wish to discuss, you may come to me." We started to climb the stairs slowly, as Mrs. Reynolds was hindered by her tight corset. "Your room was prepared yesterday. You may want an extra blanket, though the weather has been unseasonably mild."

She noticed my glances at the portraits that hung on the wall.

"That is Mr. Benjamin Eldridge," she said, stopping in front of a portrait of a languid young man in ruffles, "the great-grandfather of the present Mr. Eldridge." She drew herself straighter, basking in the long history of the family. "The Eldridges first settled here in the middle of the last century, during the seventeen fifties and sixties. They were farmers in those days, but in the eighteen thirties they started to build the mills. They own two along the river and most of the farmland in the area."

I thought their faces haughty and proud, generations accustomed to respect and the comforts of life. Judging by the quality of the clothing and the greater skill of the painters in the more recent portraits, the position of the family had only improved over time. "They look very distinguished," I said, glancing at the women in elaborate hairstyles and the men in their stiff collars.

"They are indeed," Mrs. Reynolds replied proudly. "Few families in all of New England can boast a better reputation." She panted up the remaining stairs, her ample bosom straining the corset. "Here we are. All the family bedrooms are on this floor. Directly in front of us are Mrs. Eldridge's, your room, and the nursery. Mr. Eldridge's room is on the left. Miss Millicent and Master Hugh have rooms behind us. There is also the room of Evan Roberts, Mr. Eldridge's secretary, and at the end of the hall, the uh, facilities."

Evan Roberts? I had not heard the name before. My mother had not been pleased to discover that there was one unattached gentleman, Hugh Eldridge, living in the house. Two such men would distress her greatly.

Mrs. Reynolds opened the door to my room, and I followed her inside.

"It's beautiful," I said with unintentional awe. Not even while my father was still alive and healthy had any room in our house looked so grand. The furniture was made of polished cherry, the bed covered by a thick quilt. A small green lounge stood opposite the fireplace. One flowered rug lay in front of the lounge and another by the side of the bed. The walls were papered with sprays of violets, giving the room a cheerful aspect. The white muslin curtains were open, and I could see the remainder of the hill, which ended abruptly beyond a living fence of hedges.

"I'm sure the room will be most agreeable," I said, unbuttoning my coat.

Julianne walked into the room with the towels and a pitcher of water, which she placed on the commode. Easily carrying my small battered trunk, Mr. Reynolds walked in after her.

"Put that in the corner," Mrs. Reynolds directed.

"Right," he replied, deposited it, and left.

Mrs. Reynolds regarded my trunk solemnly. It was obviously old, each passing year having inflicted its scars, and could not possibly have held many clothes. She returned her gaze to me. I looked down. Both my coat and dress were stained with mud.

"We have a laundress who works here four days a week. When you change, leave your outer clothes over the chair. Julianne will see that they are cleaned." She turned to the maid, who was nursing a small flame in the fireplace. "When you're done, take the trunk to the attic." With a nod to me, Mrs. Reynolds swept from the room.

Julianne remained, waiting patiently beside the wardrobe. "I'll take your hat," she said when it became obvious that I wasn't going to say a word.

I took out the pins and handed her my hat of blue felt, its ostrich feather, so jaunty this morning, decidedly worse for wear.

"Is there any particular way you would like me to arrange your clothing?"

"Ah, no," I answered doubtfully. No servant had ever worked for my family. I had no idea how to behave. It was one thing for the housekeeper or a member of the Eldridge family to give orders, but I was none too sure of my position or what was expected of me. "Anything will be fine."

"Very good, miss," she said. "I'll come back after you're done changing." She walked briskly to the door and closed it after her. I heard her steps as she continued down the hall.

I sat on the bed. I was tired and hungry. The cold had settled in my bones. In a few minutes I would meet Mr. Eldridge for the first time, and oh, Lord, but I hoped he wouldn't be disappointed. I came from a good family, but this household was a hundred times more wealthy than I had thought.

Mr. Veazey had seemed so unassuming when I first met him two weeks ago. His office in Providence was modest, and so was he. A slightly built young man, with innocent blue eyes and curly blond hair, he immediately put my mother and me at ease. The situation he had summed up briefly: his sister had not yet recuperated from the ordeal of having a child and, because she was bedridden, did not have companionship. Mr. Eldridge's daughter was away at college and could only come home on infrequent occasions. His son was helping with the family business.

I rose and wandered distractedly about the room. I should have known that any man who would send his daughter to college would not be like the men I knew when we lived on Pembroke Street. His family would not be like mine: their standards, their way of life, would be different. What if I said the wrong words, or Mr. Eldridge took one look at me and decided he wanted an older woman, one with credentials and experience?

I took a deep breath to steady my nerves. There was nothing to do but face Mr. Eldridge, and I would have to make myself as presentable as possible.

I unhooked my dress and laid it beside my coat on the bed. I took my second-best dress from the trunk. It had survived the journey well, but its excellence dimmed when I realized it was of no better quality than that worn by the maid. My clothes, especially my underclothes, had been mended many times, and I couldn't help but feel embarrassed about their condition. Julianne would talk about them to the other servants, as gossip was one of the few means available to a servant to compensate for the never-ending orders. A neighbor of mine in Providence had been a maid and delighted in recounting all the sordid, intimate details she had learned.

I had laughed. Now my ears burned.

Telling myself that as soon as I was paid I would augment my meager wardrobe with some better clothing, I washed my face in the tepid water, exchanged my boots for slippers, and put on the simple blue dress. That completed, I undid my hair.

It fell in thick masses to my hips. My hair was invariably unruly and much to my disgust refused to abandon its red hues as my mother had promised it would. Worse, whenever I combed it back into place, I would have to look in the mirror and see myself and all my flaws. My jaw is square, denoting stubbornness, while my chin is unaccountably pointed. My eyes were more suitable for a cat. They were really hazel, but light played tricks with them: one moment they were green as the sea, the next they reflected a yellowish light. Instead of a gentle arch, my eyebrows swept upward at the corners and were a darker shade than my hair. Having a perfectly adequate nose was not sufficient compensation. Paying as little attention as possible to my reflection, I pinned up my hair.

There was a knock on my door.

What should I say, what should I do? For the first time I realized that nineteen was young, and I, still inexperienced in the ways of the world despite all, was about to meet a man who could buy and sell the welfare of a thousand families like mine.

"Miss Hall?"

"Yes, I'm ready." I opened the door and with trepidation walked out.

Mrs. Reynolds led me back down the stairs and to the rear of the house, past more paintings and statuary and furniture. I saw all of them through a dark mist, heard her brief comments over the pounding of my heart.

She opened a heavy door.

I held my breath and followed Mrs. Reynolds into the room. A man, not particularly tall, but stocky and broad-shouldered, stood at the window. Abruptly he turned.

I jumped, so startled was I at the speed of his movement.

"Miss Hall," he said, walking toward me with quick strides, "I'm glad that you've finally arrived." His handshake was frightfully firm. "Won't you have a seat?" He nodded for Mrs. Reynolds to leave and took his place behind a massive, ornate desk that must have been many generations old.

From his blotter he picked up a sheet of expensive paper covered with flowing handwriting and carefully placed the letter in the top drawer of the desk. While he was momentarily occupied, I shot a swift glance at his office: along one wall stood a huge case filled with leather-bound books; in the corner was a smaller desk covered with neatly stacked papers; and a utilitarian potbellied stove sat upon blue Dutch tiles against the far wall. The paintings, with the exception of a large map of Connecticut with last year's date, 1887, were all of storm-ravaged coastlines.

My gaze returned to my employer. The deep lines on Mr. Eldridge's face indicated a man who frowned frequently; his countenance was stern, his mouth tight. Though he had seen his fortieth birthday some years ago, his hair had little gray. He sat very erect. Even in his superbly tailored brown suit, the muscles in his broad shoulders were not completely hidden.

"Miss Hall."

Abashed at being caught staring, I nodded weakly and blushed.

"Mrs. Reynolds informs me that my brother-in-law instructed you to be here today"—he folded his hands on the desk—"and not yesterday."

"Yes, sir."

It must have been my barely audible voice that caused him to fix his disconcertingly intense brown eyes on me, examining me in the minutest detail and causing me to withdraw as far back as possible in the chair.

"As my agent in Providence, David Veazey is a very busy man, and allowances must be made for occasional lapses in efficiency, especially in view of the fire Providence experienced last week. I read that the loss is estimated to be half a million." His voice was cold and hard. He would not be a sympathetic man. "The business district sustained the worst of the fire, I believe."

I nodded.

"Some of my interests there were affected, though not seriously. Your family, I trust, has not suffered as a consequence of this unfortunate incident."

Our rooms had escaped the flames, and although Eugenia's position was still secure, one of the companies for which my mother sometimes sewed was no longer in existence. There would be a corresponding drop in income. "My family is doing well," I said in a small voice.

"Good. Now to the matter at hand. I am certain David delivered instructions to you concerning the care of my wife. I will nevertheless repeat them to prevent any future misunderstanding.

"My wife is in a very delicate condition, though not of a nature that would warrant close medical attention. Her strength has not returned as expected, and several weeks ago she developed influenza, weakening her still further. I therefore decided that she needed a companion who would ensure as much rest as possible and see to those needs that a woman practically incapacitated would require. Quite understandably, my wife has grown restless, and your presence will help. Also, she will not permit me to hire a nurse, insisting that her illness does not require such drastic measures." He regarded me solemnly. "If there is any, any sign of distress, you are to notify me and no one else. Last night . . . was extremely difficult for her . . ." He paused, giving me the impression he was about to launch into a long explanation. "Is that clear?"

"Yes, sir."

"I'm sure I can rely on your discretion in this matter and your good services."

"Certainly, sir."

"You may have been wondering why I engaged someone as young as yourself," he continued. "My daughter, Millicent, is studying at the Society for the Collegiate Instruction of

Women, more commonly known as the Harvard Annex, and my wife naturally misses her. I hope that your presence will lessen her sense of loss." He stood up. "I trust there are no further questions?"

"No, sir."

"Good. Mrs. Reynolds is waiting for you. She will show you the house and, if my wife is awake, take you to her."

Perfunctorily dismissed, I rose, all the well-planned words of gratitude stilled by one look from those eyes. Was this how rich husbands treated their wives? A companion chosen without her express consent? But no matter: I had a job, and surely the future would be bright.

I left the room, treading carefully so as not to make any noise and give Mr. Eldridge cause to look up from his account book and fix his eyes upon me. Mrs. Reynolds was in the hallway, examining a small ornate table for dust.

"Mrs. Reynolds?" She also had a way of looking at me that made my confidence melt like a spring frost in the sun. "Mr. Eldridge said you should take me on a tour of the house and then to his wife." I sounded as if I were apologizing for causing her great inconvenience.

"Very well. Mrs. Eldridge was anxious to meet you, but she was still asleep the last time I looked. She should be awake by the time you have seen the house."

It would not have occurred to me that it could take long to show a house, but indeed it did. The reception room was small, containing two velvet-upholstered armchairs, a round table of inlaid wood, and a Turkish rug before a fireplace adorned by carved wooden panels. This was where unwelcome guests were left to contemplate their inadequacies, according to Mrs. Reynolds. The drawing room was more beautiful than any I had seen before, with a many-faceted crystal chandelier and a parquet floor. The furniture consisted of a black piano, delicate gold and lacquered cabinets, and pale blue silk armchairs and sofa. In the dining room there were a large oval table of mahogany, six straight-backed chairs, and two large sideboards.

I followed her about, feeling somewhat dazed by the opulence of this house. The two small rooms in which my family lived flashed through my mind. *Lived*. The word was too lofty to describe a habitation where the windows let the icy fingers of winter into the room on even the calmest day, where the walls were as thin as paper and the floors groaned in agony with every step. We heard each spoken word of our neighbors, smelled the food they cooked. The summers were debilitating, the heat becoming a thick stagnant pool, and in the winter we huddled together, rarely able to afford an adequate fire in the stove. There were times when we could scarcely afford a good meal and subsisted on the diet of the poor—bread and strong tea.

I was frightened of the streets. The dirt and litter accumulated, moved only by starving dogs pawing through the refuse for food and by children playing without supervision. Some families had come to the neighborhood as we had, driven by circumstance, and one could watch their decline, day by day. Almost all men, women, and older children worked at some gainful occupation, but were barely able to survive with a modicum of comfort: a small fire, a bit of meat, resoled shoes. They were usually tired in a way that only endless toil can produce, a tiredness that allows no room for compassion and gradually numbs the mind into a ready acquiescence of all that befell them.

And there were the others: women who had lost all dignity, people who had fallen into the vice of drunkenness, coarse men who loitered on the street corners. My sister Eugenia would be walking home in a few hours. In the dark.

Upstairs Mrs. Reynolds pointed out again who occupied the bedrooms and briefly showed me the servants' wing, where the maids and Mr. and Mrs. Reynolds had their quarters. From there she took me to the third floor, consisting mostly of guest rooms and a large and masculine billiard room.

I looked up the stairs that led to the tower, but to my surprise Mrs. Reynolds started to walk back down. "Is there a room in the tower?" I asked timidly, not sure I should say anything at all.

She stopped. "The tower is used exclusively by Mr. Eldridge. No one is allowed there unless invited." She continued down the stairs, opened the door to Mrs. Eldridge's room a crack, and closed it silently. "She's still sleeping," she said with relief. "In the meantime, I'll introduce you to the staff."

Mrs. Reynolds led me to the back of the house on the first floor. The servants had, for my benefit I assumed, assembled in the large kitchen. The wonderful smells, irresistibly attractive even in the hallway, almost caused me to faint. Bread was baking in the largest iron oven I had ever seen. The copper pots on their pegs sparkled, as did the porcelain-lined sinks. The ice chest was large and modern and undoubtedly well stocked with perishables.

The servants, who had been seated around a large wooden table, stood up, rather grudgingly I fancied, when I entered the room.

"Miss Hall, this is Mrs. Babbage, the cook," Mrs. Reynolds said.

The cook nodded imperiously toward me. I had heard that in many households the cook reigned supreme in the kitchen. I could well believe it. Mrs. Babbage was a large woman, possibly because she had sampled too many of her own puddings. Her hair was a nondescript brown, her cheeks, which were very plump and red, made it most difficult to judge her age, but her bearing made me think she was in her middle thirties. Her brown eyes were small and exceedingly sharp.

"Rosemarie is the waitress." She was pretty and fair and appeared bored.

A ruddy young woman stepped forward next. I was glad to see that Mrs. Reynolds did not reserve her stern looks for me alone. "Martha is our parlormaid. And Lucy."

Lucy, though dressed like a maid, was apparently without a title and looked like a tall, gangly farm girl of about fifteen.

"Arthur, the stable boy, and Ken, the groom, are outside attending to their duties." Mrs. Reynolds turned to Mrs. Babbage. "I presume that Mrs. Eldridge will wish to eat soon."

The cook sniffed. "More tea and cakes, I suppose." She shook her head, then peered closely at me. I was thin, but hardly of my own volition, and I rather hoped that she wouldn't think I was disinclined toward food.

Mrs. Reynolds glanced at the clock sitting on one of the cupboards to determine, I presumed, how long her mistress had been sleeping. "Miss Hall, I will take you to Mrs. Eldridge now."

One more hurdle to overcome. Nervously I adjusted my sleeves and went meekly back up the stairs.

Heart pounding once again, I entered a large bedroom. Under a silk coverlet lay Mrs. Eldridge, her long, once blond hair streaming across the pillows. I was shocked. I had assumed that I would be a companion to a second wife and expected a woman not much older than myself. This woman with the wan smile had to be over forty, older than my own mother.

"Won't you sit next to me," Mrs. Eldridge said softly, raising herself slightly from the pillows.

I sat on the very edge of the bed. She had once been a beautiful woman. Her pale face had skin the quality of fine porcelain, which no illness could mar. Vivid blue eyes were fringed by thick eyelashes. Her features—a straight nose, small chin, and full lips—were perfectly suited to one another. Her expression was pleasant, and when she smiled at me, two dimples appeared in her cheeks. She had lost a considerable amount of weight: that much was evident from the way the nightgown fit her. The thin hand with which she touched mine was unnaturally cold, and the nails had a bluish hue.

"I'm glad you have finally arrived," she said. "I was beginning to worry. A young woman traveling on her own has no protection. I trust it was an uneventful journey?"

"Yes, ma'am."

"That is good." She shifted her attention to Mrs. Reynolds. "I'm sure Lydia would like some tea"—she turned and smiled again at me—"and some cakes. They may be served here."

Mrs. Reynolds nodded. "I took the liberty of asking Mrs. Babbage to make the tea ready." Her face was hard to read, but I thought I detected a look of relief. "I'll bring the tray up shortly." Unobtrusively she left.

"Ruth does worry about me," Mrs. Eldridge said, before turning her full attention to me. "Now then," she said with false energy, "I want to know all about you. David communicated so little in his letters." She propped up the pillow behind her back. "I only know you are the oldest of four daughters, that your father was a clerk in a bank, and that you've lived your entire life in Providence."

"There isn't much else to say."

She surveyed me. "No, I suppose you are too young to have had many adventures. Have you ever been outside of Providence?"

"Only to Fall River," I answered.

"You must have found it disconcerting to leave the city then. I was born in Putnam, although at the time Putnam was only a string of villages, so I'm very used to places like Bradford. The train didn't present any problems?"

I shook my head.

"Good. I hope the road wasn't too bad either. Despite the short journey, the road is very rough in winter, and days pass before the ache subsides from all the jarring."

"It was not difficult. I liked traveling along the river."

"I do, too. The winters are too harsh for my taste, but in the spring and fall this part of the country is beautiful. There is a spot along Sachem River that always reminds me of a boat ride I took down the Rhine. You have the feeling that around the next bend a castle or some romantic ruin will appear. Of course, our river isn't large or of historic consequence by any means, but at that point it has charm. You can't see the mills, and the trees hide the road where they come to the water's edge. We'll go there when it becomes warm—soon, judging from the weather these past few weeks. I enjoy the outdoors very much." She peered at me. "Although the sun makes skin turn an unbecoming shade of brown, like some field hand's, I daresay that your face could use a little color."

"I've always been very pale." Deathly white was probably a more accurate description of my skin at the moment, but no one must ever think I was ill. I had only recently suffered from influenza—the same illness that afflicted Mrs. Eldridge. Still I did not think Mr. Eldridge would want a young woman who might harbor sickness employed to care for his wife. "I don't go outside very often."

"At this time of year, few people do." She looked out the window, her expression becoming somber. "Once it becomes warmer and my strength returns . . ." She stared intently at the drab winter landscape for long seconds. "Did you like the train ride?" she asked abruptly.

"It was very pleasant." My mother and Caroline had seen me off at the station. I had waved and waved as the train left until they were out of sight and I was alone in the shaking compartment. With a speed that took my breath away, the city disappeared, and we were amid fields and farmhouses. At that point I realized that I was truly alone, with no one to offer counsel or to comfort me in times of distress; no one with whom to share my excitement, apprehension, and happiness.

Of course, I couldn't tell Mrs. Eldridge these things. She would think me exceedingly inexperienced.

"An uneventful journey is usually best. Have you seen my son yet?"

I shook my head.

"He's four months old and healthier than my other two children were at that age. His name is Jon Frederick." The pride in her voice was unmistakable. "I'll have the nurse bring him to me in a short while. He's such a good baby, hardly ever cries. I've been crocheting, when my strength permits. I finished one jacket and have started on another. If you will open the cabinet over there and bring out the basket, I'll show you what I've done so far."

The cabinet, like the other furniture in the room, was white and graceful. On the large mirrored dresser, amid Belgian lace, stood half a dozen perfume bottles, as well as a silver inlaid brush and comb and a jewelry box. On each wall, in ornate gilded frames, there were paintings of bouquets of flowers. It was a very feminine room. The thought was disrespectful, but I wondered why Mr. Eldridge apparently didn't share this room with his wife. It was customary.

I handed her the knitting basket, and she took out a half-completed baby jacket of soft white wool.

"My brother said that you like to knit."

"I'm very good at it," I replied, finally feeling on secure ground. "And I do crocheting, needlepoint, embroidery, and sewing. My mother taught me when I was five, so I've had a great deal of practice."

She laughed pleasantly. "I'm sure you're better than I. Other than doing occasional embroidery, I've done very little. Hugh and Millicent were born one after the other, and I never had the time nor, I confess, the inclination until recently." She reached across the night table for a framed photograph. "This is Millicent. Did my husband tell you that she's away at college? We're both proud of her. You'll meet Hugh later."

Millicent was perhaps a year older than I. She bore a superficial resemblance to her mother in that she had fair hair and an oval face, but her eyes had the intensity of Mr. Eldridge's. She would go far in life, for confidence was visible in her carriage and her gaze. The idea entered my mind that if I had come from a monied family, I, too, would regard the world on equal terms.

"Millicent announced her engagement last summer to Alexander Lodge, with our permission of course, and they shall be married next fall. It's an excellent match," she said as she returned the photograph to its place, "since Mr. Eldridge and Mr. Samuel Lodge are old friends. It's amusing, too, because Alex and Millicent didn't like each other throughout their childhood. They hadn't seen each other in years when they met again last winter and discovered a mutual attraction." She smiled fondly. "Children do change as they grow older." The door opened. "Oh, thank you, Ruth."

Mrs. Reynolds arranged a table at the side of the bed and placed the tray upon it. "Is there anything else you would like, Mrs. Eldridge? A soufflé perhaps?"

"No, I don't think so," Mrs. Eldridge replied firmly. "Come back in half an hour and show Lydia the house."

"I've done so, as your husband instructed."

"Oh." She frowned slightly. "In that case, in a while, if Jon Frederick is being agreeable, take her to see the baby. Then Lydia can lie down before dinner." She shifted her eyes to me. "I'm sure you can use some rest."

I nodded, pleased that she was so thoughtful.

"Good. You may leave now," she instructed Mrs. Reynolds, not speaking again until the door was closed once more. "Ruth has been looking after me as assiduously as possible given her other duties, hovering about at every opportunity, cajoling me to eat, making sure I sleep. Now, dear, will you pour the tea? I'm afraid my hand is much too shaky to trust it with hot water."

We talked, or rather Mrs. Eldridge talked, while we drank the tea. She spoke chiefly of Millicent and the baby, holding the cup in her hand and taking occasional sips. She didn't touch one of the delicious little cakes. I ate four of them and only self-restraint stopped me from eating the other two.

Gradually her speech slowed until in mid-sentence she dozed off. I sat there for a moment waiting to see if she would waken. Asleep, when her features weren't animated and the force of her personality was not in evidence, she looked older. For the first time I noticed the blue circles under her eyes and the tiny lines around her lips. Something about her made me think of my mother who had aged quickly in the last several years, but that was from worry. It didn't seem possible that Mrs. Eldridge need be concerned about anything.

I took the teacup from her hand. Her eyes opened for a moment. Her lips twitched into a smile, and she turned over, sound asleep. I pulled the covers over her shoulders. Deciding it was part of my duty to keep the room as agreeable in appearance as possible, I took the tea things downstairs. I had not reached the kitchen when Mrs. Reynolds appeared in the foyer.

"Mrs. Eldridge fell asleep," I told her.

"I am happy to hear that." And for the first time she smiled and regarded me favorably, as if I had been responsible for such an accomplishment. She took the tray from me and walked swiftly to the dining room. "Rosemarie, stop dusting and take these." Having divested herself of the tray, she returned to me. "Mrs. Marsh says it would be quite all right to see Jon Frederick." Together we climbed the stairs at a labored pace, and by now I was slower than Mrs. Reynolds. One afternoon and I had learned to appreciate why servants hated the stairs, for it seemed that nothing could be done without either going up one floor or down another.

"Mrs. Marsh is the baby's wet nurse," Mrs. Reynolds explained between sharp breaths, "and has full responsibility for him. She's married to Peleg Marsh, who works for Mr.

Eldridge as a carpenter. They have a little house between here and the town. It's fortunate for Mrs. Eldridge that the youngest Marsh baby—they have four altogether—was born about a year ago. She would have hated to hire a stranger to help with the boy. Most of the employees have worked for the Eldridge or Veazey families for years." She took an extra deep breath. "Mr. Reynolds and I worked for the Veazey family in Putnam before we came here. All the maids are the daughters of the local farmers, who expect the girls to earn their keep as well as the boys." Another sharp breath. "Mrs. Babbage is the only one not from these parts. She was a cook up in Boston where the Eldridges keep another house. As a rule, they don't like to hire anyone they don't know. Except you."

I wondered why they didn't hire a companion from Putnam then. Surely there must be someone suitable.

Mrs. Reynolds opened the door to the nursery. "Maggie, I've brought you Miss Hall."

The small woman looked up from her sewing. "I'm very glad to meet you," she said quietly, rising to her feet. It didn't seem possible for her to have borne four children. She was hardly taller than a twelve-year-old, although she must have been at least thirty. Her hair and eyes were brown, her face a little too long, but still attractive.

Jon Frederick began to make gurgling noises in his crib.

"Now, what's the matter, little man," she cooed, "want to see who's here, do you?" She picked up the baby.

Jon Frederick looked like many other babies: plump cheeks, a few strands of blond hair, blue eyes that opened for a moment, little fists curled tightly. Though a stove heated the room very well, he was dressed warmly in a flannel Gertrude suit. The white crib, obviously new, was up against the wall. On the opposite side of the room was Maggie's bed, a dresser, a rocking chair, and a small table. The winter landscape was hidden by blue curtains, and a matching rug reduced the cold of the floor.

I turned my attention back to Maggie. She was dressed plainly in a striped cotton dress. Though inexpensive, it was well made, probably by Maggie herself. Most important of all, something in her expression told me that here was someone with whom I would be on equal terms. I felt a tremendous relief.

"He's lovely," I said, stroking the baby's cheek.

"And getting big for his age," Maggie replied. "I reckon he weighs all of fourteen pounds." She laid him back down in the crib and covered him with a blanket.

"We should leave you now," Mrs. Reynolds said. "I'm sure Miss Hall would like to get some rest before dinner."

Maggie smiled at me. "Come back any time you have a free moment and feel like visiting."

"I will," I promised and reluctantly left.

LIKE A DROWNING SWIMMER WHO managed to reach dry land,
I closed the door to my room, utterly grateful that the ordeal
was over and I had survived. My dress and coat were gone, and
so, I noticed, was the trunk. Opening a dresser drawer, I saw
my chemises and stockings carefully folded. My possessions
only took up three of the four drawers, and these none too
full. Julianne had placed the old photograph of my family on
top of the dresser. I took it and sat on the bed. My father had
been tall, and taller then to my young eyes, my mother pretty
and plump in her frilly dresses, my sisters all so young and
gay in their innocence.

I put the photograph aside, slipped out of my dress, and lay
on the bed wrapped in the quilt.

What was my mother doing now? Still sewing undoubtedly,
worrying about the impression I had made, hoping that I
would like it here, concerned for her other daughters' futures;
apprehensive that the extensive fire in Providence's business
district would rob her of gainful employment. It seemed that
there was no end to worries as I slid into sleep.

The neighbors were fighting again and throwing bric-à-brac
against the wall. I snuggled deeper into the quilt. The knocking
continued. It was my door. Someone was trying to wake me.
The door opened.

"Miss Hall?" It was Julianne. "Dinner will be in an hour."

"Oh, thank you," I said, but she had already left. I rubbed
my eyes. The window was dark.

I dressed quickly and entered the hallway. Not being certain whether I was supposed to go to the dining room by myself or with Mrs. Eldridge, I knocked on her door and, when she said "come in," entered. She was sitting up in bed, the baby next to her.

"Do you feel more rested?" she asked.

"Yes, Mrs. Eldridge."

"That's good." She stroked the baby's hair. "I felt well enough to look after Jon Frederick myself while Maggie went to visit her family for a few hours. She walked. The road takes a roundabout way to get here because of the steepness of the hill, but there's a path that starts at the edge of the promontory and runs along the river. It is barely a mile to her house," she added for my edification. She eased away from the edge of the bed. "Sit down beside me. The conversation will be easier."

I complied.

"I've been making plans," she continued, "as to what I should like to do now that you're here. My eyes aren't as strong as they used to be, and I should like you to read to me. You do know French, don't you?"

"Yes . . ." I had reasonable confidence in my pronunciation, but little in my comprehension.

"And you can help me with my various needlework projects. Other than that, there isn't very much to do yet to keep busy, although there are errands I shall probably send you on." She hugged her knees. "I do want to resume sketching."

Inspiration came to me. "Are these paintings yours?"

"Not all of them, but some," she replied with obvious gratification. "I wanted to be a painter when I was younger, much to my parents' horror. I spent so much time at it they took away my paints." She looked wistful. "It is a very good way to pass the hours, sitting by the river as the water rushes by, and there are a hundred different greens of the grass and the trees to be reproduced." Her blue eyes widened. "I want it to be spring again so badly. This wretched winter is getting on my nerves."

"Is something troubling you?" Mr. Eldridge asked as he opened the door.

"I was merely complaining to Lydia about the weather." The tone was polite but cold. "Nothing at all to concern yourself about."

Equally polite and distant, he replied: "You would not find the winter so disagreeable if you took your tonic as the doctor instructed."

"The two are hardly related."

I looked from one to the other and wished there were an unobtrusive way to disappear from the room.

"You should still take the tonic."

"It does no good."

"The doctor said—"

"I am not interested in what the doctor said or his theories. He isn't the one who had a baby, he isn't lying in this bed, his . . ." She stopped.

"Will you please take the tonic?" They looked at each other with suppressed anger as only well-bred people could. "Please."

Mrs. Eldridge was sick and weak and tired. In other circumstances, I could see her standing up to him, but today it was clearly not worth the effort. "Very well."

Mr. Eldridge took a green bottle from the nightstand and handed it to her. With obvious distaste she took two tablespoons of clear liquid.

"Shall I expect you to join us for dinner tonight?"

"No."

He whirled around and strode out the door.

With eyes still smoldering, she stared after him. "Dr. Patterson's so-called tonic is distressing to the stomach," she said for my benefit, "but he and my husband have the usual male assumption that they know best." She smiled apologetically at me. "Go down to dinner without me."

The prospect of dining with Mr. Eldridge was not inviting. "I could stay with you."

"That won't be necessary. I prefer to be alone with my son and then to retire early."

"Yes, Mrs. Eldridge."

Very slowly I descended the stairs. What would I do? I could not speak to Mr. Eldridge. His intense eyes would tie my tongue; his correct, rigid manner would strangle my thoughts. With the greatest of trepidation I went to the dining room and saw that I was not the first to arrive. A young man with curly brown hair and blue eyes lounged on one of the chairs. When he saw me, he rose instantly. "You must be Miss Hall," he said affably, though I sensed a certain stiffness. We both stood there regarding each other.

"You must be Hugh Eldridge."

He relaxed slightly before nodding. "Won't you have a seat." He stepped around the table and held out a chair for me. "The others will be here shortly. I take it that since you're alone, Mother won't be dining with us. Unfortunate, although these last few months as often as not she's taken her meals upstairs." A slight flush crept up his neck as if he had inadvertently revealed some family secret.

I realized Hugh Eldridge was shy and that he was trying very hard to be nice to me. I felt an instant bond of sympathy, for all too often I have found myself blushing and stammering for no reason other than my own unease, the knowledge of which made it all the worse. I looked over my shoulder at the sound of footsteps.

"I see you've met my son," Mr. Eldridge said, scrutinizing the blushing Hugh from the doorway. "And this, Miss Hall, is Evan Roberts, my secretary."

"How do you do," I said.

Mr. Roberts bowed slightly. "Very well, thank you, and most happy to make your acquaintance." He seated himself next to me while Mr. Eldridge took his place at the head of the table.

The serving girl, Rosemarie, appeared with a large tureen of beef soup and freshly baked rolls that she placed on the table before she turned to me to fill my glass with wine.

Mr. Roberts must have noticed something in my face. "Miss Hall, would you prefer Apollinaris water instead?"

"Ah, yes, I would prefer mineral water," I said with relief. I had only tasted wine at the communion table and found that quantity sufficient. My father disapproved of alcohol except for medicinal purposes.

"Would you like some bread?" Mr. Roberts asked, reaching

for the basket. "Our cook is also an excellent baker."

"Thank you," I replied.

Mr. Roberts had apparently been delegated the role of host by default, for Mr. Eldridge regarded his soup with far more attention than necessary. Hugh Eldridge was equally silent, but I felt this was due only to the taciturn presence of his father. I also had the impression that Mr. Roberts intimidated him. The secretary seemed to be an extremely competent man; in fact, had I not known otherwise, I would have taken him for the son of the house, so sure was he of himself. He was handsome, with a straight nose, soft gray eyes, and wavy brown hair, and an easy, friendly smile. That smile was the single greatest difference between the two young men. It made Mr. Roberts likable on short acquaintance, whereas the lack of one made Hugh appear sullen.

Halfway through the meal, Mr. Eldridge and Mr. Roberts began a conversation about the need to hire additional help when the sons and daughters of the farmers stayed home to work the fields. Hugh, I noticed, did not take part. He kept his head down, picked at the excellent pork on his plate, and drank several glasses of wine. I, too, remained silent, preferring to concentrate on the heavenly food.

"Miss Hall," Mr. Roberts said as the pudding was served, "I assure you that we do not always discuss such dull subjects at the dinner table."

"I wouldn't say that," Hugh said suddenly.

"Hugh." The imperative tone in Mr. Eldridge's voice was unmistakable.

"Come now, Father, you've got to admit that all these details about the mill are not fascinating to a young lady."

Deliberately, Mr. Eldridge laid aside his fork and stared at his son.

Hugh's voice faltered. "I mean, we should be discussing something other than the Bradford mill. Miss Hall can't participate in—in such a conversation when she's only seen the inside of the house."

"Hugh does have a point," Mr. Roberts said quickly. "Don't you agree, Mr. Eldridge?"

"Hugh can start to show Miss Hall about," Mr. Eldridge

commanded, "beginning with the grounds tomorrow. I trust there will be no difficulty in this?"

"No, sir," Hugh remarked in a subdued tone.

"We have an excellent view of the valley from the promontory," Mr. Roberts said smoothly. "Although the grounds aren't particularly interesting in the winter, there are several excellent trails for hiking that are usable right now. Do you hike, Miss Hall?"

"No."

"Ride?"

"I've never sat on a horse," I admitted.

"Millicent would find that shocking," Hugh said, swirling the wine in his glass and leaning back against the chair. "She thinks everyone should ride for their health. She thinks a great many things."

"I'm sure Mrs. Eldridge told you that she's studying economics at the Harvard Annex," Mr. Roberts said.

Apparently this was a topic dear to Mr. Eldridge, for he came alive. "Economics," he said with reverence. "My sisters were considered accomplished because they spoke fluent German and French. Now so many young ladies aspire to much more. Millicent feels confident enough to argue about business practices with me."

He enlarged volubly on her many good qualities. She excelled at mathematics, geography, and biology. At twenty, her business acumen was sharp enough that he would trust her to run the mill in a competent manner in his absence. I was not accustomed to hearing daughters described in such a fashion. These were the words men reserved for their sons. I looked at Hugh. His face was impassive. I waited for Mr. Eldridge to talk about him, but he did not. Poor Hugh. He must have felt the need of a good word. Finally he excused himself and left the room.

Mr. Eldridge, other than giving permission to leave the table with a curt nod, did not acknowledge his son's departure and continued his narration about Millicent until I could almost see her at his side. At length, Mr. Eldridge drew out his gold pocket watch and looked at the time. "I see that it is a quarter past eight. Shall we retire to the drawing room?"

To my dismay, Mr. Eldridge escorted me himself, and my heart thudded nervously. The room was uncomfortably elegant, and I sat gingerly on the velvet couch beneath Millicent's portrait. Mr. Roberts sat across from me, and Mr. Eldridge remained standing. During my brief glimpse of the room this afternoon, I had noted the black curio cabinet of Oriental design and the watercolors, also native to Asia. I looked to the items with curiosity.

"Are you familiar with Japanese art?" Mr. Eldridge asked me.

"I know very little," I replied, not wishing to admit total ignorance.

"An interesting people," he said, opening the cabinet. "They are not like the Chinese, content to allow the Manchus to rule them according to their ancient manner and look to ancestral wisdom to guide them in a changing world. The Japanese are most progressive and adaptable." He took out a delicate blue cup and placed it in my hand. "This is part of a tea service. Tea plays a very important part in many of their rituals. This particular service is believed to have belonged to the Heian period of their history, which occurred at approximately the time of our own Middle Ages."

"It's beautiful."

"I came into possession of this service because the captain of a trading ship that belongs to my old friend, and my daughter's future father-in-law, docked in Japan last year and was fortunate enough to secure it. Before that it belonged to a member of the Japanese nobility."

I gathered conversation was expected from me. "Why should they wish to part with it?"

"Money." He shrugged. "The family in question was impoverished after they chose the wrong side when the Emperor seized control of the nation from the Shogun, who had ruled on the Emperor's behalf for centuries."

I shivered. He spoke so casually of a ruined family.

"You shall hear more about the Japanese," Mr. Eldridge was saying, "for I am currently collecting more artifacts from their islands."

"Have you studied art?" Mr. Roberts inquired.

I shook my head.

"There is an excellent book on Japanese art in the library, but it is in French. What languages do you speak, if you don't mind my asking?"

"French and some Latin, though I have had little opportunity to use them in the last three years." Should I have admitted my deficiencies? I glanced at my employer and found that Mr. Eldridge appeared to be more interested in the tea service than me.

"There is a very good collection of French novels and poetry in the library. Mrs. Eldridge is very fond of poetry."

Mr. Eldridge returned the cup to the cabinet and closed it. "You may certainly read anything we have in the library."

Mr. Roberts explained the layout of the library to me, for it was a large room and well stocked, but in truth I heard little, for I was tired and to my relief was soon granted permission to retire.

After searching for a moment for my nightgown, I undressed and put my clothes away. There was a low fire in the grate. I sank into the soft mattress, delighted that a bedwarmer had been passed between the sheets. Thinking that it was a luxury to have a room to myself, I fell asleep.

∽ 3

Wednesday, February 22

I WOKE EARLY THE NEXT morning as the pale sunlight was just beginning to enter my window. Though the fire had died down to embers, I was quite warm. Everyone should know such comfort, I thought charitably, lying still to savor the feeling. There was a knock on the door.

"Excuse me, Miss Hall," Julianne said, opening the door a crack. "I was wondering if you'd like to take a bath before breakfast. I could get it ready for you now."

"Yes, I would." I climbed reluctantly from my nice warm bed, put on my wrap and slippers, and followed Julianne.

Baths in my childhood home had been hurried, except in the summer. It was even more of a discomfort in the tenement, for our source of hot water was a pot placed on the stove. In this house, baths were a luxurious affair. The room had been patterned on some Roman model. The tub was enameled and deep. The soap was scented and the towels amazingly thick. A stove heated the room admirably, and a red and black Persian rug covered the tiled floor. My bath was enjoyable and languid. I walked back to my room in a very good mood.

"Good morning, Miss Hall," Mr. Roberts said, passing me in the hallway. He was immaculately dressed and freshly shaven. "Did you sleep well?"

I was ready to succumb on the spot. Of all the embarrassing things to have happen to me, only meeting Mr. Eldridge in my present attire could have been worse. "Very well, thank you," I stammered quickly and fled.

Mr. Roberts appeared not to have minded the encounter, for he showed no reaction of any kind, as if meeting me in a wrap were a daily occurrence. He was probably used to female guests in the house. For me, since I had no brothers and my parents had not been in the habit of entertaining male guests overnight, it was a mortifying experience. It was just the possibility of such a situation that had made my mother have doubts about this position. Gentlemen, especially young, unmarried gentlemen, were to be treated with caution, she had explained without going into details; and she admonished me always to remember the proprieties.

Julianne's already having invaded the room to make the bed and remove yesterday's underclothes didn't help. I felt an acute lack of privacy very different from living in a two-room tenement. I dressed hastily, wondering what use my proprieties were among people who lived by other standards.

I checked on Mrs. Eldridge—she was still asleep—before going reluctantly to breakfast. Mr. Roberts, studying an account book and drinking coffee, was seated at the table. As soon as he looked up, I blushed.

"Good morning again," he said cheerfully and rose. "Mr. Eldridge has already eaten. Hugh, I'm afraid, eschews the benefits of a hearty breakfast and won't get up until nine at the earliest. Feel free to help yourself to the food on the sideboard."

I feasted on biscuits dripping with butter and sausage after sausage, unable to summon yesterday's restraint. I stopped finally, aware that Mr. Roberts was watching me from across the table. I sipped my coffee, wondering what he must think of me acting this way.

His voice was benevolent. "Are you nervous?"

"No." I felt my face burn. "Not especially."

"I remember well my first position away from home, suddenly in the midst of strangers. I don't believe I said three words in as many days. I was filled with the utmost trepidation, convinced I would make some blunder and be forced to walk the ten miles home in disgrace and face an ignoble future. In a week, I began to feel comfortable in my new surroundings; in a month, I felt as if I had lived there all my life. Give yourself time to adjust to new routines, keep an open mind, and don't be fearful of making mistakes."

"Yes, sir." I dropped my eyes, feeling I had been rebuked, no matter that his words were kindly spoken.

He came around the table to stand by my side. "No one in this household bites," he whispered in my ear, "not even Mr. Eldridge, and certainly not me."

I smiled shyly at him.

"That's better. Yes, Julianne?"

The chambermaid stood in the doorway. "Will you be going back to your room, sir?"

"No. You may proceed with your duties." He laid a hand on the back of my chair. "I shall see you tonight, Lydia, if not earlier. Give my regards to Mrs. Eldridge."

"Yes, sir." Pleasant as he was, I was relieved when I was alone.

I saw to Mrs. Eldridge next, and she immediately dispatched me to the kitchen for breakfast. Lucy was scrubbing the sink. At the large worktable Mrs. Babbage was drinking a cup of coffee. "If you ask me," the cook was saying, "that man is going to get into trou— Miss Hall?"

Who were they talking about? "Mrs. Eldridge sent me for coffee and rolls."

"What sort of breakfast is that!" Mrs. Babbage huffed. "She won't be getting her strength back with that sort of food. Meat is what she ought to be having. Ladies these days don't take proper care of themselves. When I was a girl, a woman ate a good meal instead of lying around all day on doctor's orders and then wondering why she doesn't have an appetite." She rose imperiously from her chair. "Lucy, boil some water."

I left Mrs. Babbage muttering. Julianne seemed equally displeased by the request to prepare the bath for Mrs. Eldridge.

I was still combing out Mrs. Eldridge's hair when Rosemarie carried a large tray into the bedroom.

"What is all that there?" Mrs. Eldridge asked, staring at the plate with a thick slice of ham on it.

"Ma'am, Mrs. Babbage thought you might find it tempting. If you saw it." She nervously shifted her weight from one foot to the other.

"I do not find it so. Leave the tray, but take the ham back. Tell Mrs. Babbage that when I feel myself ready to eat more, I shall inform her."

"Yes, ma'am." Rosemarie fled peremptorily from the room. Once outside, however, her footsteps slowed noticeably. She would most likely hear a thing or two from Mrs. Babbage also. I suppose I was partly to blame for not relaying Mrs. Eldridge's orders forcefully enough.

"The cook," Mrs. Eldridge informed me, "considers it an affront against civilization not to eat in amounts she considers sufficient, and she is aided and abetted by Mrs. Reynolds." She studied me. "Mrs. Babbage undoubtedly has plans for you and is at this moment consulting her cookbooks."

"I don't think I'm in need of ministering," I said.

"You are a little thin for your age," she commented. "You haven't been ill lately, have you?"

"No!" My pulse quickened.

"Then it's probably living in Providence. My brother insists cities are not conducive to good health." She smiled fondly at some memory.

Relieved that the topic of my health had been abandoned, I poured the coffee as she seemed to expect. "Why doesn't he live in Putnam?" Was it wrong to ask personal questions? She seemed not to mind.

"He's the youngest member of the family, so he could not enter the family business, and the opportunities in these parts for an ambitious lawyer are few." She spooned large amounts of sugar in her coffee before sipping it. "Since a good many of the families in Putnam have connections with Providence, it was natural that he should go there. I, too, have many financial interests in that city, and he looks after them assiduously." She nibbled on a roll. "That's why you're here. He insisted that as I wasn't getting any better, I should have someone to look after me, a nurse or a companion. I'm not sick enough for a nurse, so my husband and I settled on a companion." She laid the remainder of the roll aside. "I've had enough of breakfast. Mr. Eldridge, if he were here, would insist that I take that silly tonic to stimulate my appetite." She pushed the covers from her and reached for her wrap, which was lying across the chair. "I think you had better help me to the bath, as I'm none too steady on my feet this morning."

Mrs. Eldridge could barely manage to climb out of bed. She leaned heavily on my arm as we slowly navigated the length of the hall. It was not necessary for her to tell me she was dizzy: her uncertain steps gave her away, and she sighed with relief when we reached the door. "Have Julianne make the bed and lay a fire in the den, then you can go to the baby." My concern must have been obvious on my face. Her voice softened. "I'm fine, Lydia."

I discovered Julianne on her knees in Hugh's room, mopping the hardwood floor under the bed. I stopped on the threshold and peered inside the open door at what I imagined to be a typical man's room: a bed with an ornate headboard, wardrobe, dresser, a bookcase filled to capacity, and two dark blue upholstered armchairs. The one painting I could see was of an inappropriately fuzzy pond that was too modern for my taste. "Excuse me?"

Julianne looked up, at the same time whisking something from my view.

"Mrs. Eldridge asked me to tell you to make the bed?" I couldn't make the words carry authority. It was simply not in my experience.

"All right. This can wait." She tucked a stray lock back into place. "Is Mrs. Eldridge going back to bed . . . miss?"

I fancied I heard resentment in her voice at my orders. "No, she's going to her den and wants a fire."

Julianne settled back on her knees. She was very beautiful, even with the dust on her sleeves and her hair falling into disarray. I wondered what she was doing here working as a maid, for she seemed like an intelligent young woman who would not wish to waste her youth working as a drudge.

"Is there anything else?" she asked.

"No, no there isn't." I left her to her work and went to the nursery.

Maggie's face brightened when she saw me enter. "How is everything?" she asked cheerfully, rocking the baby.

"Very good, thank you." I pulled up the chair to sit near her. "Mrs. Eldridge plans to take care of the baby. For a while at least."

"I'm glad to hear that. She was so looking forward to the baby after all those horrible experiences, and she hasn't done much of that."

I looked at her inquisitively.

"You'll find out anyway. She lost several children," Maggie elaborated quietly. "There were three miscarriages, or so I've heard, and then the stillborn boy. That was heartbreaking for Mr. Eldridge. He had his heart set on another son to carry on the family name. He's the last male member of the family, although he has several sisters and a good many cousins."

"But he's got Hugh."

Maggie sniffed. "Men always want more boys. If they had their wishes for sons granted, the human race would end in a generation. Only one of my children is a boy," she added for my benefit. "Anyway, the Eldridge family owns so much, sons would be needed. Mr. Eldridge must have had doubts years ago that Hugh would be a good and proper businessman. That was before Millicent started to be interested in the mills. I can tell you one thing, that caused a lot of talk around here."

"It is somewhat unusual." Millicent was beginning to sound more and more like those women who were constantly agitating for the vote and that sort of thing. A lady, my mother had always insisted, didn't concern herself with such issues.

"Mr. Eldridge," Maggie continued, "was not pleased about it at first, but he's proud of her now."

"I would think she would return to look after her mother, or was Mrs. Eldridge sickly even before the baby?"

"Not as far as I know." The expression in her eyes became serious. "Dr. Patterson couldn't be found when the baby came, and Mrs. Webster ended up helping with the birth. She was my midwife, and I have faith in her even if Dr. Patterson calls her an old witch. He only wants to charge more for a baby. Anyway, Dr. Patterson was angry about that. He keeps saying Mrs. Webster did something wrong, but that's silly. What can a man know about having babies? Anyway, although she was weak after Jon Frederick was born, she really didn't start to become sick until weeks later."

"There were many cases of influenza this winter," I remarked, still feeling its shadow on me. I had almost died, huddled in the cold corner of our tenement, while to my frightened and feverish mind death took on a tangible aspect, waiting greedily to steal the last breath from my body.

Maggie stopped rocking. "She got over that quickly enough. Mr. Eldridge wouldn't let her see the baby until they were better, being afraid Jon Frederick would get sick, too. He thinks the world of this boy."

"He is adorable," I said. "May I hold him?"

She handed him to me, then paced a trifle to banish the stiffness from her joints. "I'm glad you've come here. It gets lonely having only a baby to talk to. The maids are all too busy, although Julianne sometimes finds the time to visit. I don't know how to talk to Mrs. Eldridge." She laughed. "Hard to believe I'm ever tongue-tied, isn't it? Most folks think of me as quiet. Even though you're a stranger, you're someone to feel comfortable with."

"I'm glad that you're here, too. I don't think there's anyone else that I can talk to."

She regarded me with surprise. "That's real kind of you to say. When I heard they were hiring a companion, I thought they'd hire a woman who fancied herself a lady and would look down her nose at everyone who wasn't an Eldridge."

I heard a light footstep in the hall. "Mrs. Eldridge?" I handed the baby back to Maggie and went outside. Supporting herself against the wall as she walked, Mrs. Eldridge was slowly coming toward me. I ran to her side.

"I won't topple over," she said as she grabbed my arm. "At least I don't think I will." With short steps, she managed to reach the chair I had vacated. "Spending so much time in bed has made me frightfully weak."

Maggie handed the baby to her.

"Hello, precious," Mrs. Eldridge cooed. Jon Frederick wrapped his tiny fist around her finger, and she smiled. "I have missed you so much," she told him, "and have had to content myself with making plans for when you are all grown up. Your father has already determined that you will go to Harvard, so I'm not the only guilty one." She stroked his hair. "How would you like to go to the den with me?" He opened his eyes and looked directly at her. With his head resting in the crook of her arm, he did all but purr like a kitten before falling asleep. He remained sleeping while I carried him to the lady's den at the opposite end of the hall.

"This room hasn't been used for months," she told me after collapsing onto the divan. "The cold has penetrated."

I found the room comfortable, but I stoked the small fire. It flared brilliantly.

She arranged pillows behind her back. "Give me the baby and then get a shawl from the bottom drawer of the high-boy."

When I returned from her bedroom, she was staring at the fire. I placed the shawl across her shoulders. As she seemed too mesmerized by the flames to notice me, I sat quietly in a chair.

"I absolutely refuse to become an invalid," she said at last. "In certain circles it is fashionable to withdraw from life under the guise of some malady and, if time and money permit, go to the spas in Germany where they bathe in waters with curative powers, and what is more important, sample the social life of the cities. If a voyage across the Atlantic isn't possible, there are always the mountains of our own New England, or the seaside, or wherever the air is deemed better, or the water purer, or the doctor has a more exclusive clientele." Her hands curled into fists. "Last night my husband made the suggestion that I leave for a rest cure. The weather is too severe here, he said. I will not follow the prescribed routine of Dr. Patterson, so perhaps another physician and another view would restore my health." Her eyes grew cold as she stared at the flames. "I shall not be treated as a cantankerous child who, refusing to be quiet, is banished from sight."

I fidgeted. I didn't want to be a part of domestic quarrels. They were invariably sordid and embarrassing for all parties. The way her eyes now rested on me was disturbing. Was she debating the feasibility of exchanging confidences? I was too young for her to do so willingly. Was that why I had been selected as her companion?

The remainder of the morning proceeded at a slow pace: I read a little and helped her with crocheting. When she closed her eyes, rimmed with vivid red as if she had been crying, she nearly fell asleep. Her eyes snapped open. "What time is it, Lydia?"

"Almost noon."

"A good enough time to stop. We will have lunch served here. And Lydia, make sure Mrs. Babbage doesn't attempt her culinary masterpieces. A simple soufflé will be sufficient for me, and some tea, black, not herbal tea." She looked fondly at her son. "Jon Frederick must be getting hungry, too. Take him back to Maggie."

I found Mrs. Reynolds in the dining room determining what silver needed to be polished, and upon being asked, I relayed Mrs. Eldridge's orders.

"It's an improvement," she said brusquely, "but she probably will eat only a little. What could improve her appetite? Master Hugh." A gleam appeared in her eye that I didn't like. "You'll have to persuade him to eat with his mother."

"Me?"

"He'll never think of it himself, and it would make her happy. But don't say it was my idea. It's been a few years since he listened to me."

I found it impossible to say no, not with the way she was looking at me. Anxiously trying to think of some intelligent words and failing, I walked into the library. Hugh was on the window seat, flanked on both sides by the books. "Mr. Eldridge?"

He looked up from his reading, obviously distracted by my entrance. "I'm sorry, I didn't hear you come in." Book in hand, he rose awkwardly. "Do call me Hugh—if you don't mind—" He studied my face intently. "I'm not the head of the family, and if I may, I'll call you Lydia?"

I nodded. Using first names on such short acquaintance was not quite proper, but I could see no harm. "I thought you would like to know that your mother is feeling better and has decided to eat in the den instead of her bedroom." A comment from him at this point would have been most helpful; unfortunately he remained silent. "The change in rooms seems to have done her good." There were other words, better and more interesting, that flowed smoothly into sentences but were lost in the recesses of my mind. "She plans to eat luncheon there and in general feels much better." My face turned redder and redder with each inane word.

"That is good to know. The companionship must help."

"Thank you. It's a pity that your sister couldn't be with her. I'm sure your mother would enjoy a stimulating conversation."

He closed the book. "Um, do you think she would like more company? I mean, it's not that I don't think . . ."

"I think she'd be delighted," I said with relief.

Mrs. Reynolds was correct: Mrs. Eldridge smiled with pleasure when she saw Hugh enter the room.

"Would you like some additional company?" Hugh asked her, lingering near the door as if he expected to be rebuffed.

"You know I would." She searched his face. "Sit down, dear, and tell me what you've been doing all morning."

"Nothing, I'm afraid," he replied. It was amusing to see him sit on the little armchair and not quite know what to do with his long legs.

"You should be helping your father," Mrs. Eldridge admonished gently.

"He's got Evan, and that's all the help he needs. You know how useless I am in business matters."

"If you tried a little harder . . . never mind." She gestured with her hand, waving the thought away. "Have you made any plans for the day?"

A slight flush crept up his neck. "Father said I was to show Lydia the grounds." He paused. "Is there something else you would prefer me to do?"

"No, Lydia should become familiar with the grounds and with the village." She turned to me. "Bradford has a library, not of the same quality as ours, but occasionally one finds a delightful book, two small stores—"

"Mother," Hugh interrupted, "if you continue with the description of the cultural aspects of Bradford, Lydia will flee back to Providence."

Mrs. Eldridge laughed heartily. "My dear, you are absolutely correct. This time of year we can't even regale her with picnics and drives in the woods, or even formal dinners."

There was a faraway look in Hugh's eyes. "It's not Boston."

The humor fell from her face. "No. It's not."

He winced. "We can't even take you skating," he said quickly to me. "The river isn't completely frozen—it rarely is—and at the moment neither are the nearby ponds."

"I don't know how to skate," I said.

"And Lydia doesn't ride either," he added.

"Not that many women ride," Mrs. Eldridge pointed out. "It is not so easily mastered."

"I'm sure I could teach her," Hugh ventured after a pause.

"Are you serious?" Mrs. Eldridge asked, obviously considering the idea.

Ride! I thought with dismay. "I used to go on the ice when a child . . ." I began, hoping to lure them from the subject.

"I'm a competent instructor," Hugh replied modestly. "Remember all the cousins I taught."

"My father would hold my hand," I continued, but no one was paying attention to me.

Hugh leaned forward in his eagerness. "Riding will enable Lydia to have more freedom. It's a long walk to our neighbors', and the carriage takes time to prepare."

"A valid point," his mother said. "Yes, it is a good idea."

Perhaps it was the enthusiasm in Hugh's voice that led her to agree. He was such a retiring young man, it must have been uncommon for him to take the initiative in any situation. Unfortunately I was very much like him and could not express my extreme dislike for the entire plan. When Rosemarie brought up our meal, I still had not found the opportunity to voice my reluctance. I ate in silence as mother and son plotted my undoing.

~⊃ 4

AFTER THE MEAL MRS. ELDRIDGE returned to her bedroom
to rest, giving me the opportunity to explore the estate with
Hugh. He was ill at ease, his head down much of the time
as we walked over the grounds, and mumbling replies to my
tentative questions. Not until we reached the stables did he
relax. An old horse, whose tan hair was fading into gray,
whinnied a greeting from his stall.

"This is Beauregard," Hugh said affectionately, producing a
lump of sugar from his pocket. The horse gobbled up the treat
with his lips, disclosing large yellow teeth. "His real name
is Lord Ambrois, in recognition of his bloodlines, but he
never seemed the type to me, so ten years ago I re-christened
him. Here, give him some sugar." He put a lump in my
hand.

Warily I let the beast take it.

"You're not afraid of horses, are you?"

"They've always seemed large and untrustworthy to me," I
replied.

"Not if you know how to handle them." He stroked the
horse's nose. "Treat them with some affection, and they will
repay it a thousandfold." Beauregard nuzzled his shoulder.
"He's as gentle as a lamb. You'll have no difficulty han-
dling him."

My heart sank. This was to be my mount! I stared at his
long flank and the muscles rippling under his coat. My head
scarcely reached above his shoulder. "Are you certain?"

"Perfectly. You're a good boy, aren't you?" Beauregard flicked his tail and stamped his feet restlessly. "You want to go out, don't you? Ken!"

A grubby individual in overalls and a plaid shirt appeared from behind a huge pile of straw. Though he was most likely only in his twenties, his hairline was already receding. "Yes, sir." He blinked at me. "Ma'am."

"See to it that the lady's saddle is ready," Hugh ordered before turning to me. "If the weather holds, we'll take the horse out in a day or two."

"So soon?" I was still hoping for a reprieve from this misadventure.

"When spring comes, you'll want to go riding. Mother loves to ride."

Since I found it quite likely that I would have to share Mrs. Eldridge's hobbies, if only because the force of her personality would carry me along, I decided to acquiesce again. Hugh, I suspected, would be an easier taskmaster. Besides, it was novel to be with a young man. I found him very attractive, even his personality, which I'm certain did not endear him to many women. I had never had a sweetheart, and I was not fool enough to believe that anything other than friendship would develop between this man of position and myself, but I was pleased to have his companionship.

He showed me the other horses and Jon Frederick's Shetland pony before taking me around the hedges of the promontory to view the river.

I peered cautiously. It was many feet down, and the slope was rocky and steep.

"I lost many balls here in my youth," Hugh said, the wind pulling at his hair and his voice.

"It seems dangerous." I held on to my hat as I looked in turn at the farmland directly across the river and Bradford lying to our left. "You expect a gentle slope."

He nodded. "I frequently forget that it falls so abruptly and only remember at the last moment. In the summer when I was a child, I used to climb those rocks all the time, and it never seemed steep."

I stared at the water. Not a magnificent river by any means, but it appeared fairly deep and rushed past me at a steady rate. "Weren't you afraid?"

"Of that? No. The river isn't as deep in the summer, and I'm a good swimmer. Had I fallen in, it's more than a mile to the falls and I would have had time to reach the riverbank. These days I rarely come here, except to watch Mother paint." He pointed to the woods. "Over there is the path that leads to town."

From what little I could see of the serpentine path, really no more than a trail through the woods, it did not appear easy to walk. I decided that I would prefer to take the road, even if it was longer, should the need arise.

I turned my attention back to the farms across the river. A few cows were visible on the centermost farm, as well as a man splitting wood. When a youngster climbed over the stone fence to tend to the half dozen sheep kept there, Hugh waved. The boy waved back.

"That would be one of Julianne's brothers," he said.

"How nice that she can see her home." I felt a pang of jealousy at her good fortune.

"I don't think Julianne cares particularly."

I turned around to face the Eldridge house. It was impressive, the roof rising above even the tallest trees. I found my room. And high above that, the tower loomed. "What is the tower used for?"

"The tower? That's Father's private domain. In the winter it is too inhospitable, although I might be able to persuade him to allow us to go up to it. The view is excellent."

"No, that's not necessary. This is high enough for me." I shivered.

"Forgive me for not realizing you're cold. We'll go back inside immediately." He took my arm, and we walked together in awkward silence.

By the time we entered the house, my fingers had grown stiff and my nose had become an unflattering red, so it was with pleasure that I went to the drawing room to stand before the fire.

Hugh sat down and regarded the empty air thoughtfully, obviously not about to launch into one of his talkative spurts. There had to be some innocuous way to restart a conversation. My wandering eye settled on a painting. "Do you paint?"

"Me?" He looked startled. "No, I'm afraid I don't have the talent."

"I think your mother is a good painter."

"She may very well be, even in these bucolic and uninspiring surroundings. It's a pity my parents live such provincial lives." His eyebrows knitted together. "It's the mill that keeps Father tied here, year after year. Mother could make him leave if she tried."

"Don't you like living here?"

"I prefer Boston. There was an expression they used in the Middle Ages: *Stadt luft macht frei.*"

"Pardon me?"

"Oh, you don't know German. 'City air frees.' I suppose that's the way it's translated. The serfs, when they escaped the fiefs, fled to the cities, and if they could stay away for a year and a day, they would never have to return. Until I went away to school, I never knew how provincial my life was. Being in Boston on my own, the exhilaration, the freedom—I can't explain the lure of it—it was incredible. I was there for almost three years, but unlike the serfs, was forced to return home."

"Would you go back?"

"In a minute if I had the money," he answered in an impassioned voice.

I could not feel his yearning. Whether I lived here, in Providence, or Boston, my life would not be radically different. I should still have to earn my keep at the few occupations that were open to women, and any excursions would be unadventuresome in any event.

He smiled apologetically. "Excuse me. I shouldn't discuss my dissatisfactions with you in such a manner. I am impulsive at times."

"That's quite all right." I sat beside him. He must be lonely, I thought. Other men his age would be completing their education or working, enjoying the very stimulation denied to him. Poor Hugh. I could see him growing up in this fine house, playing by himself day after day, discovering the outside world and then returning to seclusion. "Did you have any companionship when you were a child? I was wondering with whom Jon Frederick would play when he gets older."

"The Brewster children will be close enough to his age. It's a quick drive to their house. During my childhood, my tutor often took me to the Manning house where my best friend lived, and since Putnam is scarcely more than an hour away by coach, frequently enough my cousins came to visit."

My image of an isolated child evaporated.

"When I was a little older, nine or ten, we started to spend the winters in Boston. I—"

"Good afternoon, Miss Hall," Mr. Roberts said. "Hugh."

"Hello." Hugh, I noticed, said nothing.

"I trust you had an agreeable afternoon."

"Indeed I did."

Mr. Roberts glanced at Hugh, but it was to me that he addressed the next question. "How is Mrs. Eldridge today?"

"She was up a good deal of the morning."

"Good. Then she may be in the mood to catch up on her reading. I've brought the newspapers from Hartford and Putnam, a letter from her sister, and a copy of *Harper's Bazaar*." He handed me the items. "Did Hugh take you to town by any chance?"

I glanced at Hugh. "No, just the grounds and the stables."

"Why the stables?" he asked Hugh civilly.

"Mother and I thought it would be a good idea to teach her how to ride," he answered reluctantly.

"The ground is hard and the weather cold. Not good riding weather for a novice."

Hugh stiffened defensively. "My mother had no objections."

"Your mother was practically raised on a horse." He stopped to think for a moment. "I assume you are going to use Beauregard to minimize the risk of injury?"

"I know what I'm doing. I will stretch the learning over many weeks, and by spring Lydia will be able to ride the trails with Mother."

"Assuming your mother will be fit enough to ride by then and Miss Hall doesn't have any objections to learning."

Both men looked at me. I could feel my cheeks turn bright red.

Hugh's eyes were angry. "Do you presume that she was ordered to express an interest in riding?"

"Did you actually ask her," Mr. Roberts countered easily, "or did you make the decision ahead of time because it struck your fancy to play the riding master?"

Wordlessly Hugh rose from the chair and stalked out of the room.

Mr. Roberts sighed and sat down across from me. "As I'm sure you've gathered by now, our relationship is not always cordial." He looked earnestly at my face. "Tell me truthfully, did you agree to learn?"

"I did express some slight interest," I replied in a small voice.

"Mrs. Eldridge is a very good horsewoman and dotes on her favorite steed as if it were a child. That is true of the rest of the family, including Mr. Eldridge, and consequently they forget that others don't share their sentiments. As for Hugh, it isn't often that he shows much inclination for any activity, and I'm sure his mother is hoping that a new interest will bring him out of this withdrawal he has been in for months."

Now I understood that anxious look on Mrs. Eldridge's face.

"Since I presume you don't have a riding habit, you should be safe from lessons for at least several days. After that, Mrs. Eldridge will either have procured one for you, or Hugh will have lost interest."

I hadn't thought of a riding habit, and neither had Mrs. Eldridge. I had a reprieve, but it was at the expense of further companionship with Hugh. "Does Hugh have any hobbies?" I asked none too artfully.

Mr. Roberts suppressed a knowing smile. "Hugh was supposed to be preparing himself for a career in law, and at times he does seem fascinated by the legal complications that ensue when a new law is passed, but his interest is usually transitory. Other than that, he likes to read."

"I would have thought that he hunted or something like that."

Mr. Robert's laughter filled the room. "Hugh with a gun!" He sobered quickly. It was not, after all, proper that he should find the son of his employer so amusing. "Hugh is not an enthusiast of the great outdoors, other than riding. In that one respect, he is an Eldridge to the core, willing to take the roughest trails in the worst weather."

This was not reassuring.

Mr. Roberts read my mind. "Would it help if I spoke to Mrs. Eldridge about your reluctance to ride?"

I did not wish to appear a coward. Far better to wait and hope for a way to escape. I could claim to become dizzy. "I might enjoy riding a great deal."

"Very well. If you change your mind and find yourself in need of moral support, come to me. Now I must be going back to the office—the one in the house. If I can be of any service, you can find me there. Mr. Eldridge, if I'm not mistaken, will be in the nursery assuring himself that Jon Frederick is indeed as healthy as a child could be. If you'll wait a few minutes before going upstairs to Mrs. Eldridge, you can avoid him."

He bowed slightly and left the room, no doubt amused by me. I decided to take his advice. When I judged a sufficient amount of time had elapsed, I went to my room to repin my hair and to clean the hem of my dress as best I could. I hoped no one would notice.

At exactly three o'clock, I returned to Mrs. Eldridge and found her sitting up in bed, stretching. "Did Hugh show you the stables?"

"Yes, ma'am. Oh, and Mr. Roberts brought the mail."

She laid the articles aside after a cursory glance and regarded me happily. "Tell me, did you like Beauregard?"

How could I tell the truth? "He appears a gentle animal."

She smiled. "I am pleased you think so. You will find him a good mount. Now we must consider the habit."

Silently I prayed there would be no solution to this problem.

"Hmm, Millicent. Somewhere in the attic is her old habit. I do believe it could be altered without great difficulty. Mrs.

Reynolds would know. She may be in the kitchen. Look for her there and order a light tea. And please be so kind as to emphasize the light part."

My fate was sealed.

Leaning back against the pillows in her bed, Mrs. Eldridge studied the habit I held to my shoulders. "What do you think?" she asked Mrs. Reynolds.

"The alterations shouldn't take more than a day or two," the older woman proclaimed.

"Good." Mrs. Eldridge beamed at me. "I'm rather enjoying this."

My own emotions were far from joyful; nonetheless, I managed a weak smile in reply. Mrs. Eldridge did look better, I had to admit, now that she seemed to have something to distract her from her illness. There was some color in her cheeks, and her eyes sparkled, so my sacrifices were all for the good.

"Now as to the matter of boots," she mused.

"We have plenty of those stored away," Mrs. Reynolds replied, "along with hats and gloves. It might be easier to have Lydia try those on in the attic than to bring them down."

Mrs. Eldridge nodded. "While you're there, we should bring down more of Millicent's dresses for Lydia," she said casually. "They'll only be going to waste sitting up there in the attic."

"But—" I began.

"I was saving the dresses for one of my nieces," Mrs. Eldridge explained to me, "but she has gained so much weight of late that it was a useless endeavor—and you can put the dresses to good use."

I dropped my eyes down to the floor. Charity! I felt so embarrassed. Did I present such a pathetic spectacle? I raised my eyes to the mirror hanging above the dresser, and for the first time saw myself as I must appear to others. I was thin. My hair lacked luster. The cloth of my dress was obviously cheap and much mended.

I wondered what the servants thought. I was sure they had little regard for me, and once I appeared in my inherited finery, the talk would be lively around the dinner table. I longed to decline Mrs. Eldridge's generous offer, but pride has its limits. If I had learned nothing else since my father's death, I had learned that all too well. I mumbled my gratitude.

Not until nightfall did I find an opportunity to write letters. The first I wrote to Mr. Veazey, expressing my sincere appreciation. The second was for my family, assuring them of my good fortune. I placed the letter in the envelope and shed a tear that they could not share my pleasant surroundings.

5

Thursday, February 23

THE FOLLOWING MORNING, Mrs. Reynolds and I were driven into Bradford by her husband to have my clothes fitted. As we crossed the bridge, I wondered if Bradford would appear different to me today in the bright morning sunshine, but it remained just as small and gray and isolated as it had appeared before. A dozen or so adults, mostly women, waved at us, while several runny-nosed urchins stared with openmouthed curiosity. I found it disconcerting to be worthy of so much notice.

Dolly, the seamstress, reminded me of my mother: the same round shoulders, the pin-pricked hands, the evidence of chronic fatigue etching her face. Her rooms in the four-family house were cold, the rugs theadbare, the furniture scarred. Dolly's sewing room was very much like the one my mother had at our old home. The sewing machine stood beneath the window. Several scissors and a case for pins lay on the table, under which a large wicker sewing basket sat overflowing with clothes to be mended.

For each fitting I changed behind a wooden screen. I ran my hands over the exquisite materials of each garment: such fine clothes with velvet and lace and ribbon, discarded for a small stain or tear.

Our first task completed, Mrs. Reynolds took me on a tour of the town. We walked up the street a few yards and stopped in front of the dry-goods establishment, distinguished from an ordinary house by double doors that faced the street; the owner undoubtedly lived in the back. A small group of men—farmers, I judged—were gathered by the entrance to discuss the merits of a sturdy black horse evidently for sale. Deferentially they made way for us, and inside we went.

The interior was dim. Two counters ran the length of either side of the room. I saw cans of chewing tobacco, cases of cigars, and bottles containing medicinal liquids. There were several kegs for nails and a large barrel of kerosene oil. Ribbons, cotton cloth for ladies' dresses, silk threads, shoes, crockery, and an assortment of cheap trinkets rested in separate cubicles behind one counter. Behind the other stood a young boy, obviously bored, glancing through a catalogue. It was to this youth that the mail was entrusted. He scarcely looked up when I gave him the letters, including the one Mrs. Eldridge had pressed into my hand at the last minute to send to her brother.

We resumed our tour. Mrs. Reynolds pointed out the school, donated by an Eldridge as the small library had been. Both buildings looked like miniature versions of the mill.

I began to realize the appeal of a town like this, where a rich man could still be lord of manor and fief. What attraction in Boston or New York could compare to people standing respectfully, hat in hand, willing to do all that was asked without any danger of radicalism encouraging them even to question the social order? To give Mr. Eldridge his due, I had to admit that I was not here a witness to the deplorable poverty I had seen in Providence. The children running up and down the street, although their clothes were old and patched, at least looked well fed, and the mill houses in which they lived were kept in a good state of repair.

We returned to the street, passing the grocery and better houses belonging to the doctor, the mill foreman, and the minister. The white Congregational church lay a little to the outside of town, closer to the farmers who had first brought prosperity to this valley. The steeple reached high into the sky, though not as high as the mill's clock tower.

It was at this point that I had a good view of the river, the falls, and the adjoining mill. The falls weren't high, but the water flowed swiftly over the broad rocks. I looked up. The house sat high on its hill, casting a shadow on the town.

I was preparing to enter my room to freshen up before the midday meal when I heard Mrs. Eldridge call me weakly. I discovered her lying in bed, the covers up to her chin, a fine film of perspiration on her upper lip. "Oh, I'm so glad you've come back. I feel dreadful, hot one minute, cold the next. I even took some of that tonic, and it has only given me an upset stomach." She took my hand. "Don't tell my husband about this. He will only insist on sending me away to some spa, and I couldn't bear to be separated from Jon Frederick. No one is to know that I feel ill. Do you understand?"

I nodded before I recalled that Mr. Eldridge had specifically instructed me to notify him if his wife was in any distress. Mrs. Eldridge was kind to me and had asked me not to inform him. I could not follow both orders. Perhaps she was only suffering from a gastric disorder or some female complaint, which I certainly couldn't discuss with her husband. In an effort to soothe my conscience, I decided the latter was most likely to be true.

"Should I get you a wet compress?" I offered.

"That might help," she said.

I got a wet washcloth from the bathroom and placed it on her forehead, then arranged the bedclothes to make her more comfortable. I pulled a chair next to the bed and sat beside her.

"What did you think of Bradford?" she asked.

I had been brought up not to lie, so I said merely, "It's nice."

"You're a polite child. Did you mail my letter?" She looked relieved when I nodded. "One less concern then." Whatever was wrong with her, she was clearly not alarmed. This would make it easier for me to pretend that nothing was seriously amiss, and I felt no qualm leaving her alone to arrange for a light meal.

As I had a few minutes before our food would be ready, I whiled away the time in the drawing room. Giving in to temptation, I depressed the keys of the piano one at a time. My mother used to play, and she had a lovely singing voice. I heard footsteps and stopped, feeling guilty, for perhaps I had breached the etiquette of the house.

"Hello." Mr. Roberts stepped into the room. "You're alone. Mrs. Eldridge seemed so energetic since your arrival that I half expected her to be up."

"She became fatigued." I hoped I sounded convincing. "I am waiting to take a tray up to her."

"Then I will wait with you. Do you play the piano?" he asked as he walked up to my side.

"Not very well. I can play a simple tune."

"I admire the arts, perhaps because I was never exposed to them until a late age, when I no longer had the time to pursue such studies. Mrs. Eldridge plays very well. You have hands like hers: elegant, talented."

I was taken by surprise. "An unusual compliment, Mr. Roberts."

"Hands can't be disguised. They reveal your age, occupation, health." He took my right hand, turning it palm up. "An old woman who professed to tell fortunes explained that this is called the lifeline." He traced the line across my hand.

My pulse started to quicken. I was extraordinarily aware of his own hands, gentle and yet strong. He was a handsome man. Soft-spoken. Charming and confident. So different from other men I had encountered.

"According to my fortune-teller, you would have a long life. My own prediction is for happiness."

He was expecting me to speak, but I didn't know what to say. No man had ever looked at me the way he did then. "Did-did the fortune-teller's predictions come true?"

Mr. Roberts smiled wryly. "Some of them. Of course, she told all her customers the same tale."

"Do you?"

"No," he replied with a shake of his head. He took a step backward.

"Miss Hall?" Rosemarie was in the hallway, walking toward us.

"My tray is ready," I said.

"I have to get back to work, too."

"Yes, of course." My head was in a whirl. I kept thinking of his eyes and hands, his entire demeanor, as I took the tray from Rosemarie. Did Mr. Roberts treat all women of short acquaintance in such a fashion? As I started to climb the stairs, I saw Julianne on the landing above me. She looked decidedly angry, not just at me, but also at Mr. Roberts for the moment the two of us stood together.

Julianne and Mr. Roberts would make a handsome couple, I thought with an inward sigh. I, too, could easily succumb, as I suspected she had, to his charm. A pity he would have no reason to encourage me. I could hope for friendship, for I sensed he was most like me and would be understanding.

I spent the rest of the afternoon studying fashion magazines with Mrs. Eldridge to pick out clothing for Millicent's trousseau. Finally darkness arrived, and she released me from my duties, once more refusing to go downstairs, but determined that I should have a good meal.

I was closing the door to her bedroom, wondering if it was in her best interests to leave her alone for so many hours in a day as she demanded, when I saw Hugh exit his own chamber. I had not seen him all day. Mrs. Eldridge had not mentioned his whereabouts, and I did not think it proper for me to ask. I smiled at him. "Hello."

"Good evening," he said, bowing with elaborate gallantry. His face looked unnaturally flushed. "And how has the day progressed for you and my mother?"

"Quite well." I hoped he hadn't noticed my slight hesitation before answering. "She's sleeping at the moment." It was a bald lie but went unquestioned by Hugh, who seemed not at all inclined to see her.

"Then I won't disturb Mother. May I accompany you to the dining room? We can plan your riding lessons. I would think that next week would be a suitable time to begin."

"That would be fine," I replied, secretly hoping a blizzard would strike.

"I've been going over account books all day to please Father," Hugh said, leaning toward me. His breath had a minty odor, as if he had been drinking herbal tea. "Awful, boring stuff, account books." He held on to the banister as we went down the stairs together. "I hoped you would interrupt and set me free."

"I was with Mrs. Reynolds. She showed me Bradford."

"I would have been a much better guide. Mrs. Reynolds is such a practical individual. The finer, more delicate nuances of our little community are lost to her. I'm sure she did not take you to see our falls, a rival of which is not to be found within at least a mile or two."

I laughed, pleased and surprised to find him so loquacious. "Actually we went by them."

"And did she show you the library?"

"Yes."

"And a wonderful library it is. At least a hundred books, all suitable to be read by anyone over the mental age of five, and meeting the full approval of any clergyman standing in any pulpit in this great state." He assumed a haughtily dignified expression.

I had no idea he could be so clever and wondered what had come over him to put him in such a jolly mood.

Mr. Roberts approached the foot of the stairs. "Hugh." Though his manner was cordial, I sensed disapproval. "Your father wishes to speak to you before dinner."

"Oh." Hugh didn't look happy anymore. "Excuse me, Lydia." As he was about to walk past the secretary, Mr. Roberts took hold of his arm and whispered to him urgently.

Hugh shook himself free. "You don't need to talk to me like that," he snapped at the secretary and continued walking to his father's office.

Mr. Roberts's eye twitched. Whatever had been said, it had ignited a spark of anger. Just as quickly as it had flared, it was gone, and his face assumed its usual impassive countenance. He turned to me. "The meal may be slightly delayed."

"Is anything wrong?" I asked, descending the remaining few stairs, stopping on the last so that my eyes were level with his.

"Nothing that has not been of issue in this household for many months, as Hugh well knows." He deliberately began a new line of conversation. "Do you miss Providence?"

"Not very. As I shall only be here for six months, I'm sure I won't."

"Your mother must miss you. Sending a child out into the world on her own is always difficult."

I bristled. "I'm nineteen and quite capable of looking after myself."

"I remember being nineteen and discovering I could not."

"That cannot have been so long ago that . . ." It wouldn't be polite to say that he wasn't old enough to have the right to talk to me in such a manner. "That . . ."

"I was nineteen eight years ago, and eight years is long enough to appreciate the inexperience of youth. I am aware of the uncertainties facing you in this house. Because they entertain frequently and always have servants underfoot, the Eldridges think nothing of having a stranger in their midst. They will behave in front of you as if you were a long-standing acquaintance, and as most of the people they know are very much like them, they expect that you will learn their customs quickly, without need of explanation, and to understand the nature of their relationships to one another.

"Take Hugh, for example. He is an irresolute young man. This naturally irritates his father, who wishes his eldest son would make a mark upon the world. He is simply another careless young man who will eventually, after much prodding, discover what he is to do with his life. Mr. Eldridge is becoming impatient and is occasionally somewhat heavy-handed in the way he treats Hugh—he is like that with all people—but such behavior is not indicative of the way he feels. Were you to ask him, he would say that he has nothing but the strongest of affection for his son. Now take this business of trying to persuade Mrs. Eldridge to go to a spa. A couple of years ago, she did go alone to recuperate her health. The visit was very successful. Mr. Eldridge doesn't realize that he sounds as if he were trying to get rid of her; and as the baby is well looked after and will be quite all right without her for a few weeks, he cannot understand why she would object to leaving if it means she would come back healthy."

"You understand, though."

He smiled wryly. "I'm paid to listen and to observe and to make life agreeable, as you are."

"I don't know how to make life agreeable," I confessed. "I feel I am of little use to Mrs. Eldridge."

"You're doing well. Mr. Eldridge wrote to his brother-in-law the day you arrived, expressing his approval of you."

I smiled most happily at this news.

"And Mrs. Eldridge added her own letter, also favorable, of course."

Strange then, that she should send a second letter through me. "Does she write to her brother often?"

"No, not really. He comes here at least once a month, although after this terrible fire in Providence he isn't expected for some time, not until he has his new office established. Mr. Eldridge communicates with him quite frequently about business."

I felt vaguely disturbed by the information Mr. Roberts had imparted to me. On reflection there seemed to be something secretive about the way Mrs. Eldridge had handed me the letter.

Then again, we all had our secrets and hidden motivations.

Mr. Eldridge and a long-faced Hugh appeared, and we were all presently seated around the dining table. As expected, conversation soon devolved to business, and Hugh looked bored.

Mr. Eldridge looked at his son. "Hugh."

"Sir?"

"Have you nothing to say now? You said you would familiarize yourself with the equipment orders."

Mr. Roberts quickly interposed. "I'm sure he hasn't had the opportunity to do so fully."

"I can answer for myself," Hugh snapped. His eyes shifted from his father to me. "I was occupied with the newspaper. One article was particularly interesting: all about the threat of a miner's strike in Pennsylvania."

"What is that supposed to mean?" Mr. Roberts demanded.

"Your damnable relatives are probably behind it!"

Mr. Eldridge rose imperiously from the table and glared at his son. "You will not use such language in this house! Apologize!" he ordered.

Hugh stood his ground. "Why am I always the one who must tolerate ill treatment? I'm your son, and you treat your servants better."

"Then act like you belong to the family whose name you carry."

"The great name of Eldridge. You persist in indulging in a medieval notion of the family name and family honor."

"I do not find my sense of responsibility to the family and this community founded by our ancestors to be medieval. I know that doesn't interest you, since you have never shown the slightest sense of responsibility, as your misdeeds clearly show."

"My misdeeds?" Hugh squinted at his father. "What have I done that other men of my age haven't? I'm expected to behave like a saint when you're far from perfect." He was reckless in his anger. "You gave the town far more to gossip about last summer than I ever could."

I thought Mr. Eldridge would explode. His face had turned purple, and he held on to the table with both hands, as if once letting go he would throttle his son. Frightened, I turned to Mr. Roberts. He was immobile, at a loss for conciliatory words.

"Get out!" Mr. Eldridge shouted.

Hugh stood up with such force that he knocked over his chair and flung his napkin down like a gauntlet before he strode from the room. Mr. Eldridge shoved his chair back and charged up the stairs.

Mr. Roberts sighed. "They'll have a similar argument next month." He looked at me. "Are you all right? You look as white as a sheet. Here." He poured a glass of water for me. "As I said, don't attach too much importance to the family squabbles." He returned the chair to its proper position. "Don't mention this to Mrs. Eldridge, though, as it will upset her. And whatever you do, don't mention it to either Hugh or Mr. Eldridge. They wouldn't want to be reminded how much they made fools of themselves. At the moment they must both be more embarrassed than angry."

I sipped my water in an attempt to find composure.

He regarded me with some amusement. "Didn't you ever have noisy disagreements with your parents?"

"Never!" I replied with vehemence. "Members of a family should always love and respect one another. My father always said that."

"A sentiment that people always greet with approval, although that has never stopped children from being beaten. Or wives, for that matter. Some day you will have to tell more about your father. He must have been an interesting and unusual man."

"He was, I suppose," I replied wistfully. The waitress appeared with the food. "What do we do now, Mr. Roberts?" I whispered after she had left.

"We go on with our meal," he replied without any sign of distress. "And do call me by my Christian name. There is no need to be so formal."

"All right—Evan," I murmured.

I wondered about him, about his family, and how he had come to be in Mr. Eldridge's employ. To have risen from crude mining stock to an urbane secretary in so few years must have taken exceptional skills. That would be admired by Mr. Eldridge. Then there was Hugh, who was temperamentally more suited for the role of poet than shrewd businessman. Hugh, I was certain, was unreliable, whereas Evan would carry out the smallest order painstakingly. I surmised Mr. Eldridge couldn't help but make comparisons. It had to be an awkward situation for both young men.

"Why are you looking at me like that?" he asked.

I lowered my eyes.

He came to my side of the table and sat next to me, laying his hand on my shoulder. His touch was light and electric.

"Lydia, there is no need to fret. The argument meant little."

Quite different emotions were stirring within me. I had no experience in these matters. I didn't know how to separate kindness from—attraction?—to me.

"Everything will be fine," he said softly.

I wanted to believe him. I wanted to believe he meant more than sympathy and brotherly concern.

Rosemarie came in to see how the meal was progressing. Her eyes were curious, her manner a studied nonchalance, for she had seen us together. More gossip for the kitchen. The meal completed, Evan excused himself and returned to work in the office, and I went back upstairs to Mrs. Eldridge, who seemed to be feeling better. Together she and I made plans to invite Mrs. Brewster over tomorrow afternoon, or rather she talked while I listened. Within an hour she had decided on what to wear and what to have the cook make. Mercifully, she was too preoccupied with her own plans to ask about tonight's dinner.

Before retiring for the night, I decided to spend a few minutes with Maggie while the baby settled into sleep. She was pleased to have company, and we chatted amiably as she sat in the rocking chair, embroidering a dress for one of her daughters. Before long the conversation turned to the Eldridges.

"Did you ever meet Millicent?" I asked.

Maggie answered without looking up from her stitching. "Of course. I know everyone in and around Bradford. By sight anyway."

"That must be pleasant. I knew very little about my neighbors in Providence."

She carefully put the needle through the cloth and laid the dress aside. "Count yourself fortunate," she said earnestly. "If I fight with my husband, everyone knows. Within the hour. I know what all my neighbors are doing. Who's sick. Who can't go to church on Sunday because they drank too much gin. When the marriages are going to be. When the babies are coming."

"It must be difficult to keep a secret."

"Lydia, there is no such thing!"

I thought of the tenement and its constant noise and indifference. It hadn't been like that when we still lived in our house, but neighbors usually kept a polite distance that grew when my father became ill. "People care about you, though."

"I suppose we do look out for one another, although the gossip is dreadful. You'll see. This still being winter—for all the good weather we've been having—the light fails before the body, and all people do is talk until it's time for sleep. And we don't get so many strangers here that you won't attract attention."

"The gossips would find me a dull subject."

"No, they wouldn't." Maggie leaned forward. "You were asking me about Miss Millicent. When she was home last summer, she wore a dress with a square yoke to church. You would have thought it was a great sensation the way the women talked about it for days afterward. When they stopped, it was only to talk about the way she acted, her wanting to know all about the way the mills were being run. Acted very forward, just like a man. People didn't stop gossiping about her until Mr. Eldridge was seen walking with Mrs. Hamilton along the trail in the evening while a dance was held at this house, and poor Mrs. Eldridge was so ill in bed. The baby, you know. No one talked about anything else for a month."

Was this the incident that Hugh mentioned? "An innocent walk?"

"I'm sure it was, but Mrs. Hamilton is a widow, a very young widow with one little girl, money of her own, and a fast reputation. More than one man would cast an eye on her." Maggie nodded for emphasis. "She's staying with the Brewsters, Mrs. Brewster being her sister."

"Mrs. Eldridge invited Mrs. Brewster to visit," I said.

She resumed her needlework. "Mrs. Brewster should perk her up quick. She's a nice lady. So, by the way, is Mrs. Hamilton, for all her wearing powder on her face."

I nearly laughed. A fast woman indeed! Ladies wearing powder, while not common in Providence, were also not so unusual as to warrant notice unless it was some old crone trying to hide the ravages of age under an inch-deep layer of cosmetics. No wonder Millicent and Mrs. Hamilton created such a fuss here. They were probably not so exceptional at all. Mr. Eldridge was only taking a stroll with an undoubtedly charming, cosmopolitan woman. Millicent was uncommonly studious. Hugh was a spoiled young man who found the study of law required too much discipline. How simple it all really was!

We spoke for another hour, and then I went to my room. I was lying on the bed, trying to think of something helpful that I could do for Maggie, when the voices of Mr. and Mrs. Eldridge intruded into my thoughts. Clearly they were having an argument, though I couldn't catch the words. A few moments later, I heard Mr. Eldridge stalk into his room.

I opened my door and peeked outside. All was quiet. Tiptoeing, I approached Mrs. Eldridge's door. No light showed underneath. I put my ear to the door and heard nothing. I couldn't barge inside as if I were a nursery governess and she my charge, and so, hoping that all was well, I returned to my bed.

I sat at the window and looked out into the darkness. What could the Eldridges fight about at this late hour? It would seem that they had everything anyone could want: money, family, opportunity.

My mother would be sewing by feeble lamplight, her head bent, her fingers working busily. Eugenia might be talking to her young man on the stairs. I hoped they would marry soon. With two of her daughters no longer with her, there would be enough room for my mother to move in with my father's parents. The quarters were already cramped with the aged couple and Aunt Louisa, but they would find a way. If you were patient and good, all would turn out well in the end. I had always believed that.

Then why had my father died wretchedly, and why was Mother struggling? They had never hurt anyone in their lives. Hugh and Millicent, who had grown up with everything, didn't seem to care about the welfare of others and were prospering.

For the first time I knew how closely hate and pain and jealousy were intermingled. I hated the Eldridges for being free of care while I was powerless to help my family. I hated them because they could still dream and hope.

6

Friday, February 24

MRS. ELDRIDGE WAS IN A flutter all Friday morning. Hours before her guests were to arrive, we began the laborious preparation. As Mrs. Eldridge stood in layers of chemises and petticoats, I tightened the corset. Next I helped her into the dress and spent a considerable amount of time with the hooks and bows. Another hour was sacrificed pinning her hair in elaborate curls on top of her head, and when that did not please her, her hair was repinned with the addition of a hairpiece.

"Certainly an improvement over bedclothes," she said with self-satisfaction as she looked at herself in the long mirror. "I am going to enjoy this. I have missed Harriette very much." Harriette was Mrs. Brewster, and I did not fail to notice that her sister was not mentioned. "We have so much to talk about. I don't even know what is happening in Bradford—Mr. Eldridge is absolutely useless at conveying information that does not concern business." She turned around to look at the bustle. "Sometimes I wonder why these silly things ever came back into fashion." She dabbed her wrists and throat with perfume. "Come along, Lydia. You had better help me down the stairs."

No sooner had we entered the drawing room than I heard horses' hooves. I ran to the window and looked out. "They're here."

"And not a minute late," Mrs. Eldridge replied, arranging her skirts comfortably around her on the sofa. A few minutes later I heard the sound of feminine voices as the guests handed their coats to Mrs. Reynolds.

"Elaine, my dear!" Mrs. Brewster rushed into the room and embraced her friend.

I studied the arrivals from beside the curtains. Mrs. Brewster was dressed simply and was rather long in the tooth. Her sister, Mrs. Hamilton, was another matter. She was a plump, round-faced woman of about thirty, exceptionally fair-skinned, with masses of dark blond curls fashionably arranged under a hat amply supplied with feathers. Her carriage was extremely graceful, and she seemed to glide as she followed her sister.

"It is so good to see you finally out of that room," Mrs. Brewster said, sitting down without formality. She took off her gloves and hat without taking her eyes from Mrs. Eldridge. "How are you feeling? Truthfully."

"Better."

Mrs. Brewster clucked reprovingly. "I had expected you up and about long before this." She glanced over her shoulder to her sister. "Isn't that right, Susan?"

"Yes, indeed," Mrs. Hamilton affirmed, her voice as dainty as the black lace on her bodice. She did wear powder, I noticed, just enough to help hide the unevenness of her skin tone, the only flaw in her appearance. "We were so relieved when we saw your note. We were beginning to worry." Her eyes traveled nonchalantly about the room and settled on me.

Mrs. Eldridge pursed her lips when she looked at the younger woman. "I shall recover quickly from now on, aided by my new companion, Lydia."

As is usual among friends who had not been able to see each other for weeks, the conversation turned to gossip once everyone was comfortably seated. Names were rattled off with the rat-tat-tat of a Gatling gun: who did what, when, and with whom. Predictably the subject turned to children, and I was dispatched to bring Jon Frederick down. Up the stairs I hurried, retrieved the sleeping child, who nestled peacefully upon my shoulder as I held him with one hand, and with the other held up my skirts as I carefully went down the stairs with my precious cargo.

"She seems extremely young," I heard Mrs. Hamilton say as I neared the open door of the drawing room.

"I'm sure she's sweet and dutiful." This from Mrs. Brewster.

"Is she dependable?" Mrs. Hamilton again.

"Certainly." Mrs. Eldridge. "She comes from a very good family."

"Then why is she working? And that dress of hers is—" Mrs. Hamilton saw me and instantly changed sentences, her face as innocent and devoid of guile as an angel's. "Oh, there he is! Let me hold him."

I looked to Mrs. Eldridge for permission before acquiescing to the request.

Mrs. Hamilton cradled the baby in her arms, her aloof expression gone. "He must have gained five pounds since I last saw him." He opened his eyes. "You don't know how I wish I could have a little boy just like you to keep my Amanda company," she cooed, for the first time sincere.

An hour-long conversation about babies ensued. There was nothing for me to say, even had I the courage to intrude. Rosemarie brought coffee and cake. Two more hours passed in which I struggled to repress my yawns and managed to look reasonably alert. I returned Jon Frederick to the nursery. More talk. I lit the lamps as the light faded, not paying the least attention to the approaching night until Mr. Eldridge appeared at the door.

"Good evening, ladies," he said cordially. He gave scant notice of Mrs. Brewster, but his eyes settled on Mrs. Hamilton.

I did not like the smile she gave him in return.

"Certainly it isn't as late as that," Mrs. Brewster said and glanced at the clock on the mantelshelf. "Oh dear, it is. We must be going. My poor, dear husband must be wondering where we have strayed. Come along, Susan, we must be off."

"Surely we can stay a little while longer," Mrs. Hamilton protested. "It has been so long since I have had the opportunity to talk to the gentlemen of the house. I swear the last time was just before Christmas when we had that wonderful dinner."

"I see no reason why you can't remain," Mr. Eldridge said in a genial tone. His wife's expression was most certainly not genial.

"No, no," Mrs. Brewster said firmly. "It will be time for the children's meal, and my brood is anything but well behaved when not closely supervised."

Mr. Eldridge bowed slightly. "Then I'll say *au revoir*."

Amid a great deal of last-minute chatter, the women departed.

Mrs. Eldridge sighed with relief when silence had again descended upon the house. "I didn't think talking could be so strenuous."

"You shouldn't have been up for so long," Mr. Eldridge said sternly.

She looked at her husband with a measure of anger. "I was certain you would make that very comment."

"I'm only concerned about your health."

"And I have no intention of turning into a recluse, despite your efforts."

"Then you'll join us for dinner."

She arched one eyebrow. "Most certainly."

The meal began on a somewhat strained note, but I was glad of her company, which relieved me of having to find anything to say. With his wife across the table from him, Mr. Eldridge became much more talkative and less forbidding. I was rather surprised to find that she took an active interest in the mills and the farms, leading me to believe Millicent had come by her interests naturally. Hugh was very polite, and Evan seemed introspective.

I began to picture what it must be like in this house when dinners and dances were held, the women wearing glittering jewelry, the men in evening dress, the conversations flowing like wine, the luscious food, champagne.

"Lydia," Mrs. Eldridge said, "you're being very quiet."

"I was just thinking about what the ladies had said, about the dinners they had gone to in Putnam and the ones held here."

"Mrs. Hamilton dearly loves to be entertained," Mrs. Eldridge remarked. "She must be most disappointed that we have done little of late."

Mr. Eldridge came to her defense. "She's a young woman. It must grow tiresome living with her sister, a married matron. A young woman needs frivolity in her life."

"I'm sure she has found enough," Mrs. Eldridge commented dryly.

Mr. Eldridge looked perplexed. "I simply do not understand what you have against her."

"You wouldn't, no matter how many times I've tried to explain." She rose. "Don't bother to get up, gentlemen," she said, and then to me, "You had best help me up the stairs. I'm afraid the wine has gone to my head."

I felt most sorry for Mrs. Eldridge. She had done too much too soon and paid dearly, leaving me very much afraid she would faint upon reaching her room. She leaned weakly against the dresser while I undid her stays. That helped a little.

"I have heard that our modern clothing is a crime against women," she said, exhaling to expand her rib cage fully. "I have grown unused to corsets and to rich food. A dreadful combination."

"Mrs. Eldridge." I hesitated to give her advice.

"Yes, Lydia," she prompted.

"Would it not be better to admit that you are ill?"

"There's a difference between sickness and weakness. I suffer from the latter. My husband, however, does not seem to comprehend the distinction."

"Is that not what a spa is for? To regain your strength?"

She smiled wryly. "So I have heard. I did go to one several years ago and did very nicely, but that was because the winter chill had settled in my chest. I coughed constantly, although otherwise I felt fine. Some sun, the sea air, was all I needed to restore me. This isn't the same. I lost a lot of blood when the baby was born. It seems to have brought on a chronic weakness that a week or so will not change no matter how good the spa. And I would not like to be away from my son for long, even if I do no more for him than occasionally give him a bottle and stroke his cheeks."

"You could take him with you, couldn't you?"

"Mr. Eldridge would never permit that, not at this time of year. The baby could catch a chill traveling. He almost canceled the christening because a cold rain began to fall on that day." She shook her head. "I have no doubt I will get better in time." She didn't have to add that the longer she remained bedridden, the more Mr. Eldridge would press her to leave for a healthier clime.

Having made Mrs. Eldridge as comfortable as I could, I went in search of a soothing book for her to read. I slipped into the library, walking quietly so as not to be noticed by Mr. Eldridge and questioned.

"Julianne!"

She whirled to face me and quickly put a thick book back in its place.

"Isn't it late to be dusting?" I meant only that she was working hard, but evidently she interpreted my comment otherwise.

"I have permission to be here," she said, but her face looked guilty and she fled without another word to me.

I looked at the book she had taken from the shelf: it concerned Wales. "So she is sweet on Evan," I said aloud. An awkward situation, but as she was the daughter of a local farmer, the match would not be impossible. Her demeanor could become cultivated in time. Certainly I would not grow as beautiful. "Don't be foolish," I told myself. "Evan would not care for you." Any young woman with even the pretensions of breeding would desire him as a husband. I thought of the beating of my heart at the touch of his hand. It would go no further, and my brief flight of romantic fancy fell to the ground.

When I had returned to my room but not yet lit the lamp, I heard a knock. Thinking it was on Mrs. Eldridge's door and that she should not be disturbed, I started to open my door. Julianne's voice, barely audible, reached me.

"Do you think she'll tell on me, about being in the library?" she asked.

"I doubt it," Evan answered. "And what if she does? There's nothing wrong with you borrowing a book to read. Mr. Eldridge won't object."

"I don't know that he would feel that way about a maid."

"You have as much right as anybody else to read what you wish. You're just as good as they are. Don't forget that."

"Easy said, but not easy done." She sounded sulky.

"Don't worry," Evan said firmly. "But in the future, perhaps you should let me get suitable books for you."

"All right, Evan. Only—"

"You'd better leave." I heard the door shut.

I wasn't sure what to make of that relationship. I thought of her beauty and came to the inevitable conclusion.

Saturday, February 25

THE NEXT MORNING, I helped Mrs. Eldridge inventory her art supplies. She was none too strong and slept a good deal of the afternoon. The clothes arrived from the seamstress, and my wardrobe was suddenly full. An uneventful day, except for an encounter with Mr. Eldridge, who pressed me to have his wife take more of the tonic. For the life of me, I couldn't understand why he had such faith in a country doctor's nostrum.

7

Sunday, February 26

WE ALL ARRIVED AT CHURCH in the large carriage. As soon as Mrs. Eldridge descended from the conveyance, a group of women hurried to greet her, and she was quickly swept away. Hugh chanced to see some childhood companion, and Mr. Eldridge strode over to the minister, a timid gentleman with spectacles, while Evan was ensnared by an elderly man. The servants who had come down to attend the service were all with members of their own families. Ken, the groom, looked quite respectable in his Sunday suit, much to my surprise. Martha seemed intent on flirting with a young man, who in turn was trying unsuccessfully to attract Julianne's attention.

Unexpectedly alone, I drifted around the church and found myself in a very old and well-kept cemetery enclosed by a low brick wall. The headstones, carved with long verses and figures I found crude, dated back to the mid 1700s. I had bent over to read an inscription when a shadow fell across me.

I jumped. "You startled me."

"I'm sorry," Evan apologized. "I was talking to Mr. Breckinridge, the previous mill foreman, and saw that you seemed to have been forgotten. There is always a good deal of socializing before and after the service. Often it is the only time people can meet."

I wondered if Evan had deliberately sought me out. I searched his face for an answer. A flattering notion, but this was not the place for personal declarations. "Is this the Eldridge family cemetery?"

"Many of them are buried here." He pointed to an elaborately carved marker of slate. "Over there is Mr. Jonathan Eldridge, the founder of the present line. Next to him lies his wife, Millicent Eldridge, née Bradford. It was her grandfather who first settled here. He was the local judge, among other occupations." He looked at me with those intense eyes. "Lydia, I—"

His gaze made me nervous. I thought of all the words I should say, but I didn't know how to ask a man politely about his intentions, about Julianne. "Millicent was named after her?" I blurted out and was immediately angry at myself for such an inept response.

"Yes. Hugh was named after Mr. Eldridge's grandfather, the one who had the foresight to build the cotton mills. His mortal remains lie there." He took my elbow and guided me, his hand straying to my waist. I was sure he could hear my heart pound as we stopped before a miniature mausoleum, consisting of a huge carved box. "The original Hugh Eldridge, however, was the last of the family to be buried here, at which point they ran out of room and another ground was opened at the edge of town."

"There you are," Mr. Eldridge said, walking up the path to join us.

Evan took a step away from me. "Lydia is interested in seeing the cemetery, since it is historical."

A look of pride crossed Mr. Eldridge's face. "Yes, it is that." He laid a hand on his ancestor's stone.

How easy, I imagined, it must be for Evan to play up to Mr. Eldridge. The man had all the arrogance of some blooded European dynasty. He was, I saw, about to give me a detailed lecture on the subject, but the tolling of the church bell interrupted. We retraced our steps, passing in silence the stone box in which Mr. Hugh Eldridge slumbered until the Judgment Day.

The church was simple, painted white, with plain glass windows and wooden benches. All heads turned in our direction. It seemed Mr. Eldridge nodded to each and every person before we joined his wife in the first pew of the church. The servants sat two rows down, Julianne looking particularly lovely, Martha glum to be seated next to her. Opposite us sat the Brewster family, represented in force by the addition of several children ranging from age three to nine, who commanded most of their mother's attention. Mr. Brewster was a thin, dour-looking man, who took his eyes off the hymnal for a moment and nodded in our direction before continuing with his studies. Mrs. Hamilton waved gaily.

Behind us, I learned, sat Dr. Patterson and his family. He had an anemic-looking wife and two equally frail children, a boy and a girl, who must have done nothing to give people confidence in his ability as a physician. Mrs. Eldridge most deliberately snubbed him, refusing to look when he addressed her politely.

As the minister began his sermon, I found my thoughts drawn back to Mrs. Eldridge's health. Surely most women, even those of such an advanced age, would have recuperated fully from the rigors of childbirth by now, and her other illnesses could not have been severe. I chanced to note how Mrs. Hamilton was looking at Mr. Eldridge. My thoughts were far from charitable toward them. Some business was afoot.

The service over, I was introduced to a myriad of people, then once more abandoned. Seeing that Mr. Eldridge was deep in conversation with Dr. Patterson, and that we could not be leaving soon, I went to Mr. Brewster and the horde of children left in his care. The youngest Brewster son was squirming in his father's arms, tugging at the man's collar and plucking at the buttons on his coat. A little girl was pulling on his sleeve.

"And how have you been enjoying Bradford, Miss Hall?" he asked.

I was beginning to run out of polite words to describe the dreary little town. "It seems a very tranquil community."

"Marie-Astrid, stop running around," Mr. Brewster shouted. "What were we talking about? Oh, Bradford. Dull place, nothing much ever happens here, at least in the winter. We were all so glad to hear that Mrs. Eldridge has someone with her now. It can be very lonely living up in that house."

"She seems to be improving quickly, so she should be able to get about more often."

"I hope so. Mrs. Eldridge seemed well enough last month and then had another relapse. Right after Dr. Patterson had gone to see her, too. Spring should make her feel better. You'll be coming over to see us quite a bit then." He looked at me sharply. "I hope you like children."

"Very much." The little boy made an attempt to grab my bonnet.

"Naughty boy," his father said indulgently to him.

Mr. Brewster reminded me of my father, despite his dour appearance. He probably played with his children's toys and read them their fairy tales at night. I couldn't imagine Mr. Eldridge doing either. As far as I had noticed, my employer did no more than look at his infant son on occasion.

"I want to go home," a little girl said.

"We'll be going soon, Amanda."

So this was Mrs. Hamilton's little girl. Amanda looked petulant and spoiled, but she was a pretty child, and I was sure she could be a perfect angel if she chose to be.

He beamed at his small son. "This is only Harold's third trip to church and he was very good."

"I didn't hear him cry once," I said. "So many children do."

"Harold slept through most of the service. So did a few other people, judging from the snores I heard from the back pews." He shook his head sadly. "Dr. McGraw is a sincere man, but not inspiring behind the pulpit or at the dinner table, as you'll find out shortly, since it is the Eldridge family's turn to host him." He looked at the women. "I had better collect my wife, or we'll all be out here at sundown. It has been such a delight to meet you, Miss Hall." He bowed to me and departed, followed by a herd of rambunctious youngsters.

Shortly thereafter I was ushered back into the coach by Evan.

Mrs. Eldridge relapsed after seeing the doctor, she repeatedly becomes ill after taking the medicine, I thought as we jostled up the hill. I couldn't make the uneasy thoughts go away. I caught snatches of conversation: that Clive Armitage

had made another drunken spectacle of himself on Saturday
and should be talked to; that the Kincaid baby was sick. In
no time at all, Mrs. Eldridge decided I should knit a sweater
for the child, in response to which Hugh asked if I could teach
him to knit and escape the rigors of dinner with the minister.

I had seen jolly ministers, hell-and-damnation preachers,
men who could fill your soul with religious ecstasy. Dr.
McGraw was none of these. His voice was as dry as the
few leaves still clinging to the trees. And yet he tried. He
had the earnest look of a dog willing to do anything to please
his master and succeeding only in getting in the way.

I began to appreciate having to knit that sweater. As soon
as politely possible, Evan used the pretext of attending to
correspondence to excuse himself, and shortly thereafter I
was dismissed to start knitting. As I left the dinner table,
I saw that Mrs. Eldridge was struggling to stay awake, Mr.
Eldridge had a blank, stoic stare, and Hugh was desperately
drinking coffee.

I went upstairs to the den and found the material I would
need. The room was cold, and I did not have the courage to
order that a fire be laid for me on this day of rest. I did my best.
Within half an hour my fingers grew stiff with cold, and for an
hour afterward I hovered between finding a new place to work
or having a fire laid. Either way I would have to leave. I went
to the stairs and tried to make up my mind. I assumed that Dr.
McGraw would be entertained in the drawing room and should
be avoided. I would have loved to work in the nice warm and
richly scented kitchen, but I was certain my presence would
not be entirely welcome, busy as the cook and serving girl
were at the moment, either preparing more food or cleaning
up. I decided to search for one of the maids.

I approached the servants' wing and saw that one of the
maids' rooms was open. I hesitated for a moment, gathering
my courage, when I heard Julianne whisper urgently.

A man's voice whispered in reply.

I knew that voice. It belonged to Evan.

I retreated to the cold den and sat on the divan, abandoning
my knitting. What would Evan be doing in the maid's room?
A most improper thought came to mind, and my mother would

undoubtedly be distressed to learn that I even knew that men visited women for immoral purposes. Now I knew why my mother had been concerned when informed that there was an unattached gentleman living in the house, although, I conceded, Evan might just possibly be teaching Julianne how to read, judging by the previous night's conversation. Possible, but unlikely. I admitted it: I was jealous. I had no right to feel this way, and yet I was hurt.

"Miss Hall!"

I turned red as if Mrs. Reynolds could see into my mind.

"You can't sit in this cold room," she scolded.

"It didn't seem so bad at first," I stammered.

She checked the fireplace. "It will take time for the room to become warm. If you caught a cold, I'd never hear the end of it. Come with me."

I didn't protest and was taken to her apartment, past the closed door to Julianne's silent room. In the apartment Mr. Reynolds was sitting on his couch, smoking a pipe and reading a newspaper. He rose partway out of politeness when I entered, and continued reading.

Mrs. Reynolds fussed over me. "You sit here and work. Why didn't you have a fire laid?"

"I didn't want to disturb anyone. Sunday afternoon is the only time everyone has to themselves."

"A fire doesn't take long to make. You look completely chilled." She shook her head. "I'll get you some coffee so you can warm up good and proper."

I made myself comfortable, completely at home in this unpretentious room, so much like the one in my old home with its antimacassars on the furniture and a braided rug. By the time she returned with the pot, I had resumed knitting.

Mrs. Reynolds watched me work for a few minutes. "You're very fast, faster than I am. I wouldn't have expected it from someone your age."

I couldn't help but look pleased. "I started when I was five."

"I started when I was four, as all girls do who live on farms. I would have thought your family would have been more interested in teaching you book learning. You sound like you went to some fancy school."

"Most of what I learned I learned at home. My father taught me Latin and mathematics; I think he would have liked to have been a teacher. And my mother used to read to us for as long as I can remember. She loved good literature and history. She used to belong to a literary league. That was before my father died."

Mrs. Reynolds patted my hand. "It's hard for a family when the man of the house dies, at least if you don't have relatives who can look after you."

"My mother has two older brothers in Ohio. I've never met them. They left New England before I was born. They've both got families to support, and there really isn't anybody else except distant cousins."

"How's your mother doing then?"

"She gets help from my father's parents," I exaggerated. "And she sews a little to earn extra money. One of my sisters works in a dress shop. It's a very nice place." Standing for long hours, waiting on persnickety women who couldn't make up their minds, taking home scant wages because the owner insisted girls didn't need money.

"I hope you like living with us," Mrs. Reynolds said. "I was a little worried when you arrived late that you would be a flighty girl and not take your responsibilities seriously. I can see why Mr. Veazey thought you so suitable."

"Thought he would send us some battle-ax," Mr. Reynolds interjected without taking his eyes from the newspaper.

"You should see the embittered women who work as companions," Mrs. Reynolds continued. "It's enough to make a sick woman become even sicker."

"I met some of them in the waiting room outside of Mr. Veazey's office." Older women, dressed in dark clothes, looking down at me and my mother. Maybe it was understandable after long years of hard work with no end in sight, and perhaps no family to comfort them, that they should not be pleased to see another join their ranks. "They didn't look cheerful."

"No. And they are so concerned about their position. Act like they'd never seen what a broom was for. Not one of them would worry about disturbing a maid in the middle of the night to do something trivial they could have easily done themselves." Mrs. Reynolds looked grim. "Most care only about getting paid. I knew of one woman who packed her bags because she wasn't paid one month and walked out. Disgraceful it was. And do you know, the companion got another position in no time."

I found the news encouraging, and I was much more charitably inclined to the companion. I could not afford to work for nothing.

"I can't imagine finding a more pleasant place to work," I said, "and shall miss this house when my six months are up."

"You might be asked to stay longer," Mrs. Reynolds said.

"Mrs. Eldridge will be better soon," I said. "Won't she?"

"Perhaps. Some complaints come and go," she replied cryptically, lowering her voice. "In any event, I think you'll be staying longer. And who knows, with all the people the Eldridges know, you may find yourself employed by one of their friends or cousins when you do leave. Did you know that several members of the President's cabinet stayed here when they visited Putnam?"

"No!" I was impressed. For a moment I forgot my longing for home. A more delightful prospect I could not envision than staying a while longer, and knowing I had another position waiting for me. So far in my life, I had not been able to depend on luck. To find a good position through a newspaper a second time did not seem likely. In fact, had I not been desperate I would not have replied to Mr. Veazey's advertisement in the first place. For that matter, had his office not been deliciously warm, I don't think I would have waited for my interview, since the other candidates all appeared so much more likely to be hired. "I'm curious, how was I selected?"

"I believe Mr. Veazey sent the particulars of each woman to Mr. Eldridge, who then made the decision. I don't really know why he chose you, but I'm sure Mr. Veazey's recommendation had something to do with it."

"That's always nice to hear," I said slowly, feeling a chill return to my bones. All those mature and knowledgeable women—what advantage could I have had over them? I was young and inexperienced, undoubtedly the most inexperienced of all.

I did not judge Mrs. Eldridge to be difficult; I didn't think she was desperate for young company, for while she missed Millicent, she did not pine for her daughter. Then was I chosen just to prevent a potential bond from forming between his wife and the companion, to keep her from talking too freely of family matters? Was I chosen because I did not come from Putnam and would not have the opportunity to spread gossip? Or was there something worse? The image of Mrs. Hamilton came to mind. And a glass bottle, sitting in the open, the contents unlisted.

My thoughts were preposterous. I shoved them aside and concentrated on my knitting. The idea of Mr. Eldridge slowly poisoning his wife so he could marry a younger woman was a morbid fancy. I could prove it myself. All I had to do was sample the medicine. With great determination to think better of my employer, I entered into a prolonged conversation with the housekeeper as I knitted industriously.

8

Monday, February 27–Friday, March 2

THE NEXT FEW DAYS PASSED uneventfully as I gradually overcame my feelings of shyness and developed a better understanding of the house's inhabitants. There were undercurrents
of emotion: between Mr. and Mrs. Eldridge, Hugh and his
parents, Evan and Julianne. In time I would sort them out.
Already they no longer seemed as threatening.

Mrs. Eldridge occupied herself by planning Millicent's
trousseau and writing long letters to her daughter and other
relations, which were answered in kind. I got to hear a great
deal about Alex, her future son-in-law, what a studious young
man he was and how responsible. She ate better than when I
had first arrived, and once or twice I suggested she take the
tonic to comply with Mr. Eldridge's request, but she refused,
as I expected. I was not in a position to add it to her meals,
most of which were taken in the den so she did not have to
tire herself by going up and down the stairs, so I was absolved
of all responsibility there. Unfortunately I was also not in a
position to try the tonic myself and thus give myself complete
peace of mind. Julianne always seemed to be about. This was
partly as a result of Mrs. Eldridge's request that her room be
thoroughly cleaned, and partly because of Hugh.

It all started on Monday. Mr. Eldridge insisted that Hugh
occupy himself with the mill. He acquiesced reluctantly,
bringing home books with long columns of figures to study,

only to find himself distracted by the wonderful volumes in the library. Finally he decided that he would work in his bedroom. Julianne brought him food and drink, more of the latter, I think, than was good for him. Once or twice Hugh appeared a trifle unsteady, though by dinnertime, after several cups of coffee, he appeared no more than jovial.

The baby had several uncharacteristically bad days when he cried and his round little cheeks turned bright red. Mr. Eldridge hovered about earnestly, although he was assured by both Maggie and his wife that it was no more than a touch of colic. One night the baby was very distressed, and since I was a light sleeper, I slept badly, too. Otherwise, life was pleasant.

Until Hugh announced it was time to commence the riding lessons.

On the appointed day, I woke early, hoping for inclement weather. I was rudely disappointed, for though the sky was overcast, rain was not in evidence. As I looked out of my window, trying to detect a large dark cloud on the distant horizon, I saw Julianne walk to the promontory. She stopped at the hedge and after looking about for a few minutes, waved. I closed the curtains before she turned around because I did not want her to think that I was spying.

And so, at eleven o'clock, after receiving instruction from Mrs. Eldridge on the proper decorum for a young lady when seated on a horse, and with all the enthusiasm of a prisoner being led to the gallows, I went to the stables with Hugh, knowing that all eyes in the house would shortly fall on me.

Ken had the horse ready for us and stood at his head, blank faced but surely amused.

"Beauregard looks very happy to be taken out," Hugh said.

"He does?" I would have described him as being delighted to trample the closest victim—me.

"Here, you take the reins and let him know who you are."

Cautiously I did as I was told. Beauregard wouldn't hold his head still and jerked about.

Hugh quickly grabbed the reins again and stroked Beauregard's flaring nose to calm him. "Lydia, you have to be firmer with him than that. Firm, yet gentle, the way you would treat a child. Remember, an uneasy rider makes an uneasy horse."

It was on the tip of my tongue to say that he had nothing to be nervous about, that I was the one about to make a complete and absolute fool of myself, providing I was lucky enough to escape serious injury when he threw me.

Hugh handed the reins to Ken. "I'll help you into the saddle, Lydia."

"So soon?" Hadn't I made plans to avoid this situation? I couldn't remember what they were. "Shouldn't I talk to him a while longer?"

"You're not having the horse over for tea. Up you go."

His strong hands held my waist, and he lifted me to the saddle. It was an incredibly long way to the ground from atop the horse. I could feel the muscles ripple against my legs, and I swayed each time the horse moved.

"There, that isn't so bad, is it?" Hugh asked.

I took quick breaths, fearful I would slide off. "No. Not at all."

He laughed. "Lydia, I do believe that you are the worst liar in the world. It's written all over your face that you're scared."

"I am not," I replied firmly. The horse swished his tail enthusiastically, destroying my feigned composure. "Why doesn't he stand still?"

"He's anxious to go out, that's all. Believe me, he won't run away with you on top of him."

Small reassurance when I was more worried of falling. I gripped the reins for dear life as Hugh took the brute into the open air. I believe I closed my eyes. At any rate, I suddenly found myself outside with no knowledge of how I came to be there.

"I'll walk you around in a circle. I'll be very slow," Hugh promised.

"How old were you when you learned to ride?" I asked in an effort to appear relaxed.

"About four or five, I should imagine. I had a little pony named Silver. I still remember taking him out by myself for the first time. I galloped to the hedge and back. It was exhilarating. I must have thought myself all grown up and that riding was the most wonderful experience in life."

How could anyone want to ride when they could be in a nice carriage? Why couldn't Mrs. Eldridge express an interest in croquet, where you stay close to the ground?

I glanced at the house and saw Mrs. Eldridge wave at me. I almost waved back, but as that would have meant letting go with one hand, I thought better of it.

Hugh took his hands from the halter. I froze. The horse, much to my surprise, stood still, his head in the air, listening alertly. "Now what?" I whispered.

"If you're feeling exceptionally brave, you can give the reins some slack, and he'll just wander a short distance."

"Isn't there something else we could do first? I don't feel secure in having him trot about."

"He's much too old to feel like trotting as soon as he's out of the stable. He'll walk first. I'll stay with you, in case you think you'll fall, although I think you have no reason for concern. You have excellent balance."

"Thank you."

Hugh continued to chat pleasantly about riding in the woods when young and then graduating to trails and the occasional hunt in which he took part, yet did not enjoy.

And suddenly I realized that he wasn't beside the horse anymore.

"Hugh!"

"You're doing very well." He walked quickly over to me and stood in front of the horse. "Beauregard," he coaxed, walking backward, "come on, old boy."

The horse moved steadily forward.

"If you want him to stop, pull on the reins. Not too hard, though. We don't want to hurt his mouth."

I tugged. The horse stopped.

"See how simple it is? Horses are wonderfully uncomplicated creatures. You tell them what to do, and they do it unquestioningly."

I nodded dumbly. I had also heard that horses panicked easily and did the most stupid things.

"I think we've had enough of a riding lesson for today. As we go back to the stables, I'll stay by your side, and you tell Beauregard what to do. Just pull on one rein to turn him around."

With a great deal of effort, I managed to get the horse in the proper direction. Hugh walked by my side, one hand on the horse's flank until we were back at the entrance to the stable. Then he helped me down.

"I'm sure the ride wasn't as difficult as you thought," he said, leaving his hands around my waist.

"No, it wasn't." My arms and legs were trembling, my nose felt frozen, my fingers were numb. I took a deep breath. "I truly thought I would fall."

"I would have caught you," he replied. "Don't worry, Lydia, I wouldn't allow anything to happen to you."

He retained his hold on me and looked into my eyes in a way that made my heart race. He was only trying to be nice, I knew, only my heart did not appreciate the distinction.

"It's been a long winter. You've made the world a less desolate place."

Before I could phrase an appropriate reply, Ken came for the horse, and the mood was broken. Hugh, looking embarrassed, released me and directed the horse to be unsaddled.

"Perhaps you'd better see to my mother," he said with a preoccupied air.

"Yes. I think it is time." I left the stable, my thoughts in confusion, jarred all the more when the door to the house opened just as my hand reached the knob.

"The lesson went well, I gather," Evan said, stepping aside for me to enter.

I had been treating him coolly since I had my suspicions about his relationship with Julianne. "Were you watching the entire time?"

"Yes."

I was thankful that he couldn't see into the stables.

There was a speculative glint in his eye as he closed the door. "Do you wish to continue with your lessons?" he asked. "If not, I can still help extricate you."

"In truth, I'm not sure," I confessed. "Hugh enjoys being a riding master, and Mrs. Eldridge is looking forward to riding again soon and would like me to accompany her. She has written so to her family in several letters. And there may come a time when the skill will prove useful."

"And you will always be the dutiful companion and put your own interests last." His voice was not unkind. "I only want you to take care."

I could see in his eyes that he was sincere. "I'm not being asked much of a sacrifice. I only need to learn to ride enough to accompany Mrs. Eldridge, if she is once again capable of such an activity."

"She will be, no matter what Mr. Eldridge or the good Dr. Patterson may think. By the way, Mrs. Eldridge likes to take some rough trails, too. I have to return to the office. Just remember what I said." He started walking away, then stopped, and looked back at me. "I think you did very well."

I was smiling to myself when I ran up the stairs to my room to change. For the first time in my life, men were paying attention to me. My spirits soared beyond the aches I had sustained in my little adventure.

Mrs. Eldridge was in a good mood when I was once again by her side, and she spoke volubly, giving such a mass of advice on riding that I had no idea how to untangle all the information. Certainly these riding lessons were going to make my relationship with her easier, and I congratulated myself on having been wise enough to go along with all her plans. We now had something to discuss other than needlework.

I went to the library in the early afternoon while she took a nap. If I could make myself more congenial in Mrs. Eldridge's eyes, then I could do so in Mr. Eldridge's view as well. True, I had my suspicions about him, but that could easily be because I found his manner intimidating. As Evan had done before me, I would learn about what he held dear. I found a book entitled *The History of the Eldridge Family to the Year 1861* and made myself comfortable in an upholstered chair.

The family history began with the landing in Boston of George Thomas Eldridge, who had traveled from Yorkshire, England, to seek his fortune. He was a blacksmith by trade and apparently moderately successful. His second son had met and married Millicent Bradford, and together they had founded a most prominent line. The list, which must have included everyone, was extensive and detailed: physicians, legislators, educators, clergymen in abundance, traders, and then mill owners. The names of friends and distant relations were enlightening, for they were names I had read in schoolbooks and the newspapers. No wonder cabinet members chose to stay here when visiting this part of the country.

I closed the book and sat thinking in the darkening room. If at the end of my employment Mr. Eldridge gave me a satisfactory recommendation, I would have access to some of the best families in New England. And to think I had almost not answered the advertisement: only Eugenia's nagging had finally moved me to action.

I heard a heavy step in the room and looked up.

"It's getting dark," Hugh said and lit a lamp. "How's Mother?"

"Her strength is returning again." Not wishing to be too obvious in my desire to impress his father, I hugged the book so that Hugh couldn't read the title.

He dropped gracelessly into the chair opposite me. "I went riding after you went back inside. I went all the way to the outskirts of Putnam. Had to get away from the house for a while, and I most definitely did not wish to join Father at the mill." He sighed. "I didn't think I would arrive home in time for dinner, but as you can see, I am here."

He looked strangely at me, more than just tired and sleepy. "Did you know that Mrs. Hamilton will be joining us?" He didn't wait for a reply. "She should be here soon. Father sent the invitation this afternoon, Evan told me. Evan tells me many things. Does he give you advice? He must. I can't imagine why he thinks he knows so much. He's not that much older than I am. He didn't learn to read until he was eleven, never saw anything other than a miserable mining town until fifteen. Wouldn't know it now. Talented man, my father tells me."

He stared intently at my face. "Are you displeased with me?"

"Certainly not," I replied.

"Everyone should have at least one ally in the world." He shook his head like a dog shaking off water. "I shouldn't have ridden so far. I'm much too tired." His head fell back against the chair with a thunk.

"Hugh!" I bent over him. His breath was unpleasant, the result of some drink, I fancied. "Hugh?" I nudged him gently, but he only mumbled incoherently in reply.

Tiptoeing needlessly, I left the library and went to my room to leave the book by my bedside before looking in on Mrs. Eldridge. She was sitting up in bed, tickling her small son, who gurgled appreciatively.

"I was about to call for you, Lydia. See what I drew." She reached for a piece of heavy paper lying on her night table. "A good likeness of the baby, I think. I'll send it in the mail tomorrow to my father, since he has been too enfeebled to visit the baby for months."

I held the sketch next to Jon Frederick. "It's excellent."

"I ought to sketch you next. In your riding habit." She tilted my head up. "Your face has interesting angles. In a few more years, you will be a most attractive woman."

I glanced at the mirror, wondering what she was seeing.

"You don't think so," she said.

"Eugenia is the prettiest girl in the family."

"There are different kinds of pretty. In youth some have a glow and vitality that makes you forget their flaws. Age can leave them looking like a faded flower. Others have maturity or character stamped on their features at an early age. They don't look fresh or innocent the way we expect them to be; time gives them grace. I'll warrant that you haven't looked in a mirror in the last five years without listing all your faults."

"Well, yes."

"Millicent was like that. Her complexion was rather unattractive, as I recall, and that was all she saw when she looked in a mirror. She was absolutely convinced that no one would ever marry her."

"Every schoolgirl has those worries. Unattractive women don't have many chances." I was penniless. I was not beautiful. To be a poor, plain woman was to be cursed. My only advantage in life was a certain amount of wits. A pity that I could not now be older and more experienced so that I did not fall into awkward situations that I could later regret at my leisure.

"I've always thought it wrong to judge anyone by his appearance," Mrs. Eldridge said. "Remember my prediction, but also cultivate both intelligence and talent, and the years will be kind."

"Would you like to paint Mrs. Hamilton?" I asked. "She seems very attractive."

"I've never fancied that kind of woman," she replied firmly. "What made you think of her?"

"She's been invited to dinner."

Mrs. Eldridge groaned. "Again. How I wish she would visit her husband's family in Hartford. And stay there. That not being the case, I suppose there is nothing to do but get dressed and go down to dinner. Mr. Eldridge is capable of standing up against anything and anyone except a young woman who bats her eyelashes and looks helpless. She will insist on staying half the night to discuss her difficult life. If I have to put up with this much longer, I swear I'll give her the money so she can go husband-hunting in Hartford, or better yet New York." She got out of bed and flung open her wardrobe. "Take Jon Frederick back to the nursery. Oh, no. I told Maggie she could spend the night with her own family."

"I'm sure Jon Frederick could spend a few hours unattended."

"You and I might think so, but Mr. Eldridge would have a brain hemorrhage from worry. Get Julianne. She can look after him for a few hours until Mrs. Hamilton has been sent on her way. I'm going to need you to lend me support."

Mrs. Eldridge dressed with haste, and together we entered the dining room. Mrs. Hamilton was already there, gazing adoringly at Mr. Eldridge. "Elaine, I didn't expect to see you here," she said sweetly.

Mrs. Eldridge glared at her husband as we sat down. "I do have meals with my family occasionally," she stated with barely concealed venom. "Where's Hugh?"

"I don't know," Mr. Eldridge replied. "I haven't seen him since early this afternoon. Perhaps he's with Evan."

A most unlikely event, I thought, and wondered if I should say that he had fallen asleep in the library. Before I could say a word, Evan appeared, alone.

He nodded to his employer, then said, "Good evening, ladies."

"You haven't seen Hugh, have you?" Mrs. Eldridge asked.

Evan seated himself. "As a matter of fact, I did see him go upstairs."

"He told me he was tired from riding," I added.

"I suppose it doesn't matter that he's not here for dinner," Mr. Eldridge replied. "He might even get up at an appropriate time tomorrow if he sleeps ten hours."

"And what do you consider a decent hour?" Mrs. Hamilton asked him coyly.

"Seven at the latest."

"Frightful. I would think that would be a more appropriate time to go to bed."

"We can't all dance throughout the night," Mrs. Eldridge commented. "Some of us have better things to do the next day than sleep."

Mrs. Hamilton looked at me, most obviously rejecting me as useful to her. "And Mr. Roberts, how do you feel?" Her voice was seductive.

"I agree with Mrs. Eldridge," Evan replied dryly.

She pouted. "You're too young to think like that."

Mrs. Eldridge gripped the nearest piece of cutlery as if she planned to use it on Mrs. Hamilton.

"Responsibility is indifferent to age," Evan replied graciously.

"You all take your responsibilities too seriously. Life ought to be enjoyed." She turned her attention to Mr. Eldridge. "I do hope David will visit shortly. He is always good company."

"He'll be here often enough once traveling becomes easier."

Her smile was dazzling. "Oh, good. You'll have those enjoyable parties again like you did last year, I hope."

"Of course we shall," Mrs. Eldridge announced with sugary politeness. "I'll see to that. I'll also attend them."

"Oh." She looked blankly at Mrs. Eldridge. "How nice for you."

Although Mrs. Hamilton's charm was insincere, her personality without true warmth, I could see her appeal, for she could engage in lively conversation. Throughout the course of the meal, the chatter never deviated from Mrs. Hamilton, her likes, her dislikes. She made cutting remarks at Mrs. Eldridge, presenting them with such an innocent face that it was hard to respond in kind.

At a quarter of eight, Mrs. Eldridge had had enough. "My dear," she said pleasantly to Mrs. Hamilton, "you haven't said why you joined us for dinner."

Mrs. Hamilton's eyes opened wider. "I merely came for more congenial company than my sister and brother-in-law could offer."

"In that case, since the meal is over, you can join Lydia and me in the drawing room and leave the men to themselves."

Her eyes strayed to me and then back to Mrs. Eldridge. "You must be tired."

"A bit, but not enough to prevent me from talking a while longer. And of course Lydia isn't tired in the least. You would have a chance to get to know her better."

Taking my cue, I nodded.

Mrs. Hamilton looked at me with an expression bordering on dismay.

"Unless there is something you need to discuss with my husband."

"Ah, yes. I mean no. I mean . . ." She was obviously in a quandary. "Yes, I do need advice. I'm sure you'll think it trivial, but I've been made an offer of a thousand dollars for the house poor Jeffrey owned."

"The late Mr. Hamilton," Mrs. Eldridge said to me.

"Accept the offer," Mr. Eldridge told the poor grieving widow without hesitation. "You are not likely to get many better offers for that property."

"Are you sure? I simply can't make up my mind, but then I don't understand business in the least." She looked properly helpless for the two men.

"I'm sure," Mr. Eldridge replied, and smiled.

"Now that that is settled," Mrs. Eldridge said brightly, "we can go to the drawing room. I would love to show you what

I have planned for Millicent's trousseau."

"I can show you the jacket I'm knitting for Jon Frederick," I added.

For a wink of the eye, Mrs. Hamilton looked alarmed at the prospect, then her usual charmingly innocent expression returned. "Actually, if you don't mind, I think I would rather return home."

Not until Mrs. Hamilton was safely in her carriage did Mrs. Eldridge breathe a sigh of relief. "It is barely a quarter of nine, and she is gone. That is the best I've ever done." She suppressed a yawn. "I am tired. I'll just tell Julianne to put the baby's cradle into my room, and Jon Frederick can sleep with me."

We had no more than reached the top of the stairs when we saw that Julianne was just coming out of Mrs. Eldridge's room. I wondered why she wasn't in the nursery.

Mrs. Eldridge, I'm sure, didn't see the distracted look in her eyes. "Julianne, bring the cradle into my room."

Mr. Eldridge walked up behind us. "Why do that, my dear?"

"With Maggie gone I want the baby to sleep with me."

"He can stay with Lydia," her husband replied, much to my own surprise.

"I think not," Mrs. Eldridge stated, her back rigid. "I haven't looked after my son very much and I wish to spend more time with him."

They stared at each other. An expression I didn't recognize passed over Mr. Eldridge's face. It might have been anger or disappointment. "Very well. I'll be in the tower for the next hour, should you need me." He continued up the stairs.

"Julianne, what are you waiting for?" Mrs. Eldridge asked crossly.

"The cradle is too heavy for me, ma'am."

Mrs. Eldridge walked to Hugh's room and opened the door after tapping lightly. "He's asleep," she said. "Julianne, get Evan. He's somewhere down . . . oh, there he is now. Evan, we need your help."

Until this moment I had never thought of Evan as being particularly strong, for he wasn't a massive man, yet he effortlessly transported the baby's cradle, with Julianne at his heels, carrying the infant in her arms. He wished us good night and retired. Most uncharacteristically, Julianne fussed about Mrs. Eldridge's room, arranging and rearranging the bedclothes and checking on the baby.

Angry, her face stern, Mrs. Eldridge sat in her chair while I brushed out her hair. "How dare he invite that woman to this house and then expect me to treat him with affection," she fumed. "I have had just about enough of his behavior." Julianne hovered near us. "What is it?" Mrs. Eldridge snapped.

"Is there anything else that you need?" she asked in a subdued tone.

"No. I won't need you."

Julianne left, her countenance one of worry. I heard her cross the hall and knock on a door. Whichever it was, no reply was forthcoming.

By now the baby was sleeping soundly, and since Maggie said he usually slept through the night, Mrs. Eldridge felt she would need no more assistance. I helped her undress and then went to my room. I was tired from riding, and yet my mind was abuzz from all the coffee I had consumed. Knowing that I couldn't sleep yet, I decided to sit by the window and knit. The light was feeble, but I needed no more, for I did not watch my hands as I knitted. The long-familiar click, click, click of the needles filled my room and led my thoughts to home.

I had the feeling that I almost fell asleep. My head nodded. Rousing myself, I stretched and happened to glance out the window. A lamp was still on downstairs, and it cast a circle of light on the ground outside. In that light, Julianne stood swathed in a cloak. Farther away, I saw the merest outline of a man, facing away from the house. He gestured. Julianne walked toward him. I blinked, and there was nothing left to see.

9

Saturday, March 3

WHEN I AWOKE THE NEXT morning, my arms were abominably
stiff and sore; sitting up, I found other areas of my body
equally distressed. It was just past seven, and I doubted that
Mrs. Eldridge would be up and in need of my services. My
bed was so tempting I had a strong desire to retreat back under
the covers; nevertheless, I persevered and put on my slippers
and wrap.

I had just started to brush my hair when there came a rapid
knock on the door. Before I could respond, Maggie burst into
the room and collapsed into my arms.

"What is it?" I asked with alarm.

She could only sob and gasp for breath in reply.

"Is something wrong with your family?"

Maggie shook her head. "It's . . . it's Julianne. She's at the
bottom of the promontory. She must be dead."

Papa can't be dead. Louise had screamed over and over.
We couldn't calm her down, because we all wanted to scream
but the words couldn't come out; there was only this feeling
of helplessness, of abandonment, followed by a numbness, a
disbelief that insisted the doctor couldn't have said, "dead."

"What?" Surely the voice I heard belonged to a stranger and
not to me. "What did you say?"

"She must be dead, Lydia. Her head is lying in the river."
Maggie started to sob again, the tears flowing freely down her
cheeks. "I didn't want to wake Mrs. Eldridge with the news,
and you're the first person I thought of after her. Who should
we tell?"

"Evan," I said automatically, not sure if anyone else would
be dressed yet. "He'll know what to do. Maybe it's not too
late."

I rushed to his room and knocked, opening the door before
he finished mumbling, "What is it?" Evan was standing bare-
foot, leaning over the washbasin, having just finished shaving
and not yet wearing a shirt. He looked at me with astonishment.

"Julianne is at the bottom of the promontory. Maggie thinks
she may be dead."

Evan dropped the razor and ran past me. By the time I
returned to my room, he was already down the stairs. I grabbed
my quilt. "Maggie, if anyone else wakes, tell what you saw."

I hurried after Evan, holding up my nightgown with one
hand and dragging the quilt with the other. The front door was
open. The cold air bit my lungs with each breath as I ran. Evan
was far ahead, and I did my best to catch up. Long before I
reached the hedges, he began his climb down to the river.

I didn't want to look—I had had enough of death and agony
and tragedy—but I might be able to help. I dropped the quilt
over the hedge, stepped through the shrubbery to where the
ground fell away, and looked down.

Evan had just reached Julianne's side. Her long hair streamed
out into the river, her head submerged, her dress and petticoats
splattered with mud. Her legs were bent unnaturally, and one
black stocking was torn. Evan lifted his head to me, shook it,
and knelt down. He smoothed down her skirts so that she no
longer looked indecent. Carefully he slid his hands underneath
Julianne and tried to lift her. The attempt failed: her body was
stiff and awkward in death. He braced his feet and finally with
great effort raised her out of the water. Her eyes were open,
looking for all the world like white marbles.

I felt my stomach churn and looked down at my feet.
The ground had been disturbed, I saw, starting just outside

of the hedges. There was barely more than a yard's width between the hedges and the drop. Was this the point from which Julianne fell? Had she tumbled over the shrubs and kept falling? I looked more closely. Evan had gone down the slope on my left. His trail was clear to see. I had breached the hedges in almost the same place he had. So why the many deep impressions in the soft soil that could only have been made by a woman's shoe, one print clearly facing the house, and the prints of a man's shoe overlaying those?

I summoned the courage to look at Julianne again. Evan had placed her on the brown grass beside the embankment. Her arms and legs were straight, and her head lay slightly to one side as if she were sleeping; except for the color of her skin, except for those white eyes. My hands came to my mouth. I felt as if she were staring at me.

I had disliked her because she had been lovely, forgetting that her lot was not better than mine, nor likely ever to be. I had never bothered to say a kind word to her during our short acquaintance, and all the remorse I felt now could never be expressed.

Evan stared at her—I thought he whispered something—then he closed her eyes.

Like a man in a trance he returned, climbing slowly over the rocks, using the clumps of vegetation to pull himself up. Finally he stood by my side, shivering in the cold wind.

"Evan." He didn't answer me. I put the quilt over his shoulders. "Evan, you can't stay out here. You're not dressed properly. You'll get sick."

He looked down to the river, as if to reassure himself that Julianne lay there. I thought he was going to cry, then he mastered his emotions again. "It might be easier to reach her from the path," he said to himself. "Reynolds can help." He noticed me at last. "I'm sorry, did you say something?"

"Please come inside. You can't do anything more out here."

I took his hand and led him back to the house. He favored his foot, and I saw that he had cut himself on the sharp rocks. He was oblivious to the injury. His teeth began to chatter from the cold and of that, too, he seemed unaware.

I wondered what he was thinking now: did he regret the

liaison with Julianne, and had he been in love with her? I looked at his face. I wanted to tell him I was sorry, anything to make him feel better, yet no words ever suffice in the face of death. I held his hand more tightly. It was the best I, or anyone, could ever do.

Mr. Eldridge and Hugh, both evidencing signs of hasty dressing, met us at the door. They didn't have to ask about Julianne—our expressions revealed all.

"Oh, God!" Hugh said and stepped back against the door as if he had been hit. He froze in place.

Mr. Eldridge's face settled into a blank mask, and then he went to see for himself.

Once Evan was back inside the house, his mind cleared. He let go of my hand. "Stay inside, Lydia. We'll take care of—of everything."

I started for my room.

"Lydia." He gave me a searching look. "Thank you."

I nodded and reluctantly left him alone.

Maggie was sitting on my bed, crying softly into the pillow. I sat down beside her. "Are you going to be all right?" I handed her the handkerchief I kept on the nightstand.

Maggie blew her nose. "Yes. It wasn't like we were close friends or family, but it was a shock finding her like that. Oh, my." She took a deep breath. "I was walking up the path. There's a place where it's close to the river and the trees aren't too thick. Your eye naturally goes to where she was lying. I couldn't believe it at first and then I just ran. I should have run to her instead. I might have been able to pull her out of the water, and she might be alive."

I shook my head. "She went there last night." With someone. Evan? But it didn't have to be him. I had seen Hugh speak with her anxiously more than once. And Mr. Eldridge, too, for that matter. Any of the three men could have been out there, assuming, of course, that I hadn't imagined the scene because I was half asleep.

"You saw her?" Maggie asked.

"I thought I did." I looked out of my window, trying to recapture last night's image. I shook my head. It didn't seem real in the morning light. "I could be wrong. It was late and I was tired." I glanced at the clock. It was almost eight. "I had better break the news to Mrs. Eldridge. If she's awake. She'll be wondering what the commotion has been all about."

Mrs. Eldridge was nestled beneath the covers, only half awake. The baby was quietly studying his hands, oblivious to all. "Why has there been so much noise this morning?" she mumbled and opened her eyes. At the sight of my face she bolted upright.

"Julianne is dead." I rapidly explained what had transpired.

She got out of the bed and paced back and forth, shaking her head. "Dreadful, dreadful thing to happen." She wiped a tear from her eyes. "Poor child. I'll have to go to her parents. As early as possible. You'll come with me. First you had better have a warm bath and turn your soiled nightgown over to the laundress." She sat down at her desk and began to compose a letter. "This is for the minister. He'll talk to Julianne's family."

The baby was returned to Maggie, and the servants were informed of the events in the midst of their morning duties. By the time I had dressed, Julianne's body was being brought up. Ken, Mr. Reynolds, and Evan rigged a small sled with rope and used the pony. I closed the curtains so that I wouldn't have to see her body appear, and I whispered a quick prayer.

To die in such a manner, so easily avoidable, when there were so many other means of death, seemed terribly capricious of fate. I thought of her yesterday, beautiful as ever, unaware that it was to be her last day on earth.

Julianne had been disturbed last night, about what I could not begin to guess. She had wanted to speak to someone. Then the image stole upon me of a man, faceless, who had indeed spoken to her. For the last time. Had he killed her, brutally thrusting her over the edge and onto the rocks below? She had not been afraid of him, else she would not have ventured out at night. Who, then? Mr. Eldridge, Evan, or Hugh? They were all roughly the same height, and in a coat their builds would not be distinguishable from one another.

As I felt that first tremor of fear, I rushed from the room to where I would not be alone.

A very unhappy household was assembled in the dining

room. Mr. Eldridge looked as grim as death himself. Evan was drinking liberally of whiskey, a task at which Hugh had surpassed him some time ago, judging from the dazed look he gave me when I entered the room. While serving the food, Rosemarie sniffed constantly, and I swear I could hear Mrs. Babbage wail in the kitchen. I looked at the faces, wondering to whom I should confide last night's account. All seemed unapproachable: I wanted neither to interrupt the grief nor make a potential murderer aware that I was a witness to his abominable crime. Not knowing what to do, I said nothing.

Mrs. Eldridge, still wearing her wrap, was seated over a cup of undoubtedly cold coffee. "Sit down, Lydia, and have something to eat," she directed without looking at me.

"What happens now?" I whispered, seating myself next to her. "Do you notify the police?"

"We don't have any. Since it was an accident, there isn't really anyone to notify."

"How do you know it was an accident?"

"What else could it have been? Julianne often used to go there early in the morning. Her people would be up early to begin the chores, and she'd wave to them. If something was wrong, they could always shout to her that they needed her help. It gets muddy there sometimes, and as she stood there, she slipped."

I hadn't thought Mrs. Eldridge would notice such details, what with her own concerns.

"I've known her from the time she was a little child, barely able to walk. Now and again she would come with her father when he brought us meat and the like. Julianne always liked to see the house. When she was sixteen, she started to work here in the winters. Her father couldn't spare her until then, and she still returned home to help with the harvests. We took her with us to Boston last winter, and she loved it. It is difficult to believe that I saw her yesterday evening and now will never see her again."

I waited for one of the men to speak, to say that they had seen her just before retiring, and I could dismiss what I had seen as an innocent encounter.

No one spoke.

"I believe I shall make a piece of mourning jewelry from her hair," Mrs. Eldridge continued. "I'm sure her mother doesn't have the time."

"Can't we talk about something else?" Hugh pleaded in a thick voice, his words slurring. "I don't want to think about her lying there."

"It is difficult to think of anything else," Mr. Eldridge said. "Do you consider the ground workable in the cemetery?" he asked rhetorically of his wife. "We should have them start digging soon, as it can't be an easy job."

Hugh pounded his glass on the table. "Good God! Will you shut up!"

"Perhaps you should lie down," Mrs. Eldridge told Hugh calmly, "until you feel less distressed. Jonathan, I think it will be an excellent idea."

Hugh stalked from the room as his parents continued to discuss funeral arrangements. I went over to Evan. "Are you all right? You looked very distraught."

"There's nothing wrong with me." He held his liquor well. "I've known a number of people to die when a mine collapsed, known more than one woman who didn't survive bearing a child. It's just that this was so unexpected." He looked at me. "You seem to bear up well."

"I didn't know her very long. Did you?" I asked disingenuously.

"Two years. Ever since I started working for Mr. Eldridge. I was teaching her to write. Gave her advice. She almost had enough money to go to Boston. She told me only a few days ago."

Where would Julianne get that much money? Not from Evan.

He got up and replenished his glass from the decanter on the sideboard. "I can't seem to get warm."

I nodded. "Is your foot all right?"

"It was only a small cut." He resumed his seat. "Some of the rocks are sharp."

Julianne didn't have a single cut on her face, I remembered with disturbing clarity. "Hugh told me that he used to climb those rocks in the summer."

"It isn't difficult. The slope is only sixty degrees and a fall not likely to be fatal. She must have hit her head very hard and fallen in such a way that she couldn't hold onto anything." He swallowed the entire contents of the glass. His eyes were no longer focused, and I wondered if he was seeing an image of Julianne.

"Is she here now?" I asked.

"Uhm?" My words registered. "Oh, no, Reynolds took her directly into town and by now will have gone to Putnam for Mr. Fenn, the undertaker." His voice was completely flat. "They'll probably bury her on Monday."

"A doctor won't examine her?" I had to know.

"Dr. Patterson has enough trouble with the living and has nothing to offer the dead."

So the body was to be buried without more than a cursory examination by the undertaker. "Shouldn't there be some sort of an investigation?" I ventured.

"Mr. Eldridge will take care of any such matters. He always does, although the death is straightforward. Unless her parents insist, no further steps will be necessary."

How easy it was to commit murder under these circumstances, I thought. I laid a hand on Evan's arm. "Forgive me for asking so many questions at a time like this, Evan. I just need to know for my own peace of mind—since my window faces in the direction of the promontory, why didn't I hear her cry out when she fell?"

"The wind may have carried her voice in the other direction, or everything could have happened too quickly, or you could have been asleep."

"I suppose so. I'd hate to think that she called for help and no one heard."

"Someone on the staff probably would have. Ken feeds the horses very early. And if Ken wasn't about, Arthur would surely be cleaning the stables."

"Evan . . . Evan, her body was already stiff, wouldn't that mean that she'd been dead some time?"

"The water was extremely cold and the air not much better. She wouldn't have had to be there long before all the warmth was drained from her."

She wasn't completely submersed, I wanted to remind him, but I didn't want to hound him with the wretched details.

"Lydia," Mrs. Eldridge said as she rose, "we will be paying our respects to Julianne's family as soon as Mr. Reynolds has returned. I think you should wear something dark."

I heartily disliked visiting bereaved families: I never knew what to say, and the trip only brought back unpleasant memories, made more unpleasant by my impression, growing stronger by the minute, that Julianne had not met her death naturally.

We rode in silence to a typically small farm owned by the Lippit family. There were chickens in the front yard, a pen for sheep and goats, a lone milk cow sticking her head out of the barn, and another enclosure for pigs. The smell was worse than any factory could produce.

I walked carefully over the ground, lifting my skirts high, following Mrs. Eldridge to the plain saltbox house in urgent need of a new coat of red paint. A child, the very image of Julianne, opened the door for us. "Hello, ma'am," she said earnestly to Mrs. Eldridge and looked at me with unabashed curiosity.

Mrs. Eldridge patted the child's head. "Hello, Pauline. I have something for you." She reached into her bag and produced a profusion of cookies, which the child snatched eagerly. "You have to share those."

I had no doubt of that, for I saw three other youngsters appear almost immediately to claim their portion.

A woman, who might have been beautiful once, shuffled toward us. She was fat and muscular, her gray-streaked black hair artlessly arranged, her dark green dress covered with stains. "Step inside before you catch a chill," she said without preamble, ushering us into a smoky room.

"How's Mack?"

"Chopping wood. Doesn't know what else to do. He'll have another cord chopped within the hour at the rate he's going. Doesn't figure that she could die like that. Doesn't seem right when she grew up along that river."

"No. Oh, this is Lydia. She's my new companion."

"Miss," she said. "I saw you last Sunday at church. Guess we'll be meeting again sooner than usual." She gestured to the chairs. "No need to remain standing." She settled herself in the chair nearest at hand and addressed Mrs. Eldridge. "You've been sick, I heard."

"It hasn't been anything serious, merely awkward, and to be expected at my age." They exchanged knowing looks.

"It can make you awful tired at times." Mrs. Lippit looked down at her callused hands.

As the two women were soon busy discussing the upcoming funeral—the ordering of a coffin for which the Eldridges would pay, the writing of the eulogy, the refreshments to be served for those attending the service—I occupied myself by looking around. The central room was cozy, the furniture simple. There were no books on the shelves, not even a Bible. Possibly no one read well enough to be interested in books or newspapers. On the stairs that led to the upper floor, four little urchins sat staring at me with wide gray eyes. The house was neat, especially when you considered that there were half a dozen children underfoot in the wintertime and no place to send them. I could smell food cooking in the kitchen and caught glimpses of a young girl of about fifteen walking back and forth, carrying items. Through the window I could see a seventeen-year-old boy carting feed.

I saw why Julianne preferred working in the Eldridge house. No matter how constant the demands there were, they would never be as great as those on a farm. Even death didn't interrupt the chores.

The children whispered behind my back. I got up and went over to them. "Hello." My awkward smile encountered blank stares.

"We liked the cookies," the older of the boys finally said. "Do you have any more?"

"I'm afraid not."

"Julianne used to bring us cookies and cakes when she came to visit," Pauline said. "She didn't come very often, though. She didn't like us."

I was taken aback by this admission. "I'm sure she did."

"No she didn't," the boy answered, his brother nodding in

confirmation. "She liked being at the big house a lot better. Told us so last Christmas. Said that if she had her way, she'd never come back here, no sir."

"Pa wanted her to help out 'cause Ma was sick, but she wouldn't do it," Pauline said.

"Julianne had a lot of work of her own to do at the house," I explained.

"She didn't want to get her new dresses dirty," Pauline said.

"She spent her extra money on them," the smallest boy said.

"Shush," Pauline said, punching him on the shoulder.

"Well, she did," he wailed. He stuck out his tongue at Pauline.

"You ain't supposed to tell," Pauline hissed.

"But it's true!" he insisted.

"Stop making so much noise," his mother commanded.

The children were instantly still. Although I did my best to lure them back into conversation, they said little more. I returned to my chair to think.

Evan had little money. A serious liaison between them would not necessarily get Julianne to Boston and could, if Mr. Eldridge took a dim view of such things, ruin the career Evan had so laboriously built.

Mr. Eldridge and Hugh had money and could afford to be more liberal with it. Hugh drank in excess, of which his father disapproved. When Julianne cleaned his room, she would be in a position to remove empty bottles surreptitiously, or for that matter supply him with liquor. That was good enough reason for Hugh to bribe Julianne, but not to kill her. After all, even if she told Mr. Eldridge, what would he do to Hugh? And in all truth, I could not imagine Hugh capable of killing a hare, much less a human being—unless he lost his temper. He was certainly ready to snap at Evan for trivial things, and alcohol did affect Hugh's personality, for good and for ill. He had been drunk that night, had he not?

Mr. Eldridge was another matter. I felt sure that if he ever made up his mind to kill, he would do so efficiently and without qualm. The only motive I could imagine was

Mrs. Hamilton. An older man doting on a young woman wasn't uncommon—it was possible that Julianne had found Mr. Eldridge and Mrs. Hamilton in a compromising situation. A man like Mr. Eldridge would never tolerate a scandal; he would much rather pay and then kill Julianne if she became a nuisance.

I looked at Mrs. Eldridge talking animatedly. What if Mr. Eldridge wanted a young wife, one who could give him more children? Divorce would be too scandalous, and murder could be so quiet. As quiet as a deadly dose taken over and over again until she died.

Maybe I should tell Mrs. Eldridge my concerns. But I couldn't do it here, not in front of this grieving woman and the children.

Mrs. Eldridge stood. "We should be going. Do tell Mack how sorry I feel for this tragic occurrence." After saying good-bye to each child by name, we left.

Mr. Reynolds, whom I presumed was talking to Mack, was not at the carriage. Mrs. Eldridge didn't seem to mind in the least. "Lydia, when we are in the village, I'm going to have Mr. Reynolds stop at the seamstress—there are some alterations I wish to discuss with her—and while I'm there I want you to mail this letter." She handed it to me quickly. "It's nothing important, just a letter to relatives in Putnam." She stopped talking the moment she saw Reynolds walk toward us.

I wondered about this new letter. If she was mailing letters to relatives, why all the secrecy? Why not give them to her husband to take with him when he went to the mill? What was happening that would require her to mail letters discreetly?

How easy and simply all my concerns would disappear if all I had to do was ask questions and receive appropriate answers. I shouldn't have to worry that Julianne was murdered or that Mrs. Eldridge might die. More than likely my fears were mere fancies. To express them could cost me my position and be the ruin of me: but what if they were true?

I wanted to speak to Mrs. Eldridge, here, while we were alone, but I waited too long to find my courage, and soon Mr. Reynolds appeared. He shouldn't have caused me to falter, yet I could not bring myself to say what was on my mind for fear of looking foolish over something I was not sure of myself and because he might tell Mr. Eldridge. I longed desperately for another chance while we rode in the carriage. Mrs. Eldridge chatted of inconsequential matters, whether to take her mind off the death or to keep me from asking about the letter I could not determine. The minutes passed, my courage grew dim, and we reached Bradford.

I looked at the letter before I entered the store: it was addressed to Mrs. Henry Moore of Putnam. Short of opening it, I had no hope of guessing its contents. I gave the letter to Ned, who, without looking at it, put it with others waiting to be picked up. If he were asked, he would quite truthfully say that he hadn't taken a letter from Mrs. Eldridge.

No peace was to be found for the remainder of the day. I was kept busy helping Mrs. Eldridge, ensuring she took some rest despite her funeral plans, and trying to calm Maggie, who still felt that Julianne might have been alive when she first saw her. I spent half the night in the nursery offering what consoling words I could, and then tumbled into my own bed and instant sleep.

10

Sunday, March 4

SUNDAY WAS A SOMBER DAY, with none of the festive spirit and trivial gossip of the previous week. The church service was brief. After the noon meal, everyone went their separate ways: Evan to work obsessively; Hugh to sit in the library, an open book in his hands that he did not read; Mr. Eldridge to his lofty tower; and his wife to bed, where she lay wide awake but uninterested in conversation. The servants were all talking about Julianne, she had done this and that, and I heard her name wherever they gathered. Words of death, thoughts of death, were all around me. I felt oppressed and watched, as if the ghost of Julianne stood at my elbow, while her body rested at her parents' home for the last time.

Monday, March 5

THE NEXT MORNING WE ENTERED Bradford for the funeral. With the exception of Mrs. Babbage and Lucy, who stayed behind to prepare the food, and Maggie, who remained with the baby, the entire staff attended, as well as a large portion of the town, for Mr. Eldridge had given his employees two hours off to pay their final respects.

Dr. McGraw managed to give a creditable eulogy at the church, as several people commented, although there was little to be said about a young woman of twenty-two who had spent most of her life in one small town and left the world nothing to remember her by. I was glad the coffin had been closed for the ceremony. I had been disturbed enough at the wake when I passed by the bier and saw Julianne lying amid white velvet in her new satin gown that was to have served a happier purpose.

The new cemetery stood back from the community where the hill sloped sharply upward and good farmland was not to be had. All round the barren trees stood solemnly, as sentinels for the dead. A neat gray stone wall enclosed the premises, which had not so many slumbering within as yet. Most of the markers were modest, with little elaborate carving, just a name, a date, and sometimes a pertinent verse. Crumbling leaves littered the ground. Everything was so gray: the markers, the ground, the winter sky.

The coffin was carried by half a dozen men, cousins of Julianne, I had learned, to the midpoint of the cemetery. As they lowered the mortal remains of their kinswoman into the open pit, tears welled up in my eyes. The minister took his place at the grave. He said a few short words commending Julianne to God. I watched her father, Mack, his cragged face perfectly passive while his hands twisted and twisted his hat into a shapeless mass. His wife bore up well; she was dry-eyed and only slightly more stooped than when I had first met her. The children, who had not been distressed when I had seen them, now cried, the smaller ones clinging to their mother's skirts. Until now, it must have seemed to the children that their sister wasn't really gone forever. How could she be when they saw her young and vital, waving at them only a few days before?

I looked at Evan to see what he was thinking. He seemed properly somber and nothing more. Hugh never raised his eyes from his boots. Mr. Eldridge looked straight ahead over the heads of the people. Mrs. Eldridge sniffed on occasion.

Dr. McGraw closed his Bible. It was over and done, and the crowd dispersed quickly, driven by a cold, wet breeze.

The Eldridges went to pay their respects to their dead family members in a small granite mausoleum, a miniature Doric temple complete with columns and a heroic decorative frieze.

A small fortune had been lavished on this monument to death. The other monuments would crack, the names become illegible, but the mausoleum would remain. Julianne would be forgotten soon. I wondered if there was even a photograph of her.

A man with violent red hair limped toward me. He had to be Maggie's husband, Peleg Marsh. I hastily wiped my eyes.

"How do you do, Miss Hall," he said in a low tone. He appeared to be an agreeable man despite his intense green eyes that at first glance made him disconcerting. His body was thin and wiry, his hands broad and strong. "Maggie's been telling us all about you." He thought hard for a moment and continued on with his rehearsed speech. "And I'd like to thank you for the jacket you knitted for our youngest. We really appreciate that you took the trouble."

"It was no trouble, Mr. Marsh, and Mrs. Eldridge supplied the wool."

"Call me Pete if you don't mind. I was named Peleg for my grandfather, and to this day the name still belongs to him."

"All right, I will, providing you call me Lydia."

He nodded in agreement. "I was wondering how Maggie's taking the funeral. She was very upset yesterday when I talked to her."

"I haven't seen much of her this morning, but I'll make sure to look in on her this afternoon."

"I'd appreciate that a lot. She feels she might have helped Julianne if she had stayed instead of running away."

The image of Julianne, lying like a broken doll at the bottom of the promontory, came to mind. I could see open eyes, accusing eyes. I shuddered. "I don't think so. I would say she had been dead for some time."

"Maggie said you were pretty calm and knew just what to do." There was admiration in his voice.

I nodded. "My father used to say that you can always panic after the fact, but never, never lose your head during an emergency."

"Lydia," Mrs. Eldridge called, "we're leaving in a minute."

"Have Maggie bring you by our house sometime. The girls all want to meet you." He put his hat back on, nodded to me, and left.

"Nice man, isn't he?" Mrs. Eldridge commented as she walked toward me. "You'll be seeing more of him around the house soon, which I'm sure will make Maggie happy. We've decided to replace the hedge with a fence. It will be safer for all concerned."

Especially for the murderer if there was any evidence of a crime, I thought. "Wasn't this the first time there was an accident?"

"Actually no, though this is the first with fatal results. A good headwind once plunged Hugh's tutor over the edge, and Hugh of course toppled over at least three times when he was a boy, but he held on to the grass and didn't fall far. My husband is concerned that Jon Frederick might not be so lucky."

It was hard not to smile. "He won't even be walking for many months."

She sighed. "That minor point carried no weight. He's concerned that Jon Frederick's nurse might slip at some future date with him in her arms—as if that were likely—or that a horse may mistake the hedge for a jump, which is equally ludicrous. He wasn't in the least like this when Millicent and Hugh were young, and I do hope that he soon ceases this silly preoccupation with Jon Frederick's safety. A pity we didn't have a large family. He would be much more reasonable with half a dozen children to distract him."

As promised, after dinner I looked in on Maggie in the nursery.

"I saw your husband at the funeral." I pulled up the chair to sit beside her. "He asked me to see how you were."

"Fine, I suppose," Maggie answered, listlessly rocking the baby in her arms. "Tired."

I looked at her critically. The dark circles under her eyes were new. "Have you been getting enough sleep?"

"Have you?" she countered. "You've been up more than once in the night and paced."

"I didn't think anyone heard."

"I don't think anyone else did. I was only up because Jon Frederick was fretting, not because I was having nightmares. I don't think about Julianne at night, just during the day. I've seen her stand there waving to the farm, but it was never so close to the edge."

"Maybe she felt dizzy and fell forward over the hedge and then kept going." I stopped.

"What's the matter?" Maggie inquired. "You look strange suddenly."

A picture of Julianne's body had been forged into my mind, and until the day I died I was sure I could recall every detail of her appearance. "Her face wasn't scratched, and the front of her clothes weren't torn, except for her stockings. Wouldn't that mean that she fell backward without tumbling?"

"As you said, if she was dizzy, she could have turned around," Maggie suggested, "or maybe she had got done waving at her folks and had turned around to come back."

"No one said they saw her on the day of her death. I have the feeling someone would have mentioned it at the wake or after the service."

"Don't look so worried, Lydia. What difference does it make how and why she fell?"

"Because it doesn't make sense. What time did Julianne usually go outside?"

"Early, and only when the weather was tolerable."

"Dawn?"

"I don't think so. At least not often. Julianne didn't like to get up that early."

"The sun doesn't come up until after six. What time did you start walking up the path?"

"I don't know exactly. Not long after dawn. It takes a good three quarters of an hour for me to climb the hill. Lydia, what are you thinking about?"

"I was just wondering if there is a way to find out what time Julianne went outside."

"Martha would probably know."

Martha unfortunately avoided me and would undoubtedly prove uncooperative. As Mrs. Reynolds had said on our tour of Bradford, strangers were viewed with suspicion. There had to be a subtle way for me to find out what I needed to know. If Julianne had not spent the night in her bed, then her death was likely the result of murder.

Mrs. Reynolds was not in her apartment, and all the misty plans I had made to gain her aid in the interrogation of Martha vanished. Not only was the apartment quiet, but the entire servants' wing appeared to be empty.

A trunk, not much larger than mine, was standing in the corner.

I took a step toward it and halted. It would be thoroughly wicked of me to snoop among Julianne's possessions. And yet how was I to get the answers I needed if I didn't? There wasn't enough time to wrestle with such philosophical arguments. I took a deep breath, told myself that I was doing this to ease Maggie's mind as well as my own, and knelt beside the trunk.

I found several dresses of exceptionally good quality for a maid. Next I discovered a copybook with exercises laboriously written out. My heart ached. Poor Julianne, trying so hard to better herself. Beneath that was a carved wooden box with a cheap velvet shelf containing a locket of little value and a few other trinkets.

The interior of the box seemed too shallow. I examined the inside carefully and discovered a false bottom. Lifting up the partition, I found seventy-two dollars.

I sat on my heels, dumbfounded. This was too much money to have been casually saved. It was more than three times my monthly salary, and I was sure it was much more than that to Julianne. Was money like that ever handed out except for blackmail?

Servants were in a most advantageous position when it came to learning secrets, and blackmail paid well. Yet it also carried the risk of being murdered, or so some of my less than proper reading literature had led me to believe. Julianne would never have walked to the promontory if she feared this mysterious man. Why, why, why had she gone there willingly? Was it an assignation? Was she due to be paid again, and the lure of money overcame her prudence?

Expecting to be caught if I didn't hurry, I searched quickly through the remaining chemises and stockings and combs and found nothing more unusual. Finished, I put my ear to the door and, not hearing any footfalls, walked into the hallway, sure that my guilt would be visible to anyone I encountered.

There was no one there, no sounds issued from any of the rooms.

I started to breathe more easily. This trip had proven one other thing to me: no matter how crowded this house appeared at times, with people forever going up and down the stairs, it was possible to move about without being seen, if only the routine of the servants were known.

The light was fading, and I decided this would be the best time to visit the hedge. The servants were busy preparing the evening meal and completing the other routine duties that had been interrupted by the funeral, and everyone else was preoccupied by their own concerns. I got my coat and slipped outside.

My breath hung in the air as I walked rapidly, now and then stealing glances behind me to see if I was being observed. The windows were as empty as the eyes of a blind man.

I retraced the steps Julianne must have taken. Did she stay here a while, pacing back and forth in the cold to keep warm? Was that why there were so many prints? I looked down at the base of the hedges. The ground had been thoroughly trampled, obliterating the previous prints. Had this been done deliberately or by accident?

I was furious with myself for not having mentioned the footprints. Would they not have added weight to my claim that Julianne had been out at night? If I mentioned the incident now, after the lapse of a day, no one would believe me. Why should they, when I was the stranger?

Somehow I would find out for myself what the truth was. Most likely I would convince myself that Julianne's death had indeed been an accident and would congratulate myself for having the foresight to keep my mouth shut. This assessment of the situation would have pleased me more were it not evident that the sled and the men accompanying it had gone down the path and then along the river were not likely to have trampled the ground here. The alternative was that the murderer had done so.

I examined the hedges more closely, which necessitated that I crouch. Several branches were broken where the ground had been disturbed. If Julianne had fallen into the hedge, she would not have plunged to her doom. Had she been pushed, I could very well imagine that she would pass through the shrubbery and from there into eternity.

I stood up, again looking at the house. Was it my imagination, or did I see a figure move? I strained my eyes. It might have been a servant brushing against a curtain, or someone merely glancing idly out at the approaching night. There was no reason for my heart to beat in alarm. No reason why a solitary walk on the grounds should arouse suspicion in anyone.

I walked back, my pace increasing with each step. In my mind's eye, I saw Julianne going out to meet the man, thinking she was secure until she took that fatal plunge, her arms reaching out to the dark house for help. I looked up. Even the most feeble light in my room would have been obvious to someone walking back this way.

He would know the possibility existed that he had been seen.

I ran the final yards to the house, rushed up the stairs, flung my cloak over the bed, and put on my slippers. I stared in the mirror, willing my face to compose itself, as I repinned my hair.

Dinner was not pleasant. Mrs. Eldridge did not join us, and the three men were silent. I kept thinking that there had to be some telltale sign that one of these men might be a murderer, and yet nothing was betrayed. Did he think himself completely safe, or was he unconcerned that I might be aware of his crime? We each went our separate ways the moment the meal was over. Outside the wind began to pummel the house, and an occasional flake of snow descended.

It was still early, and as I had no desire to read or knit or go to bed, I went to the kitchen for tea and a word or two with Mrs. Reynolds. She was seated at the kitchen table with the cook, while the little kitchen wench scrubbed the last of the pots.

The cook saw me first. "Did you know that Mrs. Eldridge hardly had anything to eat tonight?" Mrs. Babbage said in an accusing tone as if it were my fault. "She needs good wholesome food. A nice calf's-foot broth would do her a world of good."

"She was very tired," I replied.

"She's always tired. How does she expect to get better if she doesn't eat?" Mrs. Babbage asked rhetorically.

I sat at the table. "Excuse me, Mrs. Reynolds. Maggie is still upset about finding Julianne."

The housekeeper pursed her lips. "There was nothing to be done about that."

"She knows, but it would put all her worries to rest if she knew that Julianne had fallen a lot earlier. Her body was stiff, as if she had been dead some hours." I wasn't sure if I should continue and concluded that it didn't matter whether Mrs. Reynolds was alone or not, since she was bound to discuss whatever I said with Mrs. Babbage. "I thought I saw Julianne at—"

Mrs. Babbage raised a finger to her lips to quiet me. "Lucy, why don't you stop now."

Lucy, obviously piqued at missing out on something interesting, shuffled from the kitchen.

"She's a little young to be hearing everything," Mrs. Babbage said, nodding sagely, "especially when it concerns Julianne."

"Mustn't speak ill of the dead," Mrs. Reynolds said automatically.

Mrs. Babbage sniffed. "That doesn't change what she was. She would do just about anything to escape her lot in life. Scandalous is what I would call her, a minx, playing up to anyone and everyone who was useful to her."

My discovery of the money gave me the impetus to speak. "I thought I saw her at night, sometime around eleven o'clock, walking away from the house."

"You're not certain?" Mrs. Reynolds asked.

"I would say yes, but I was sleepy and saw her so briefly. In all honesty, I could have been mistaken. Perhaps she just went out for a moment for air."

"You were mistaken. Martha is fairly certain that Julianne left the room very early in the morning," Mrs. Reynolds said.

"I'm sure that it's none of my business," Mrs. Babbage said haughtily, "but Julianne wasn't quite the good girl she should have been. She used to come back late and disappeared for long periods from her work."

Mrs. Reynolds turned to me. "Martha had complained on more than one occasion that Julianne was, ah, restless."

"I think she sometimes went down to the library for books," I said. "I found her reading once."

Mrs. Reynolds relaxed. "I hadn't been aware she did that. That explains a few of her stealthy habits. Books are unimportant in her family. She might have been afraid that we would have made fun of her learning."

"That young woman was not afraid of what we thought of her." Mrs. Babbage took a sip of her coffee, looking as if she were prepared to defend herself to the death should either of us disagree.

Mrs. Reynolds continued. "To return to the subject at hand, Martha sleeps very heavily. When I questioned her, she said Julianne had come into the room just as Martha was falling asleep some time around ten-thirty. She thought she heard Julianne undress. That's all Martha remembers until dawn, when she was cold and discovered her coverlet had slipped from the bed. She glanced over to the other bed, and it was empty. I can guess what your next question will be. Julianne had not made the bed the day before so there is no way of knowing that she actually slept in her bed throughout the night. Since I found no sign of her having performed any of her duties, I assume that she went to the promontory at dawn. I wouldn't think that the accident happened just before Maggie saw Julianne in the river. Maggie must have arrived at least half an hour after Julianne died."

"That will be reassuring. Thank you."

I left the kitchen, hearing Mrs. Babbage's tongue wag the moment I had closed the door behind me.

~ 11

Tuesday, March 6

I MENTIONED TO MRS. ELDRIDGE that I wished to post a letter to my mother and grandparents—I had not heard from either and I was growing worried—and would it be possible to take the path into the village? Her eyes lit up at the suggestion, and she pretended to be anxious for a magazine when I knew she was waiting for a letter. Maggie and I were dispatched in extreme haste, for if I was to reach the mail before Mr. Eldridge or Evan, I would have to hurry.

"Whatever gave Mrs. Eldridge the idea to send you to Bradford?" Maggie asked as we walked toward the promontory.

"I did. In all truth, I've become tired of the house and felt the need to get away for a short time." And to see if the path could be navigated at night, to rule out the remote possibility that an outsider had visited Julianne.

Maggie nodded. "To think that Mrs. Eldridge has been inside almost day and night for over six months, except for the baby's christening, with nothing much to do. My wits couldn't stand it."

"Hasn't she had a lot of visitors?"

"Not for a while. Mr. Eldridge and the doctor thought visitors were tiring her out, showing up for days at a time." Maggie glanced involuntarily to the edge of the promontory. "They won't stay away for long. Another month, there'll be hoards of them. Believe me, you'll have enough to do then, running up and down the stairs, fetching this and that, helping Mrs. Eldridge change her clothes half a dozen times a day."

"I think it will be exciting."

"You won't for long. A lot of them are like Mrs. Hamilton with their noses stuck in the air. Hold on to me," Maggie ordered, reaching for my hand. "It's slippery here sometimes, and we don't want you to fall."

I was about to comment that I was a grown woman, capable of taking care of myself, when my boot sank into the half-frozen mud. With my other hand I picked up my skirts.

"It never really dries out here because of the trees and the puddles. In the spring it's easier to go around the path in places rather than through it."

I could well believe it. The path was a deeply rutted trail, steep, full of bits of root that could trip you and perilously smooth rocks. The path turned sharply to follow the river, leveling in the process, and we walked upon a carpet of pine needles. Even with a full moon, visibility would not be good. You could, however, use a lantern until almost at the top of the hill and not be seen.

Maggie let go of my hand. "From here on, there are only a few rough spots. Every other year or so the path gets fixed, trees chopped down, gravel poured into the holes. I expect that Mr. Eldridge will have it done in April. He likes to walk sometimes when the weather is nice."

"I can't imagine why Mrs. Eldridge thought I could get lost."

"A huge tree fell down in a storm last month, right across the path, and you have to go into the woods to go around it, and the woods are thicker down there."

"Why are the trees so small up here?"

"There was a big fire, about the time I was twelve or thirteen, and a large part of the woods burned down. The big trees that were close to the house were cut down so it wouldn't burn. You see, part of the roof was burned by blowing embers, so they had to rebuild. That's when Pete got hurt falling from the roof. He was only a boy, out helping his father. His leg never did grow properly after that. It was broken in a couple of places. Mr. Eldridge, being the kind of man he is, promised that Pete would never have to worry about a job. That's how badly he felt about it."

In a surprisingly short time, we reached the fallen tree. The crown reached into the water. There was no way we could climb over it. "Mind you don't slip on the leaves," Maggie told me, "and watch out for roots."

"Do you know that you're talking to me as if I were a child?"

Maggie laughed. "By the time Jon Frederick is old enough not to need a nurse, I won't remember what it's like to talk to another adult." She slipped gracefully between the saplings, and I followed suit, not quite as gracefully, and managed to impale my skirt once.

I was winded, and a fine sheen of perspiration covered my forehead despite the coolness of the day. "This isn't an easy walk," I commented breathlessly, as I traversed the last stretch of ground before reaching the path again.

"Doesn't seem that bad to me. A few more trips and you won't think anything of coming this way. There's my house." Maggie ran ahead of me as fast as her skirts would allow. It seemed that from nowhere several little girls appeared and ran toward her with outstretched arms. By the time I arrived, she had completed kissing each of them.

"Lydia, I would like you to meet Becky, Charity, and Ann." All the little girls had their father's red hair and green eyes but their mother's small face. They smiled at me shyly.

"Pete's parents live across the path." Both houses were typical saltboxes with small front yards and chickens in the back. Two black dogs romped enthusiastically behind Maggie's house. "Clara, that's Pete's mother, she's been looking after the children while I'm gone. Come inside and meet her." Maggie and the girls led me into the warm kitchen where a stout gray-haired woman was busy baking bread.

"Maggie!" The older woman embraced her daughter-in-law affectionately. "You're the last person I expected to see today. And you must be Lydia." She pumped my hand. "Sit down, sit down. Pete's out chopping wood. Charity, run and get your father." She watched as the child scampered from the room.

"Maggie, you can stay for a while, can't you?"

"I can. Lydia is going into the village to mail a letter."

"What a pity. I'll have a nice cup of chocolate ready for you when you get back, then. Do you like fresh bread? That should be ready, too, by then."

"As a matter of fact, I do."

"Good. And I have some wonderful jam."

She reminded me of my own grandmother, ever anxious to feed any guest. She was always disappointed that my father never gained an ounce of weight no matter how often she fed him sugar cookies or rich pies, and it wasn't as if my mother didn't do her best on her own.

"Before you leave, you have to see my youngest," Maggie said. She went into the next room and brought back her son. "Say hello, James."

James was eleven months older than Jon Frederick and had curly brown hair. "You must miss your baby dreadfully." James looked at me with curious brown eyes, but said nothing.

"When you have had three already, the fourth baby isn't that exciting."

The door burst open, and Charity reappeared, followed at a slower pace by her father. "Nice to see you again," he said to me.

I smiled at him. "I'd better post my letter. I should be back in a few minutes."

Back outside, I surveyed the two houses. Carrying a lantern would draw attention, if not from the inhabitants then from the dogs who barked energetically at me. Going around the houses would take you much deeper into the woods, and they looked difficult to cross. It could be done, of course, but why would anyone undertake such a journey not even knowing if Julianne would appear, even if she had an interest in any local boy?

Whoever had killed her had to have come from the Eldridge house.

I walked on to the village in a black mood. How preferable it would have been if Julianne had died in some bizarre accident. She had been no friend of mine, and had I known her better, I'm sure I would have liked her even less. I had been brought up to be decent and honorable and would never stoop to accepting bribes and the like.

But I was lying to myself, I realized with disturbing clarity.

I had learned what it was like to be desperate. What would I have done if I were beautiful and courageous? Would I be so proper and righteous then? I wasn't sure, for I too had learned the value of deceit.

I sighed and went to post my letter. As nothing was waiting for Mrs. Eldridge and Ned had yet to look up from his perusal of the catalogs, much less talk to me, I returned quickly to Maggie's home.

The entire family was gathered in the kitchen, and as promised the warm bread and chocolate were waiting for me. As soon as I had eaten, Maggie bade *au revoir* to her family, and we trudged up the hill again.

"Do you think you can manage to find your way down the next time?" she asked me.

"Easily. I was wondering, does the path ever get used in the evening for strolls and the like?"

"It does in the summer, but I wouldn't say that happens often. It really is just used as a shortcut for the help going between the Eldridge house and Bradford."

"I don't think I've seen anyone use the path except you."

"The girls and the stableboys use it all the time. Mrs. Babbage wouldn't walk unless the house were on fire. Mrs. Reynolds gets into town often enough without having to use the path, although in the summer she'll take it when Mr. Reynolds is busy elsewhere. Of course, the winter wind does keep people indoors."

"What about now, though? Wouldn't it make you nervous to walk all alone? The woods are dark in the afternoon."

Maggie looked at me uncomprehendingly. "Why should I worry? We don't have bears or wolves or tramps. I've never heard anything bad happening here until Julianne's accident. You'll soon get used to it. Then it will be just like walking on the streets of Providence."

"I've never walked very far alone in Providence either and

never at night unless I absolutely had to. We do have tramps and a lot of other unsavory people who would take advantage of a woman alone."

Maggie shook her head. "I can't even imagine what Providence must be like, then. I've never been farther than Putnam, and that isn't very different from Bradford, just bigger. What can you do in Providence that you can't do here?"

"Not much," I confessed. "At least, my family never did much. You can go to theaters and lectures at night. There are church activities and club meetings. On Sundays we would go to a park. My father on occasion would go see a boxing match or a horse race."

"That doesn't sound much more exciting than Bradford."

"We had a lot of stores, though. You could spend an entire day just going from store to store."

"I wouldn't like that unless I had a lot of money to spend as I pleased."

A valid point, I conceded. "Well," I said, conjuring up Providence in my mind, "the streets are almost always busy. At night there are so many lights that it's hard to see the stars. There are all sorts of restaurants with different kinds of food and bakeries, and the smells spill onto the street. You have the feeling that you can meet interesting people just by walking on the downtown streets. Or if you just want to walk, you can do so, just walk for miles and miles and still be in the city, still surrounded by people and homes."

"Lydia, you're beginning to sound homesick."

"I don't think I was until this minute. It seems so strange to live in such a fine house, standing in the middle of the woods, the nearest neighbors a mile away."

"Didn't Mr. Veazey say what it was like?" Maggie asked.

"He did say that some women didn't like to go so far into the country. I didn't think anything of it, but it was a shock to see Bradford for the first time. Why doesn't Mr. Eldridge move to Boston?"

"This is his home. That makes it sort of like family. My relatives, by marriage or kin, they're not grand or always nice, but they're still family. I think that's what it's like for him. It doesn't matter that it isn't exciting or that there aren't a lot of fancy places. Even if he were in Boston all the time, I don't think he would just go to balls and operas and theaters. He likes reading and looking at that queer stuff from the other side of the world. He can do that just as well here as in a great big city."

"Are you afraid of him?" I had to ask.

"No." She smiled at me. "I've known him, at least by sight, all of my life. Both my parents worked for him. So does my brother, in the mill."

"Mr. Eldridge makes me nervous," I confessed. "He looks so stern."

"He's always looked that way. I'll admit that I don't know what to say to him when he comes to see Jon Frederick. It's not that I could talk to him about cooking or sewing or babies."

"He doesn't talk much about his children, except for Millicent."

"He dotes on her something awful. The baby, too, although he doesn't show it very often."

I couldn't contain my curiosity. "What's wrong with Hugh that Mr. Eldridge holds him in such disregard?"

"He got kicked out of Harvard, you know, for gambling and drinking and a few other things, but don't say I told you or I'll never hear the end of it."

"I'm sure he's not the first one."

"No, but he's the first Eldridge not to be fine and proper. I'm sure he will be when he's a bit older, but Mr. Eldridge is impatient. I like Hugh myself. He's a kindhearted young man, and if his father weren't so rich and powerful, no one would think it odd that Hugh isn't ambitious. Maybe if he knew he had to earn a living, he'd try harder."

"What about Evan? He doesn't talk much about himself."

She gave me an appraising look. "What, are you sweet on him?"

I blushed. "Certainly not!"

"He likes you. He told me so."

"You're teasing."

"I am not. He told me that a couple of days ago when he came into the nursery looking for Mr. Eldridge. Now, if you don't like him, why ask about him?"

"I'm merely curious. I get to hear about everyone in the household except him. Besides, I asked about a few other people as well."

"That was only until you got around to Evan. I know he's from Pennsylvania. His parents are Welsh. I don't think either of them is alive, at least he never talks about them. Probably doesn't want to, if you ask me. His father worked in a mine and I guess was a rough sort who cuffed his children around. Evan may have always had food on the table, but little else. From what I've heard, he's got to where he is all on his own with no help from them. He's sharp as a whip, I can tell you that much. My brother said that Evan didn't know much about the way a mill is run, but in no time at all he knew everything."

"Maggie, you're of little help."

"Sorry. You stand to find out much more about him than I ever could."

"He has yet to tell me anything personal about himself. You hear all the gossip."

"Oh, is it gossip you want to know about? He doesn't have a steady interest, if you get my drift."

I needed to banish a small wisp of doubt. "Was he ever fond of Julianne?"

"A bit, perhaps. Once."

That explained why he had reacted so strongly to the news of her death and ran half dressed to the river. And then what about Mr. Eldridge, deliberately going to see for himself, when he knew the situation was hopeless? Was that the murderer returning to the scene of the crime? If I had killed someone, I knew that I would never go near that spot again, could not bear to look at the dead. Hugh had not gone farther than the door and then proceeded to get drunk.

"Maggie, what had Julianne been like? Her personality has completely receded from my mind. Mrs. Babbage doesn't seem to have liked her, and Mrs. Reynolds made excuses for her, so I feel that she wasn't the best maid."

"Nobody likes being a maid. After about a year you get very tired of it, at least that's what Martha tells me. Julianne was tired of living here and would have gone to Boston if she could have gotten work."

"Couldn't she work as a maid there?" I asked.

"It's a bit hard, I hear, what with all the Irish still coming there in droves. They work cheap. So she had to have money to tide her over, and it wasn't like she had family or friends up there to help her. She thought she might find a job as a seamstress."

I laughed bitterly. "She would soon be wishing she were back here making the beds."

"Julianne had high hopes for a well-to-do husband and thought she had a better chance in Boston. There's nothing but farmers and mill help around here, unless you count people like the Brewsters and Eldridges, and they always marry their own kind. Not that she aimed that high. She was no fool who believed in fairy tales."

"Did you like her?"

"I can't speak ill of the dead," Maggie replied evasively.

"I've never known why that should make a difference. When you're alive, you can't defend yourself against gossip either. At least when you're dead, it can't hurt you."

"I'm not as sure as that myself," Maggie replied. "Who knows what it's like to be dead, what they know and don't know? If they can't see and can't hear, why have a fancy funeral, why bother with one at all? Anyway, I don't like to talk about them. It seems wrong."

"I'll assume you didn't like her, then."

Maggie sighed. "You won't give up, will you? All right then, I got along with her well enough, but she always seemed to be sneaking around. Waiting for the hallway to be empty before using the stairs, things like that. I have never liked anyone behaving like that. I don't know what she expected to hear or see."

But she *had* seen or heard something incriminating, I thought. The money indicated as much.

"Tell the truth, Lydia. Why do you want to know so much about her?"

I was silent for a moment while I debated how much to say. What I had found out about the money I had better not reveal, as it would put me in a bad light. "I keep thinking that I saw someone with Julianne that night."

"If you weren't dreaming. And what difference does that make? Julianne died in the morning."

"No one really knows for sure. Martha was in bed and half asleep when Julianne came into their room the evening before. What if she went out again to meet someone from the house and didn't come back?"

"That's a big if. You haven't told anybody else this, have you?"

"Not really."

"Well, don't talk about it. You wouldn't keep your job long if people started to think you thought them capable of murder. Besides, I know all the people in that house. No one would kill anyone."

"How can you be so sure?"

"When you get to know them longer, you'll understand."

"You haven't known Evan that long," I pointed out.

"No, I suppose not, but I know him well enough. Maybe in the city you could be mean and still show an angelic face to the world because people wouldn't know all about you. Here they do. Remember, I told you that there is no such thing as a secret, that everyone knows everyone else's business."

"Just possibly that's what got Julianne killed. She learned something she shouldn't have."

"If that's true, it'll come out in time. I have no doubt of that. If you're wrong, it'll do no one any good to talk."

"It could have been an accident," I grudgingly conceded.

"I'm glad to see you can be reasonable. I won't say a word to anybody concerning what we talked about."

I would have pursued the matter further had we not reached a difficult stretch in the path that demanded all my concentration. We reached the house close to the noon hour. The meal would soon be served. I all but flew to my room to change and into Mrs. Eldridge's room to report the lack of mail. She was visibly disappointed.

"I expect it was too soon," she said. "Never mind. I shall sketch you instead. We'll go to the den and have luncheon served there."

She made me sit perfectly still for upwards of two hours while she worked with her pencil, producing a very good likeness of me, although she was dissatisfied. She gave the sketch to me to send to my mother. Mrs. Eldridge was halfway through another sketch, by which time my neck was exceedingly stiff on account of having to look over my right shoulder, when Mr. Eldridge appeared unexpectedly.

"Good afternoon, ladies," he said congenially. "Lydia, would you excuse us for a few minutes? I'll inform you when we're finished."

I left, but the few minutes stretched well beyond an hour, and when I returned to Mrs. Eldridge, her mood was none too cheerful.

"We will be going to dinner soon. Help me get dressed."

"Are you sure you feel fit enough? You look weak."

"I feel weak, but I will not eat in my room again." With each word she sounded increasingly angry.

She was barely polite to me as I helped her into a beautiful green gown. Twice she admonished me to be careful as I combed her hair when I knew very well that I had not caused her injury.

We had our usual excellent meal. For once, Mr. Eldridge played the genial host, while his wife sat moodily, picking irritably at the food and answering in monosyllables until he gave up. Hugh had walked into the room in the best spirits I had seen him in many days, until he noticed how morose his mother was. He was instantly subdued. Only Evan was his usual unperturbed self, quickly engaging Mr. Eldridge in conversation to avoid any unpleasant periods of silence and then turning to me.

"Lydia, did I happen to see you in town this morning?" Evan asked.

Mr. Eldridge stopped chewing to look at me.

"Ah, yes, I went to mail a letter to my mother. I used the path." I felt Mrs. Eldridge's eyes upon me. "Maggie showed me the way."

"You could have waited for us to take you," Mr. Eldridge said.

"Nonsense," Mrs. Eldridge snapped in a disagreeable tone.

"That would put her at the mercy of your schedule."

"A carriage could have been prepared," Hugh said. "It would not have taken long."

"It was just a short walk," I said quickly, "and rather pleasant. I'm sure it will be lovely a few months hence."

"Saratoga offers—" Mr. Eldridge began.

"Nothing!" Mrs. Eldridge interrupted, eyes blazing. "I said I won't go there!"

"I wasn't about to suggest that you do," Mr. Eldridge replied, keeping his anger disguised by a mild voice while his eyes betrayed him.

"Then why bring it up?"

"Because the last few days have been an additional burden," Mr. Eldridge said quietly.

"Julianne was hardly an intimate friend or member of this family, and although her death was most regrettable, I am not likely to suffer great despair. If I go anywhere, it will be no farther than Putnam or Hartford and then only for the briefest of visits. I should not like to be absent from home for long, especially since you won't let me take Jon Frederick with me."

"The weather is far too difficult to undertake such a journey with an infant."

"You could visit Millicent," Hugh suggested.

She turned to her son. "You would, of course, escort me."

"If I have to," he answered slowly.

"It wouldn't be the lure of Boston that prompts such a gallant gesture?"

He looked helplessly at his father. "Since whatever I say will be misinterpreted, I might as well stop talking. I only wish I knew what I have done incorrectly this time."

"You've been riding rather far lately," Mrs. Eldridge commented dryly.

"Riding, Mother, only riding. Perhaps you think I need an escort." He looked at me. "A few more riding lessons and Lydia can serve in that capacity also."

Evan looked as if he were about to say something on my behalf when Mr. Eldridge cleared his throat.

"Shall we declare a truce?" Mr. Eldridge requested.

"Anything you wish, my dear," his wife replied acidly.

The ensuing silence was most uncomfortable. Evan studied the people around him appraisingly. He turned to me. "I presume you met Maggie's family."

I nodded.

"Clara Marsh used to help look after Mr. Eldridge."

A flicker of a smile passed over Mr. Eldridge's lips.

"I have heard that she was a veritable bully in the nursery."

The smile reappeared. "She was most definitely that. I was four when she started to work here, and I believe she was only ten years older. Originally she was to help look after my sisters, who were rather inclined to be mischievous."

"Among other things, they used to go sliding down the banisters," Hugh said. "It is most difficult to picture Aunt Isabelle being able to do that. If she tried it now, the banister would break. To put it mildly, her appetite exceeds her height." He lowered his eyes, anticipating a rebuke for talking of his elders in such a manner.

Mr. Eldridge overlooked the remark. "Clara was always putting my toys away just after I had gotten them out to play with. She used to have to chase me to put me to bed, and then when she was done with me, there were my sisters still running about. When my parents were entertaining, she used to put us in one room and then stand guard at the door, to guarantee we didn't escape and disturb the guests."

Evan, as usual, had done his job well. Mr. Eldridge spent the rest of the meal talking about his sisters and seemed to have completely forgotten his wife.

After dinner we adjourned to the drawing room. Mrs. Eldridge sat at the piano and played a few melancholy Russian pieces while Mr. Eldridge had a new book about Japan and was quickly immersed in his reading. Hugh got out the family album and showed me pictures of his aunt. Isabelle was, I most plainly saw, rather wide, somewhat like a ship. In contrast, her husband was thin and balding and very dry-looking, but Hugh assured me that Samuel Coldwell was a fascinating man who taught history at a college.

I saw old and faded photographs of the Eldridge sisters, all dressed in ribbons and ruffles, their long hair held back by bows, and in the middle, looking exceedingly glum, was Mr. Eldridge, easily recognizable even when he was still wearing dresses and had long hair himself. He looked much happier on his pony.

Then, as Mr. Eldridge became a young man, photographs appeared of Mrs. Eldridge and her family. There were several large portraits of Mr. and Mrs. Eldridge in their wedding attire. She had always been a beautiful woman, and I had to admit that Mr. Eldridge looked handsome. Perhaps he still was, and only my comparative youth made me blind. I glanced at him. His eyebrows were knit together in concentration as he read. He was a robust man, something I kept forgetting, for I automatically thought of him as a settled, elderly gentleman. I realized with a start that age was not absolute. Other men might have accomplished all they would at his age and laid aside the dreams of youth, but Mr. Eldridge would continue to nurture his ambitions. He would plan and scheme and achieve, for in his heart the same fire burned as in his youth.

"Here's a picture of my uncle David," Hugh said, turning the page.

I smiled at David Veazey as a child, sitting like an angel on Mrs. Eldridge's lap.

"And here I am, with my sister, of course."

They were the usual childhood photographs: the children posed together, the children with their parents and cousins and toys. I noticed that as they approached adulthood, it was Millicent who appeared more often. Millicent posed at a grand ball. Millicent posed with her horse. Millicent posed with her fiancé. Before my eyes I noticed how she grew in confidence and grace, while Hugh seemed to retreat further within himself and become more shy and insecure.

I would love to have had photographs of my father working at the office, his sleeves rolled up, a thoughtful expression on his face; of Aunt Louisa baking her delectable Christmas cookies; my grandparents reading to my younger sisters just before bedtime; of my mother when she wasn't careworn, when she could still laugh.

I felt like crying suddenly. I wanted to go home where I

belonged. But I belonged to the house on Pembroke Street, and that was gone, lost forever.

That night I felt unaccountably restless. I could not sleep. I could not sit by the window for fear that I would see Julianne's ghost standing there, beseeching me for help when I didn't know what to do. I climbed out of bed, put on my wrap, and went downstairs to the library to seek solace amid the books.

I sat on the sofa, staring at nothing, not wanting to think, and yet unable to banish thoughts of my mother and sisters who would be huddled in the cold and the dark. I fought the childish impulse to sob wholeheartedly, but couldn't completely stop the tears from coming.

"What are you doing here?"

I hastily brushed the tears from my eyes and blinked at the light cast by the lamp that Evan was carrying. "I couldn't sleep, so I came for a book."

"It's not easy to read the titles in the dark." He put the lamp on the nearest table and sat down beside me.

Why was it that I was always getting myself into embarrassing positions with Evan? I pulled the wrap more tightly around myself.

"You haven't been crying because you're feeling homesick?"

"Of course not. I've only got about five and a half months left. Why should that distress me?" The forlorn note in my voice betrayed me.

Evan put his arm around my shoulders in a brotherly fashion. "The months will go quickly enough when the warm weather comes. Now tell me why you are upset."

I should keep my own counsel, I thought, but Evan's eyes were filled with such compassion and understanding that I could not help but blurt out my thoughts. "I'm worried about my family. I haven't heard anything and I don't know if they're all right." A sob shook my body, and I laid my head on his shoulder the way I had with my father when I was a little girl and afraid of the dark. I suddenly felt small and helpless again, and it didn't matter that in the morning I would think myself a fool for behaving this way. All I wanted at the moment was to be held and comforted.

"I'm sure they are all right," Evan said, stroking my hair. "They would have let you know if something was wrong."

"No, they wouldn't. They wouldn't want me to worry. My mother's health isn't very good and . . . and—" I bit down on my tongue. I couldn't tell him how afraid I was that they didn't have the money to send me letters, that Eugenia could get hurt coming home late at night, that my grandparents' charity was virtually exhausted.

"You have an overdeveloped sense of responsibility. They'll be fine without you."

"I would like to believe you. It's just that my family has always been protective toward one another. Louise, my youngest sister, never found out how sick Papa was until the day he died. I know that if anything was wrong, they would do the same toward me, to spare me pain."

Why did I have to think of my father now? It only made the tears burst out. Wordlessly Evan handed me his handkerchief and waited patiently for the emotional storm to subside.

"I noticed your expression when you were looking at the album," he said when I had stopped crying. "Each time you turned a page, your eyes became sadder, and I knew you were thinking of home."

I brushed the last tear away and handed back the handerchief. "Don't you ever long for your home?"

"There isn't very much to remember fondly in my case. The mines are grim places to work, and the people are equally grim. That makes it easier to leave."

"When was the last time you saw any of your family?"

"Three years ago. They weren't glad to see me."

"I'd have thought that they would be proud of you."

Evan shook his head. "I suppose they were jealous. Jealous that I had escaped when they couldn't. It isn't, after all, as if I had suddenly become a wealthy man and could help them all to a better life."

"Don't you ever feel lonely, surrounded by strangers?"

"No. I'm very comfortable."

For the first time I caught him in a lie. He was lonely and adrift from all ties, caught somewhere between the Eldridges and the servants. That was why Julianne had been displeased with me: she knew, as I had not, that an attraction could develop between Evan and me because we held analogous positions and would rob her of his help.

"In a few months, you'll stop feeling like an outsider. Mrs. Eldridge will be going into Putnam soon, and she'll be taking you with her. I think you will feel better. You'll have other people to talk to, including a few girls your own age."

I thought of the condescending look Mrs. Hamilton had given me. "What would we talk about? I don't have fine clothes. I didn't go to a fancy school or attend balls. I'm sure they wouldn't be interested in someone like me."

"Self-pity?"

"I'm merely the daughter of a not particularly successful bank clerk."

"You are kind and thoughtful and intelligent." His eyes swept over me. "I also think you're pretty."

Suddenly his arm didn't feel so brotherly. His hand slipped beneath my hair, and I could feel his fingers on my bare neck. A shiver ran down my spine. I have to go back to my room, I wanted to say—and didn't. From somewhere far away, I heard my mother's shocked voice, but it went away amid all the unfamiliar sensations. My heart was beating fast, and my breath came rapidly. I was hot and cold at the same time.

"Evan," I began.

He tilted up my head and kissed me gently on the lips.

I didn't move. His hands traveled down my shoulders to my waist, his lips to my ears, down my neck. He pulled me close. I could feel him breathing, his own heart beating faster.

I pushed him away. "Don't. It's not—" My thoughts were in confusion. I ran from the room.

For a long while afterward, I lay in my bed, wondering how many other women had been a part of Evan's life, or had none been a part of his life, existing merely on the periphery? He couldn't possibly be falling in love with me! I bolted upright. How could I have run from him when he was willing to risk rejection, when he was willing to put himself in an awkward position by revealing his intentions? I was suddenly inordinately and most improperly curious about just what he would have done had I let him.

I buried my head under the covers and sought refuge in sleep. As it happened, I lay awake long enough to hear Mr. Eldridge's door open and his footsteps slowly and with stealth ascend the stairs. He did not return before I fell asleep.

∼∽ *12*

Wednesday, March 7

THE NEXT MORNING DAWNED AGREEABLY, without a thought of Julianne until after I had performed my ablutions and had dressed. I had just closed my door and was turning toward Mrs. Eldridge's bedroom when Mr. Eldridge quickly stepped out of his room and walked in my direction. He had to have been waiting for me.

"I just checked on my wife," he said in a low tone, standing so close to me that my back was literally pressed against the wall, "and she seems to be sleeping."

"It is still early."

"Yes, that's true." He stared at me. "How much of the tonic has she taken over the past several days?"

"I don't know, sir," I replied, keeping my voice steady. "I have not had the opportunity to find out. Or to give her any."

He scratched his chin. "Yes, things have been hectic lately."

His tone infuriated me. Hectic! A young woman had died a violent death! Outwardly I remained still, too afraid to speak my mind.

"You'll have to try harder."

"Are you sure the tonic is so good that it is worth all this trouble?" I asked timidly.

"Most assuredly," he answered coldly, making it quite clear that he expected no more such comments from me.

I swallowed. "I will do my best, then, to see that she takes it."

"How has she been feeling? She insists I am exaggerating her condition."

Just then a sound, as if Mrs. Eldridge had turned over in bed, came from within her room.

He grabbed my arm and propelled me toward the stairs as my heart fluttered with alarm at this unexpected treatment.

"Well?" he demanded.

For a moment I looked at him dumbly, my nervousness increasing at his scowl. "I would say that she is pacing herself well, sir," I blurted out.

"Not so loud," he cautioned and pulled me down the stairs. "My wife and I have had enough disagreements about her health without her hearing me questioning you. I just don't understand what is happening. That fool Patterson comes up with one excuse after another to explain why she lingers in her present condition. She hardly talks to me about her health. I merely want to know what is going on. That is not unreasonable, is it?"

"No, sir."

"Evan told me that I should stop talking about sending her away. What difference can two weeks make? The baby will be just the same when she returns, and he is much too young to miss her."

"She would miss him," I replied quietly.

"Uhm, I suppose so. Still, it would be so much better for all concerned if she got her health back as quickly as possible. Don't you think so?"

"Yes, sir."

He walked toward the dining room, and I followed at his heels like a frightened dog. "See to it that she takes the blasted tonic. At least then if it doesn't do any good, I can tell Patterson that it didn't work."

"I will—" I stopped and stared openmouthed. Hugh was in the dining room! For breakfast! His face was puffy and his eyes still sleepy, but he greeted us with enthusiasm.

Mr. Eldridge looked at him with some amazement and, I fancied, with some approval. Evan arrived just after we did.

I blushed when he said good morning.

"I thought we should go riding together," Hugh told me casually as he buttered his bread, "if you think you're up to it." He laid the bread aside and looked at me with imploring eyes.

I quickly swallowed my oatmeal. I thought that Hugh might be Julianne's murderer and, fearing I had some inkling of the events, wished to lure me to my own doom. "I do not feel comfortable undertaking such a step."

"We wouldn't go far, really just around the outskirts of the property. I would be with you at every step, and we would go no faster than a walk."

"I don't know." I looked beseechingly at Evan.

He came to my aid. "The last lesson was several days ago."

A bright red spot appeared on Hugh's cheeks. "Lydia did very well. She has a natural ability. Please, Lydia," he implored, his assurance obviously crumbling.

His plight touched my heart. I was sure to be observed the entire time and thus quite safe. "I shall have to ask your mother's permission," I replied, knowing all too well that she would acquiesce.

And so at ten o'clock, with the usual audience secreted behind the curtains, I again mounted Beauregard.

Hugh was on a black stallion that could barely contain its energy, yet he sat nonchalantly in the saddle, guiding the horse with the lightest of touches, his face confident.

I experienced nothing but trepidation as he led Beauregard out beyond the stable. I thought the wind was strong enough to knock me from the saddle, even if the jostling of the horse didn't.

"Relax, Lydia," Hugh commanded. "Your back will be stiff enough as it is without adding more discomfort. You can't fall off. Horses are very large. Like ships almost. You know what it's like. At first the rolling and pitching are awkward, and then you get used to it and it's nothing at all."

I did not mention that I had never been on a ship and had no intention of ever being on one if I had my way. I smiled halfheartedly, not really listening to the instructions he was giving me. "I don't believe that this will ever be easy."

"Certainly it will. In another few weeks, you will be cantering through the pastures. You'll have lots of company, between my mother and my sister, and think how quickly you can visit the Brewsters by taking the shortcut through the woods. It will give you the opportunity to spend more time with Mrs. Hamilton."

"That is not much encouragement," I pointed out.

He looked at me with bewildered eyes. "So you don't like her. Neither does my sister. In fact, I don't know of any woman who likes her except Mrs. Brewster, and I'm sure she has her reservations."

I smiled. "What do you think of her, then?"

"She is a delightful creature." His voice was filled with admiration. "I only wish I could help her. Father likes her and feels sorry for her, too, being left a widow at such a young age." He grinned. "Mother once said that Mr. Hamilton's death spared him a far worse fate, being married to her."

I couldn't help but laugh. "Your mother didn't say that."

"Yes, she did. I've forgotten what it was that made Mother so angry at the time. It was last summer. Mother was seriously thinking of forbidding the house to her, but Father dissuaded her. She had only been a widow for a few months then, and he thought she needed people to help her with her grief."

"Was she grief-stricken?"

He thought for a moment. "She bore up rather well. Anyway, Mother has been so annoyed with Mrs. Hamilton that visits to or from the Brewsters have all but stopped."

I looked at her window. "That's sad."

"It's not that Mother's in good enough condition to receive many visitors or to travel. She has terrible spells at times, and it would be most awkward if they were to occur in the middle of a trip."

"But she's going to Putnam, isn't she?"

He halted his horse and reached over to mine to do the same. "This is the first I've heard of such a proposal. I suppose that means she is feeling better." He thought for a moment, then we resumed riding. "I've been expecting the family to inundate us at any moment, what with this mild winter weather we've been having. Once she has visited them, nothing will keep them away. Turn the horse slightly so you don't end up in the woods."

I did as I was told. "Wouldn't you like that? You could go riding with your cousins." I didn't know what else young men would do together.

"They are not enthusiasts." He smiled wickedly at some secret thought. "At least not for horses."

"What would you do, then?"

"You're being very curious."

"I don't have any brothers or uncles who live close by, so I don't know what men do. My father didn't like to spend time away from the family and only socialized with like-minded men, who also preferred the company of their families."

"We go to sporting events. Like horse racing." He patted his horse's neck affectionately. "We play billiards. That sort of thing. Turn up there, Lydia, then go back to the stables."

Sweeter words I could not imagine. The horse, most unhappily I thought, responded to my tugging at his reins.

"Remember to be gentle. A horse's mouth is sensitive."

"Yes, Hugh," I replied meekly. The ordeal was almost over.

Just outside the building, Hugh dismounted and turned to help me down. His horse, who stood a little ahead of mine, flicked its tail. The long hair brushed across Beauregard's face. He jerked his head up and took an abrupt step backward.

To my horror, I began to slide down his rump. Suddenly I felt Hugh's hands around my waist.

"Are you all right?" he asked anxiously, lifting me down from the horse.

I nodded mutely, having lost my breath. "Just let me sit down for a moment." I stumbled to a bale of straw and collapsed on it.

Hugh knelt beside me. "Are you sure you're all right? You've gone deathly pale."

"Don't worry." Though it would not do to admit this in front of a gentleman, corsets made it hard to breathe just when you needed to the most. "It was merely the surprise to find myself slipping. I wasn't holding on very well because I didn't think the horse would do anything silly at this point."

"It's my fault. I should have immediately turned my mount over to Ken."

"No harm was done, and I don't think anyone saw the mishap." I heard footsteps. "The groom is coming. There is no reason to start talk now by looking so worried."

He stood up. "Thank you, Lydia," he said softly. "I can't express—"

Ken came out of the stable. "Sir?"

"Take the horses," Hugh said. "We're finished for the day."

The man nodded, grabbed the reins, and took the brutes away as Hugh stared after them.

"Can you stand?" Hugh whispered to me once he decided we could not be overheard.

"Of course. I didn't really fall. You caught me just in time."

Nevertheless, he helped me to my feet. "I must not be as good a teacher as I thought I was. I'm not really any good at anything else, so it should come as no surprise."

"That's not true."

"You could have been frightfully injured."

"But I wasn't. Stop worrying and stop looking so guilty."

"You undoubtedly never want to go riding with me again."

I would most certainly have loved to agree with him, but I couldn't hurt his feelings. "We can continue. Give me a few days to overcome my nervousness."

He looked at me closely. "You don't mean that."

"Yes I do."

"I'll ask you again in a few days to see if you still feel that way. I wouldn't get mad at you if you never want to ride again, and neither would anybody else. Are you going to tell my mother about this?" he asked apprehensively.

"I see no reason to."

He looked immensely relieved. "If there is ever anything I can do for you in return, you will tell me, won't you?" He didn't wait for me to answer. "I know. When Mother goes to Putnam, I can go with you. Putnam is still a small town, but we could find something interesting to do."

"Hugh, that's not necessary."

"Perhaps I could persuade Father to let you go to Providence for a few days. I know that you'd like that very much. Uncle David will be visiting in a few weeks—you could go with him."

My family. I could see for myself that they were well. It would never happen, though. "Your mother would still need me." I couldn't keep from sounding dejected.

"If you only stayed away overnight, no harm would come. My mother has bushels of friends and relatives, all of whom would be delighted to look after her for a short duration."

"It's a wonderful idea," I said, for a minute believing that it was possible, but reality intruded. "What would your father say to such a proposition?"

"I could talk him into it; not too quickly, or he'll refuse. As you know, he sets great stock in family, and so your concern about the welfare of your mother and sisters would be understandable."

My only reason for hesitating further was that if I were gone, Mr. Eldridge might realize his wife had little need for me and decide to dismiss me, or if she were to become ill while I was gone, he could very easily be furious at me for daring to leave and take equally drastic steps. "I don't know."

"Leave it to me. This arrangement will work perfectly."

The rest of the morning passed quickly as my head was filled with thoughts of home. I ran up and down the stairs, fetching books and coffee, completely unmindful of the exertion. I only hoped that Mrs. Eldridge's health would show steady improvement, so that the idea would not be rejected outright. I forgot about Julianne.

Evan, Mrs. Eldridge, and I had the noonday meal together. Evan, for once, was not talkative, perhaps because he had not had the opportunity to apologize for the incident in the library and felt badly. Mrs. Eldridge was displeased that her husband had gone riding again and was equally silent. I wondered if he had ridden toward the Brewster house. Hugh was also occupying himself with the horses and apparently didn't feel like eating.

Dinner was equally uneventful, everyone maintaining a polite façade. We all retired to the drawing room after dessert and continued to expend as little conversation as necessary. Mrs. Eldridge and I occupied ourselves with needlework, she on an elaborate piano scarf while I preferred to embroider a silk coverlet for the baby. Mr. Eldridge and Evan played tireless games of backgammon. Hugh read. At nine Mrs. Eldridge decided it was best for the two of us to go to bed. Not until I returned to my room did I realize that I had left the coverlet downstairs. I yawned several times, not really wanting at all to go back, but equally determined to have my handiwork safely in my possession.

I went down the stairs. Long before I reached the partially open door of the drawing room, I heard the voices—the volume suppressed, but not the anger. Evan and Hugh again. I stopped, about to retreat, when I realized they were talking about me.

"Yes, I do question your behavior toward her," Hugh was saying.

Evan's sigh was loud. "And in what manner have I offended your sensibilities now?"

"I don't know. I just have the feeling that something's happened. The way she looked at you at breakfast this morning. She's suddenly acting differently when you're around."

"Damning evidence by all means."

Hugh almost snarled. "I'm being serious."

"What is it that you're expecting me to confess? That I've taken advantage of her? Lydia is far too intelligent for such behavior and she has far too much at stake, as you very well know. And what about you?"

I heard Evan rise from where he had been seated and walk swiftly across the floor.

"Should I start to speculate as to your motives? Question your behavior at the stables after that near mishap?"

So Hugh and I had been seen after all. Now I knew why Evan had been so silent at our meals.

"You don't have the right to spy on me," Hugh said angrily.

"Yes I do. Remember, your father requested that I keep an eye on you. Why this sudden interest in a young woman you normally wouldn't look at twice?"

"That isn't any of your concern, but it so happens I find her company agreeable. If you were a gentleman, you wouldn't stoop to spying on me, even if my father requested you to do so. I haven't done anything wrong."

"Oh? You may have been forced to leave Boston, but you haven't given up all the vices you acquired there—"

"Shut up."

"—drinking, and gambling, not to mention the whor—"

"I said shut up."

Just in time to avoid detection, I secreted myself in the dining room. I had a glimpse of Hugh as he stormed up the stairs, two steps at a time. Shortly thereafter, Evan extinguished all the lights and went toward the office.

I retrieved my coverlet and tiptoed to my room, afraid that I would encounter Hugh. Not so much as a flicker of light showed under his door. I sat on my bed and considered the two men.

Hugh liked me because I was like him, quiet, unobtrusive, and easily overlooked; Evan because he didn't have to be on guard with me, afraid of revealing himself. And whenever one took an interest in something, I was sure the other would quickly follow suit. They were like brothers, trapped in childish rivalry.

Eugenia and I had been like that from the time we were little girls, each worried that the other had a prettier dress or received more sweets at Christmas time. I spent an inordinate amount of time trying to assert my authority over her as the oldest sister, and she spent an equal amount of time proving that I couldn't control her; all of this done, of course, behind our parents' backs. Then we grew up and became very different: I enamored of books, she of handsome young men; and both beset by more serious problems than an extra bow on a dress.

Hugh, until the last few years, had held a cherished position in his father's eye. There had been no brothers, no comparisons with which he had had to contend until Millicent proved to be a formidable young woman and Evan entered the household. Jealousy and anger, aroused after childhood, are not always dispersed quickly. I was sure that Evan was also jealous of the carefree life Hugh had led and of his lack of responsibility. In any event, I seemed to have been inadvertently added to their list of rivalries.

∽ 13

Thursday, March 8

JULIANNE WAS BROUGHT BACK TO my mind with full force the next day when I saw the strands of long black hair wrapped in tissue paper on Mrs. Eldridge's nightstand. "As soon as we're done eating," she said, "I want you to see if I have enough pins to mount the wreath. And also dried flowers. I need small ones, and they have to be light-colored to contrast with Julianne's hair. I can't remember where I put them last, but they are somewhere in the cabinet."

I felt guilty that I had neglected my investigatory duties. It could not have been helped—there were too many people about when I was free—but I could at least have given Julianne more thought. I needed to talk to the Lippits, to ask if they knew about the money Julianne had hidden; and Martha, to find out more about Julianne's whereabouts during the night of her death. I also needed to find out about the tonic and to visit the tower, where Mr. Eldridge had gone the night of Julianne's demise, if I could find the opportunity.

I thought a lot about that tower as I breakfasted with Mrs. Eldridge in her room. Just what was he doing up there late at night that he couldn't do elsewhere in this vast house? Why was that room tacitly forbidden? If I were to hide information from family and servants, I think that would be the place I would choose. After all, the first-floor office was not really private, nor was his bedroom safe from curious eyes.

I had learned in my short stay here that it is better to be patient, devious, and circumspect than to be direct and forthright. It took me a good hour and a half to work the conversation toward the tower.

Mrs. Eldridge took a sip of her coffee before answering me. "He keeps all sorts of things up there—souvenirs from places he's been, his telescope, for when he feels like observing the stars. He claims that when we have company, it is the only quiet place in the house where he can read. He also enjoys the view immensely."

"Do you ever paint in the tower?"

"I wouldn't want to unless I felt compelled to paint the mill. The hills look monotonous from there, and so does the river, especially this time of year. The only use I've ever found for the room is to look down the path to see if anyone is coming, if I'm waiting for someone."

"I imagine it's also cold there, what with all those windows."

"Like deepest winter. That's why it's practically shut up now. There is no way to keep the cold out. You have never experienced the full effect of draftiness unless you're in the tower when the wind is howling."

I thought of the tenement. I knew far better than she.

"Mark my words, one of these days that room is going to be blown away." She sounded cheerful at the prospect. "I never did like that addition to the house, and I know the servants hate it when he uses it because they have to climb up an extra flight of stairs. It was built when the children were small and tended to cry rather noisily, and like all men, Mr. Eldridge found it extremely distracting. Besides, in those days he still had friends who were not married or so newly married that they had not had children yet, and they would play billiards, then smoke and play cards in the tower. I suppose it was better than to have that foul cigar smoke all over the house. It used to make Millicent wheeze." She nibbled at her roll. "I can scarcely wait for us to be together in Boston."

This was a baffling change in attitude. "I thought you didn't want to go there."

"Of course I do. Just not now. Let me give you a piece of advice for when you are married. When a husband begins to become too insistent to do things his way, you persistently reject his suggestions, even if you want to do them, until you are ready to acquiesce. That way he has the illusion of having succeeded in getting his way, and you get to do what you want in the first place. Then, should he propose to do something you actually don't want to do, he'll feel guilty about bullying you previously and back down more readily. Besides, by summer—and I won't travel to Boston earlier— so many difficulties will have resolved themselves. One way or another."

What was it that had to be resolved? I wondered. Would Mrs. Hamilton finally be gone or was Hugh to be sent back to school? Some decision had been reached, I felt, when I was not about. Considering how free they felt to discuss family matters that I would never have broached with a stranger, I felt that this decision was not as innocent as the lightly spoken words.

She pushed the tray of food away. "Help me get dressed," Mrs. Eldridge commanded. "I have many plans for today. I wish to become active in the Bradford Literary Society again, and they will meet tomorrow."

She had not so much as hinted at this before, and I immediately suspected an ulterior motive.

"I will need the brown dress back from the seamstress. You can get it today and any mail that is waiting. I have to catch up on my reading and choose a suitable book to bring to the meeting. There must be something new in the library by now, other than that dreadful one sent by my sister-in-law. The French can be so vulgar."

"Is the carriage going into town, or should I take the path?"

"You cannot possibly carry a dress all that distance. I'll order the carriage prepared for you."

Her toilette was completed in such haste that I had the suspicion she wanted me out of the way. In no time at all, I found myself in the carriage heading for town at a leisurely pace.

I called on the seamstress first.

Her hair was escaping in long tendrils, and her face was drawn. She shooed her small son away irritably. "I got the dress done this very minute," Dolly told me.

"I'm sorry you had to rush."

"It's not your fault, is it?" She hurried to her workroom, with me at her heels.

I cleared my throat, very reluctant to intrude on this busy woman's time with my ill-conceived plan better left to a Wilkie Collins tale. "Do you have a lot of work to do?"

"Enough to keep my hands going most of the day." She carefully started to fold the dress.

"I'm sure you can't wait for the warmer weather. It makes it so much easer to sew when your fingers aren't stiff from cold."

"I can't but agree," she said, glancing down at her worn hands.

"I was wondering, do you ever sew for anyone at the house, the servants, I mean?"

"Sometimes. Not too often, though, except for Julianne. She must have put every penny into clothes."

That confirmed that Julianne's additional source of money was long-standing. The dresses I had seen could not have been made quickly. I also had the impression that she paid up, for the seamstress would have mentioned money owed.

Dolly handed me the package. "Did Mrs. Eldridge say she will be needing anything else in the near future?"

Somewhat disheartened that she didn't want to talk further, I shook my head. "She hasn't mentioned anything to me."

"I'll have time in the next week."

I could hear a note of anxiety in her voice. Feast or famine was the usual cycle. "I'll be sure to tell her."

I left in a thoughtful state and almost forgot the mail. Ned was waiting on a customer when I entered the establishment, but he quickly stopped talking. "You calling on mail for Mrs. Eldridge?"

I nodded.

"These came." He handed me a newspaper, a magazine, and a letter from Millicent. "Your name's Hall, right?"

I ceased my perusal of the magazine. "Yes, it is."

Even before he handed the envelope to me, I recognized the writing. My mother had written! I tore open the envelope anxiously.

Darling Lydia,

I am glad to hear that you like your position. We are doing well, although Caroline has developed an annoying cough. It is no more than a cold, but her illness presses upon my time, and I cannot write more at this moment. I will write you a longer letter within a week. I am counting the days until we will all be together once more.

Mother

I was relieved. Caroline's condition did not seem unduly serious. Still, the letter brought back to mind that while I spent my days in luxury, they were living in poverty. I prayed the days would pass swiftly until I was paid so that I could arrange for money to be sent to them.

Upon returning to the house, I discovered that Mrs. Eldridge was not in her room. I did a quick search of the floor and found that she was nowhere about. Everyone else was apparently busy. This was my chance. I opened the cabinet. Beside the tonic, there were several old letters written to her by Mr. Eldridge, and a diary. I skimmed through the late entries; there was nothing personal, merely the barest mention of the events that transpired: my arrival, Julianne's death, but nothing even remotely helpful to me in my investigation. I put them back.

I looked at the bottle. I wished I had the slightest faith in Dr. Patterson. My father always said that someday, when they knew much, much more, physicians would be a boon to the human race, but right now they were ofttimes a hindrance to recovery. I took off the cork and inhaled deeply. The smell was not agreeable, and I was sure the taste was not any better. The remnant of a cold cup of tea was on the nightstand. I poured the tea into the saucer and a dose of the tonic into the cup. I listened. There was no Mrs. Reynolds marching along the hall, and since Martha still had all her duties downstairs to which she must attend, I knew she would not disturb me. I raised the cup to my lips. I braced myself. I took a swallow.

The liquid burned horribly all the way to my stomach. I gagged. It was undoubtedly among the most noxious-tasting substances ever devised. Worse, within a few seconds I felt the strangest sensation in my head, as if all the blood were rushing there. I developed heart palpitations, whether from nervousness or the liquid I could not tell. My palms were sweating.

I shut the cabinet with haste. My stomach was rebelling at the intrusion, and I all but flew down the stairs to the kitchen in the hope that a slice of bread would return me to my normal state.

After having received a lecture to eat a larger breakfast before going off in the carriage and being informed that lunch would be ready within the hour, I escaped the kitchen and Mrs. Babbage's scolding, a fresh scone in my hand—and discovered Mrs. Eldridge walking toward the stairs.

"Oh, it's you!" She was obviously startled.

I didn't think she had been in the library or drawing room, which were being cleaned. She had to have been coming from her husband's office, and not on some routine errand, I fancied.

"I've been looking for a book of poetry and thought my husband might have taken it."

The lie was poorly told and, of course, unnecessary, unless she thought I might mention the visit to Mr. Eldridge. This gave me my chance.

"Perhaps he took it to the tower to read."

"He wouldn't do that." I could see her mind working. She wanted a chance to think things over, alone. Dispatching me to the tower was a good way to insure I was gone for a few minutes at least. "You might as well check. Don't stay too long, or you'll catch your death of cold up there. You'll find me in my room when you come back."

I climbed the stairs, then stopped on the landing to look down the many floors. This was an isolated place, I thought. No noise reached my ears save the mournful sound of sweeping wind. I turned the knob. The tower was not locked: had I had the courage, I might have gone to the tower at any time. I opened the heavy door. The room was dark and cold, the fire having long since gone out. Heavy curtains blocked the windows. I pulled them back to let in enough light to see. Below me was the path, the river, the mill, and a good deal of

Bradford. In the distance, I saw another large house that had to belong to the Brewsters.

It was certainly a good position from which to note the comings and goings of people at the house, made better by the large telescope that was pointed not at the stars but toward the Brewster house. I took a peek.

I had never looked through a telescope before and was amazed at the details visible. "So the prince can indeed survey his fief," I mumbled.

I inspected the room. It was slightly dusty, explained no doubt by the few opportunities the servants had to clean it. Old maps hung on the walls, as well as an assortment of weapons, ranging from sabers to old rifles. Whether or not they were usable I could not ascertain. There were bits of interesting rocks, very old photographs of young men, and old journals. I tried the drawers. They were not locked. They were, however, crammed full of papers, too many for me to sort through quickly.

Before leaving, I glanced at the books. There was not one volume of French poetry among the lot. Some, I noticed, were in Latin, but they did not seem religious in nature, as the ones downstairs were. I opened a book of poetry written by a man named Catullus and glanced casually through the pages until one passage caught my eye. It began with a description of travels to India, Arabia, Egypt, and the Rhine, but turned to the poet's message to a woman: *"Cum suis uiuat . . ."* I read.

My Latin must have been faulty. Surely it couldn't actually say that a woman should thrive with her adulterers—three hundred of them—embracing them all at once and apparently much more!

And to think that Mrs. Eldridge called the French vulgar! I slammed the book shut and shoved it back into place. No wonder it wasn't kept downstairs.

My indignation about the passage assuaged my guilt somewhat when I reported to Mrs. Eldridge.

"Never mind, I shall settle for one of these." She waved her hand at the pile of books now on the nightstand.

She read Millicent's letter and glanced through the magazine. We ate in her bedroom, after which I read to her while she lay in bed. At the end of three hours, I thought my voice would succumb from wear, and she finally dismissed me so that she could nap.

I decided to pay a visit to Peleg Marsh, who was sinking fence posts into the ground in front of the hedges.

"That must be very hard work," I said as I approached him.

"It would have been a lot harder if the winter had been bad," he answered cheerfully. "What do you think of my work so far?"

"It shall be a vast improvement over those hedges." I bent down to pick up a strangely grown piece of stray wood. It looked like a caterpillar. As I glanced at the farm across the river, my eyes strayed to the spot where Julianne had stood. Stood and fallen. I could see her face the house, feeling strong hands upon her, her eyes widening: then the fall, unable to catch hold of anything, knowing the river and rocks were below and no one would hear her scream in time, falling . . .

"I liked the hedges myself," Pete was saying.

"If the fence had been there, Julianne might have lived."

He took off his cap and wiped the sweat from his forehead onto his sleeve. "You can grab onto a bush just as easily as you can a fence, if you ask me." He, too, looked at the place where Julianne had fallen. "I still can't understand how a healthy young woman like her could have slipped so fast and hard that she couldn't save herself." He shrugged. "It happens, I guess, and I should know, considering how I fell from the roof of the house. One minute I was standing and the next I'm on the ground."

"You were lucky."

"I landed on a thick mat of grass. She must have hit her head pretty bad on a rock, not to come round when she went into the water. That's what causes people to drown, you know."

I could see her hair wafting about her head as if it were seaweed.

Just then Pete looked back at the house, and his face brightened. "There's Maggie at the window." He waved at her.

I thought an act of kindness would mitigate some of my more disreputable behavior of late. "Perhaps I can look after the baby for a little while. That way you can talk for a few minutes."

"I can't ask you to do that."

"There's no one in the house to object except Mrs. Eldridge, and she's resting." I ran back to my room, flung my cloak on the bed, and rushed into the nursery.

"Maggie, I've been overcome with the desire to look after Jon Frederick. Why don't you go out and see your husband."

She protested—though not for long. Although the baby was still not very happy and fidgeted, he did not seem to mind having my company for a change. I amused him by holding a rattle in front of him.

"Hello." Hugh stood in the doorway. "Mother's door is closed. Is she sleeping?"

I nodded. "I've been looking after your brother while Maggie gets something to eat." My ability to lie had improved, at least when I could avoid looking directly into someone's eye.

Hugh bent over to look at Jon Frederick. His hand went out to touch the baby, but before doing so fell limply to his side.

"I imagine you wish he had been born a lot earlier. Does he even seem like your brother?" I asked curiously. "Or is it almost as if he were a nephew?"

"No, I know all too well that he's my brother. And yes, my life would certainly have been different had he arrived in a more timely fashion." His voice sounded bitter.

I looked at him sharply.

"Never mind me. I was trying to please Father by working on the books and got hopelessly muddled as usual. I tried to broach the subject of giving you a couple of days to see your family, and never even got the chance to finish the sentence when Evan interrupted. I tried."

I smiled my gratitude at him. "I'm sure you did."

"I'll try again." He looked at me with sad eyes. "I don't suppose that after Mother is well, you'd consider staying on to look after me? I could do with someone of your kind nature."

I did not know how to interpret what he said. "Hugh?"

"Forget what I said. I'll see you at dinner." He was gone from the room, and I heard him enter his own.

Maggie returned not long after. "I saw Hugh come out of the nursery. What did you say about me?"

"That you were getting something to eat. Did he see you talk to Pete?"

"Hugh wouldn't notice anything like that, and no one in the kitchen would tell him I wasn't there, should he even bother to ask." She sat down on her bed, looking flushed from rushing up the stairs. "I've missed Pete. He's not too happy that I'm working here and the children are without me, though his mother is the best caretaker I can imagine. It helps that we can see each other more often."

"You know that any time I can I'll gladly look after Jon Frederick for you. I really don't mind."

Maggie plucked a piece of shrubbery from her dress. "Neither did Julianne. It got her away from chores." She smiled wryly. "Strange, isn't it, the way you miss a person? What I miss is her asking how the baby was doing and her way of humming when she was happy. I never think of her not cleaning the rooms properly. Once she hid behind the door when Mrs. Reynolds was looking for her to scrub the tub."

I thought I heard the floorboards squeak in the hallway and half expected someone to enter the room.

"It didn't make her popular with Martha," Maggie continued. "She is hopeless with babies. All she does is bounce them around so hard they cry. Mrs. Reynolds was never fond of small children and was relieved when her boys were grown. Poor Julianne."

I nodded in agreement. "I was talking to Pete about her. It seems that it happened so long ago that she fell. Oh, you'll never guess what I found out by the hedges."

Before I could continue, Mrs. Reynolds made her way toward us, her heavy breathing heralding her arrival some time before she actually appeared. "I was hoping Mrs. Eldridge was in here. There's a young woman to interview for maid."

"Mrs. Eldridge should be up by now," I said. "She's been resting for some time." I handed the baby back to Maggie.

My knock on Mrs. Eldridge's door brought an immediate response.

Mrs. Eldridge was sitting up in bed, her knees raised beneath the covers, several crumpled pieces of paper scattered around her. For a moment she looked blank at the mention of the applicant. "I had completely forgotten about her. I swear I must be getting old." She looked at her wardrobe with a certain distaste. "There must have been a time when it was not an ordeal to dress." She kept mumbling to herself. "Damn all corsets. Damn all—"

I was shocked by her swearing.

"Sorry, Lydia. As you can see I am in a bad mood, and I have every intention of staying so until tomorrow. I do hope this young woman is suitable. If there is anything I hate, it is interviewing people."

I got her comfortably arranged in her den and then went to fetch the woman. In the meantime, I had learned that her name was Annette Ronceau, her parents were employed at the mill, that she was seventeen years old, had worked two years for Dr. Patterson and his wife, and had received suitable recommendation. Her reason for leaving had been the privately expressed desire for better wages and the equally fervent desire to escape the tiresome physician. Annette had apparently complained to her mother, who had mentioned it to the laundress, who in turn passed on the information to Mrs. Reynolds. Such is the common way for jobs to be filled.

Upon first seeing Annette waiting docilely in the foyer, I felt an immense sense of superiority. She was nervous, shy, and obviously eager to please. Her coat was not stylish, the material cheap. Her hair was pulled straight back in a bun, which did not suit her square face. Her complexion was not good. Her speech was halting. My word, but I could swear that she looked at me with respect.

I led her upstairs, noticing how she looked around so obviously impressed, curiosity in her eyes, while I told her about the people in the portraits. It was amazing how quickly circumstances change.

"Good afternoon, Annette," Mrs. Eldridge said when we entered the room. "Now I place you. You do remind me of your father." Less than an hour later, I handed Annette over to Mrs. Reynolds, who would inform her of her new duties in greater detail. Martha would be most pleased.

I was coming back from the servants' quarters when I saw Evan leaving his room. "Have you just gotten back from the mill?" I asked, for it was almost dinner time and the men were not usually gone so long. He seemed too distracted to notice that I bore him no ill will for his advances in the library and that I very much wished to talk to him to discern his feelings.

"No. Hugh, Mr. Eldridge, and I arrived almost at the same time. We continued working in the office downstairs."

"Evan, I—"

"Some papers were disturbed. You wouldn't know anything about that."

"No."

He looked to Mrs. Eldridge's room. "I think I can guess. It should be an interesting evening. I would recommend that the two of us retire as quickly as possible after the meal has been completed."

"Why, what is going to happen?"

"It would appear that Mrs. Eldridge has been studying the accounting entries."

"What could she find out about all those scribbled figures?"

"Mrs. Eldridge is no fool. She knows almost as much about the family finances as Mr. Eldridge, which is why she is going to be a little bit upset about where some of the family money has gone. You go ahead to the dining room, and I'll go in search of Mr. Eldridge and inform him of the situation."

Mr. Eldridge, however, was already seated at the dining table when I entered the room. He saw me and rose quickly. "And how is my wife today? She hasn't been ill again?"

"Oh, no. Did Evan—"

"Did she find Annette suitable?"

I nodded and tried again to speak, but the swish of skirts announced Mrs. Eldridge. She entered, along with Evan. I shook my head at his mute question.

Dinner progressed with agonizing slowness. I waited for angry words. None were forthcoming, but the feeling of disquietude mounted steadily. At last the dessert was finished.

Evan put down his napkin. "Lydia, would you be interested in seeing the newspaper? They had some news of Providence."

"Yes, I would," I replied quickly, and rose without asking permission to leave.

Mrs. Eldridge didn't say a word, didn't even look up from her plate.

Evan steered me out of the room, much to the astonishment—and I believe dissatisfaction—of Hugh.

"So far so good," Evan whispered to me when we were out in the hallway. "I have the feeling this is going to be a first-class row."

I was tempted to ask the exact details, but it was none of my business, and in any case I doubted Evan would tell me. He was loyal to Mr. Eldridge. "Is there really anything in the paper about Providence?"

"Nothing much, I'm sorry to say."

"I suppose it is unlikely that any newspaper article would have a direct bearing on my family anyway." I sat on the couch and listened for angry voices. "Shouldn't they be shouting?"

"It isn't going to be that kind of an argument." He sat beside me, but at a discreet distance, after searching my face for permission.

Were the Eldridges arguing about Mrs. Hamilton? I couldn't voice my suspicions, no matter how dearly I yearned to confide in him. Or could I?

"Evan, why does Mr. Eldridge spend so much time in the tower? I was sent there today to fetch a book. The place seems most unpleasant."

"He's interested in astronomy, has been since he was a boy. He thinks nothing of staying up half the night."

Was he really only viewing the stars? I wondered. He could see the Brewster house. One if by land and two if by sea. I saw no reason why an arrangement of lights could not be worked out which could indicate the time and place to meet.

"I would think that Mr. Eldridge would be too tired to pursue such a hobby after working in the mill all day."

Evan laughed softly. "He sits behind a desk and weighs the price of cotton against that of cloth, or ponders where to invest his money next. That is not a tiring occupation. Occasionally the mill foreman consults him on some matter. That is the only reason he maintains an office down at the mill. It's easier for the foreman to reach him. Besides, he likes to know personally what is happening at the mill, go riding, or visit the other factory that he owns farther downriver."

"Farther downriver. Closer to the Brewster house?"

"A little beyond that. You seem uncommonly curious about his workaday routine. Is there any reason for that?"

"He's the first person I've met whose occupation is novel."

He leaned toward me. "I would much prefer to discuss you, how you spent the day, or how you would care to spend the evening."

I found myself drawing closer to Evan. I could almost imagine his kiss and being held tightly in his arms. My friendship with him was changing into the deepest affection, my misgivings melting, for no murderer could be so solicitous toward me or maintain a façade of sincerity. Evan had to care for me. I knew he was going to kiss me, and this time I would voice no objections.

"Am I interrupting?" Hugh asked stiffly.

I hastily pulled back. "No, you're not." Evan looked as if he were quite willing to say otherwise.

"It would appear that my parents have some matters to discuss privately. You two seemed to have known that this would happen."

"I merely pointed out a few items of interest in the newspaper to Lydia."

Hugh looked around. "I don't see any paper. I was interested in looking at it myself."

"I put it back in the office," Evan said.

"So quickly. I can never find anything in the office. Would you please be so kind as to get the newspaper? That wouldn't be any trouble, would it?"

"No trouble at all," Evan replied coolly. "I should be gone no more than a minute."

There was hate in Hugh's eyes as he studied Evan's retreating back. "Someday I must learn how he manages to extricate himself so quickly from every unpleasant scene."

"Your mother isn't too upset, is she?"

"She's in a positive tizzy about money being spent unwisely, and I very much feared to be caught in the middle again. While they were preparing their arguments, I left, but not before having been rather curtly ordered to be prepared to work at the mill all day tomorrow. This is one instance where I don't dare disobey my mother."

His last statement came as a surprise. Why would she order him to the mill? Was it to keep an eye on his father? I had to get to the tower again, for I had the feeling that Mrs. Eldridge had been there before me and discovered more than just the casually spent sums of money.

Pleading a headache, I left the drawing room as Evan returned with the newspaper. I dozed in my room for an hour or so, until I heard Mrs. Eldridge open my door.

"Are you awake?" She almost succeeded in keeping the anger out of her voice.

"Yes, I am." I quickly stood. "Do you wish to go to bed now?"

She nodded. Her anger was not directed at me, but elsewhere. Twice I tried to engage her in conversation while I helped her, but as she ignored me completely, I, too, became silent. I returned to my room and waited for the house to become silent. Hugh came up next, followed by Evan within the hour. Mr. Eldridge, his steps much heavier than usual, was the last to climb the stairs. I waited another hour before lighting a candle and slinking up the stairs as quietly as a cat. I hesitated at the tower door, half hoping to hear someone up so that I would be forced to turn back. All was quiet save for the unaccountably loud beating of my heart and my labored breathing.

I entered. Everything looked eerie in the weak light and had I not been here earlier, I wouldn't have known where to begin. First I looked in the direction of the Brewster house and saw nothing save the blackness of night. A light in the window at this late hour would have been too much to ask; nevertheless, I felt a childish twinge of disappointment. I looked down the valley. The village was quiet, although here and there a light glowed, one, I thought, at the doctor's residence. I dropped the curtain back into place.

Setting the candle on the desk, I began my search. Long, nervous minutes later, I found letters from Mrs. Hamilton, hidden in the desk in the back of a drawer full of ship designs. The letters looked very much like the one in Mr. Eldridge's possession the day of my arrival.

Dear Jonathan, the first began. This was scandalous. It was not proper for a young woman to call a man many years her senior, and married at that, by his first name. It confirmed familiarity. I felt angry for Mrs. Eldridge's sake.

I cannot tell you how much I appreciate the comfort you have provided me these many long and lonely weeks. I wish there were some way for me to repay you other than with words and devotion.

An ardent love letter it wasn't. Of course, I had never received one myself, and Eugenia only read me the passionate parts of her letters, which she undoubtedly embellished. The next several letters were similar, useful only in that they hinted at meetings. Caution and prudence would dictate more explicit letters be destroyed or, even more intelligently, not be written at all. Most of the letters had a cryptic word or two scrawled in the corner by Mr. Eldridge that were unreadable in the feeble light.

I searched quietly a while longer without success before stopping to consider what I should do next. As Mrs. Eldridge had said, the tower was a drafty place, and it creaked loudly in the wind. Now I heard sounds issuing from the direction of the stairs. I blew out the candle and held my breath. I didn't hear footfalls.

Slowly I expelled the air from my lungs. A guilty mind rests ill. Still, it would do my future no good to be discovered up here. I crept to the door—no sound greeted me—and cautiously made my way in the dark. There have been few times when I climbed into my bed with such utter relief.

ಲ 14

Friday, March 9

MY RELIEF WAS SHATTERED THE next morning when I looked
at my candle. It was tilted, and the wax ran all the way down
the holder. In my haste last night, I hadn't noticed whether I
had left a telltale trail of wax in the tower room. I thought fast.
One of my brooches, valueless save to myself, had a loose pin.
I could say that I wore it and might have lost it while in the
tower. To produce evidence, I pulled the pin away.

I went in to Mrs. Eldridge's room. "Good morning," I said
cheerfully. "How do you feel today?"

"Determined," she replied dryly. She noticed me peer about
the room. "Have you lost something?"

"Yes, a brooch that my mother gave me. I wore it yesterday."

"I don't remember it. Are you sure you wore it?"

I nodded.

"Where have you looked so far?"

"My room, the hallway, most of the stairs."

"Try the tower then," she said, as I had hoped. "That is one
room where the servants aren't likely to find it. You might as
well go now, which will give me the opportunity to wake up
more fully."

Pleased with my cunning, I ran swifty up the stairs. It
was fortunate that I had returned, for fat drops of wax had
dribbled across the desk. Using my fingernail, I began to

scrape the evidence away. I noticed the telescope. It was pointing to the grounds. Strange, I was positive the telescope had been pointing toward Bradford last night. "I hope no one noticed the wax," I said fervently out loud and finished scraping it away. I did wonder who had been in the tower.

Mrs. Eldridge congratulated me on my good fortune at finding the brooch and then suggested that I give it to Mr. Reynolds to fix, as the man had a great talent for such things. Our meal was brought to us, and while I ate, Mrs. Eldridge pawed through her wardrobe. She seemed determined to look her best when she gave Mrs. Hamilton a piece of her mind. She fretted and fussed, rejected the brown dress altered by the seamstress, and settled on a sensible tweed suit. It took a full two hours to complete the toilette, coiffure her hair, dress her to perfection, and gather all the books.

The Bradford Literary Society most appropriately met at the library. We were the last to arrive, by which time the women had drawn their chairs into a semicircle near the small stage set with a lectern.

Mrs. Brewster looked earnest, her sister bored. Mrs. Patterson sat uncomfortably, and the minister's sister glanced about unhappily, looking for a means of rapid egress once she saw the expression on Mrs. Eldridge's face. There were four other women to whom I had been introduced at church and whose names were now unclear in my mind.

Mrs. Brewster called the meeting to order. The women discussed what they had read and the activities they had planned for the library. I listened to them, struggling to stay awake, regretting that I had chosen last night for my adventure. Mrs. Eldridge, an hour or so into the discussion, spared me by asking me to get the mail.

I left gladly for the fresh air and sauntered down the street, wasting as much time as possible. There was another letter from David Veazey, as well as an assortment of reading material. There was also a letter written on cheap paper addressed to Mr. Eldridge in a masculine hand. I decided that since I had been so uncharitable to my employer, I should take the letter to his office at the mill, which would also keep me away from the discussion a while longer. Virtue, I thought, does have its occasional rewards.

Fortunately Evan had told me how to find the mill office, and without hesitation I walked down a narrow corridor and sought the first door on my left. I heard only the humming and clanking of the equipment, which while not loud was omnipresent. Since I found the door ajar, I entered without knocking, assuming no one was inside.

Mr. Eldridge had his arms around Mrs. Hamilton's shoulders. "I'm sorry to intrude," I said, checking my first impulse to retreat. "I really am sorry. I brought you a letter." I held it out to him.

"Yes, I've been expecting that," Mr. Eldridge said coolly, taking it quickly from me. "Anything of interest for my wife?"

"Only magazines."

Uncharacteristically at a loss for words, Mrs. Hamilton looked from him to me, her eyes wide.

"Perhaps you should be returning to the meeting," Mr. Eldridge suggested to her.

She nodded and fled.

I turned to follow her.

"Lydia, I can tell by the expression on your face that you misinterpreted what you saw. Mrs. Hamilton has been going through a distressing period in her life and as you know comes to me for assistance. I was merely comforting her."

"Certainly," I replied. "The door was open, and any number of people could have walked in."

He nodded as if that hadn't occurred to him. "Thank you for bringing the letter. Please don't mention this to my wife. She does not approve of my helping Mrs. Hamilton."

"I understand." I left hastily from this unpleasant scene and almost collided with Hugh in the hallway.

"A bright face on an otherwise dismal morning," he said cheerfully. He lowered his voice. "I saw you enter the mill and thought I could find out from you how my father is. In a good mood?"

"I don't think so," I whispered back.

He winced. "Then I won't disturb him." More loudly. "Would you like to go on a tour of the mill, or do you need to get back to Mother?"

"I should return."

Hugh looked genuinely disappointed. "I was hoping for a diversion, since Evan is a hard taskmaster. He is trying to teach me the intricacies of keeping accurate books. I suppose it must be done, but I do wish I didn't have to be involved. In all truth, my reluctance isn't so much a matter of laziness than an inability to understand figures."

"I'm sure there will come a time when you will appreciate what you're learning."

"I'm only doing this to please my parents, biding my time until I receive a settlement so that I can live in New York. I'd like to go farther, to London, even Paris, travel in interesting literary circles, but that is not likely for many, many years, but I do so wish to be gone."

"You'll be married by then and won't want to leave."

He smiled wryly. "I'll still want to leave. The question is whether this hypothetical wife of mine would want to see the world. She probably will be stubborn and refuse."

"Marry someone just like yourself."

"That might be hard, for I'm sure my parents have some-one practical in mind—a stern New England spinster from a renowned and prosperous family, of course."

"Hugh!" Mr. Eldridge summoned.

"I shall see you tonight." Squaring his shoulders, Hugh entered his father's office.

Did he realize that in the not too distant future I would be a stern New England spinster? That is what happens when you don't come from a renowned and prosperous family. It was a silly thought, but I wondered if I would be better situated if Hugh would consider courting me. I shook my head. I couldn't imagine Hugh courting any woman. I had the feeling that if he married—and Mr. Eldridge would most certainly see to that—it would be an arranged match. Poor, dear Hugh. If he could only see himself in a better light and display a little courage occasionally, his life would be so much better.

I had reached the library and picked up my skirts, ready to ascend the steps, when I looked up. There in the window stood Mrs. Hamilton, her back up against a bookcase, and hovering around her like a bird of prey ready to attack was Mrs. Eldridge. She turned so sharply that the younger woman jumped. Whatever was said, it was enough to cause Mrs. Hamilton to flee.

I hurried up the remaining stairs and pushed through the doors. Mrs. Eldridge, putting on her gloves, came toward me. "We're leaving now, Lydia." Her voice was curt. "Any mail?"

"Only from your brother."

I barely had enough time to pull it from the magazine in which I had the letter secreted before she grabbed it from me. Her lips moved as she read. "For once my brother has failed me." Without another word she marched from the building.

I had hoped that she would calm down once she reached home, but she did not. She barely picked at her lunch and paced impatiently in the parlor all afternoon, hardly paying attention to the baby. More disturbingly, she grew visibly paler and more drawn as the day wore on. She was hot and cold by turns and threw open or closed a window to match her mood, while I sat dutifully nearby, trying my best to appear insignificantly small, not even daring to suggest that she rest.

I heard a carriage arrive, and looking at the clock discovered it had reached three. She stormed to the door before anyone else could answer. "I wish to speak to you," I heard her snap.

"And I to you," her husband replied coolly. "You had no right to talk to Mrs. Hamilton in such a manner. Everything that needed to be said was said last night."

"Evidently not, since she immediately went running back to you. Hugh, don't you dare leave now."

"I thought I would go riding while there was a little daylight left," he replied ineffectually.

"You can go riding tomorrow. Right now I want to talk to both of you. Things have deteriorated for too long, and I will no longer put up with it."

"Mother, please, it isn't good for you to become excited."

"I think I shall be the best judge of that."

I would have liked to escape, but I was trapped in the parlor. I tried to concentrate on the view out the window, but I couldn't manage to shut out the angry words like *impropriety* and *hussy* that were flung about, interspersed with denials from both men. I couldn't tell if she was angry at just her husband or also at Hugh for apparently siding with his father. They moved away toward the back of the house where I and the servants would have less to hear.

I turned, hearing Evan's quiet approach. "I had thought of staying at the mill to work. I should have followed my instincts." He collapsed onto the sofa. "Sit down, Lydia. There's no place where you can run."

I sat in the armchair across from him. "I gather you did not have a pleasant day."

"Quite bad. I was supposed to teach Hugh about accounting practices, and even while I'm talking to him his mind wanders away. Mr. Eldridge frets constantly about Hugh, writes long, unhappy letters to his daughter, and then never mails them. We're having problems with the mills. One is in sore need of more modern equipment, and the prices are not high enough at the moment to warrant the expenditure. At another mill there is labor unrest, and the foreman walked off his job today, announcing that he was leaving for Indiana."

"I might have made things worse. When I walked into Mr. Eldridge's office, he had his arms around Mrs. Hamilton. It upset them both."

Evan was nonplussed. "She cries on his shoulder a great deal. Mrs. Hamilton fancies herself a very delicate creature struggling bravely in the face of adversity."

"What does she know about adversity!" I said scornfully. "If she sold only a fraction of her jewelry, she would be kept in decent lodgings and food for a year. She has a family that can help. All my mother could do was pawn her wedding ring and shepherd her daughters to their grandparents so that they could eat adequately, at least on Sunday!"

All the color drained from my face. I hadn't meant to say that much. "I mean, I mean—"

"It's all right, Lydia."

"I'm exaggerating."

"Of course you are."

I could have bitten off my tongue. "I mustn't let you think—"

"Lydia, there's no reason to deny that your family has been in difficult circumstances. People see through pretenses quickly enough." He came to me and gathered me into his arms. "There is nothing wrong with having to face hardship. It isn't your fault. You have no reason to feel ashamed. You're as good as anybody else, don't forget that."

I pulled away from him. He had used those very words, that same tone of voice before. "You needn't talk to me as if I were Julianne."

For a moment he simply stared at me uncomprehendingly before realizing what I had said. "Just how much have you been in the habit of overhearing?"

I didn't know what to say. I didn't know what I was seeing in his eyes. "Please, just leave me alone!" I cried, embarrassed that I had disclosed my family's true state, upset that I might have misinterpreted his intentions, that after all he did not love me as I loved him. Shocked at the depth of my emotions, I admitted the truth to myself, and at the very moment of realization Evan replied to my request and strode from the room.

I blinked away tears. How had the day unraveled so completely? I didn't want to stay where I was. Evan might come back, and I really didn't want to see him at the moment, not until I had my own mind settled. I didn't know where else I could go and not risk meeting someone else who was upset. I decided to leave the house and walk on the grounds, letting the cool wind blow away all my ugly thoughts.

Inevitably I was drawn to the very spot where Julianne met her death. A stout fence now marked the location. "Julianne," I whispered, "can't you help me?"

The only answer was a blast of cold wind, heavy with the promise of rain.

I looked back at the house. It was becoming dark—the windows looked like the eyesockets of a skull. Again, as I had so many times before, I tried to imagine how she could have slipped. I slid awkwardly through the fence and uprooted bushes and stared down at the rushing water. I could easily pace back and forth without difficulty. "How? How, unless you were pushed?"

I circled toward the back of the house, where the garden would be blooming in a few more months. I stopped and tried to picture what it would look like. I could have sworn I had heard someone approach. I glanced over my shoulder. The silence felt menacing. "Hello?" Who would be out in the evening, standing for some reason on the other side of the house? "Hello?"

I strained my ears. There, a step on the cold, hard ground. Who could it be—who would not answer when I called?

The murderer, a small frightened voice within me answered.

Keep calm, I told myself. Don't give yourself away. I bit my lower lip to contain my apprehension; I increased my pace. The door was an eternity away. What would happen if I started to run? Would he assume that I was cold? Would he fear that he had been discovered? I reached the door. I was again safe in the warm embrace of the Eldridge house. Running to the nearest window, I peered outside. I could see no one on the grounds, but to hide from the windows wasn't hard.

I went upstairs to the nursery. Maggie was knitting quietly in her chair, the baby asleep in the crib.

She laid her work aside as soon as I entered. "What has been going on? People have been walking up and down the stairs, and yet nobody's talking."

"There's been a big disagreement between Mr. and Mrs. Eldridge."

She was instantly relieved. "Is that all?"

"Maggie," I said and knelt by her chair. "You know how I said I thought I saw someone outside with Julianne that night?"

Maggie nodded. "I mentioned it to Mrs. Reynolds a day or so ago, and she inquired of Mr. Eldridge whether anyone had fallen into the habit of coming up the path. He told her he hasn't seen anyone through the telescope."

I stood up. "Oh, no!"

"Wasn't I supposed to mention it to anyone? I didn't say you thought Julianne was pushed to her death."

"Maggie, I think someone has been following me because I've been trying to find out how she died."

She pursed her lips and looked at me with indulgence, as if I had insisted the bogeyman lurked in the house. "It's your imagination."

I took a deep breath. "Julianne had a lot of money. I found it hidden among her belongings."

"Lydia!"

"I only looked because I thought it might help—somehow. I'm not proud that I snooped, but she had seventy-two dollars hidden away."

"What!" Maggie was dumbfounded. "She could never get that kind of money unless—"

"Unless she was doing something she shouldn't."

Maggie thought for a moment. "No one has mentioned that much money, just small amounts she got here and there from the Eldridges as Christmas presents and the like. I don't think her parents know it exists, so it can't have been gotten all aboveboard. But don't start thinking that she got it from anyone here. There were a lot of parties last year. Overnight guests. They could have given it to her to look the other way now and then. Julianne was always very helpful when there was an advantage to be so."

"But it's so much money!" I protested.

"To you and me, but not to the likes of the people Mr. Eldridge invited over. Ask Evan about the money. Julianne used to confide in him."

Unbidden, I imagined Julianne asking Evan to step briefly outside, to discuss some sensitive matter. My doubts aroused, I could not banish them, leaving me with no one other than a disbelieving Maggie with whom to share my suspicions.

Saturday, March 10

MRS. ELDRIDGE SCARCELY STIRRED FROM her bed all day. Her meals were sent up, and to insure her quiet, the room was prohibited to both her husband and Hugh. Whatever she had said, it had subdued Mr. Eldridge greatly. I was confined to her room, though this did not bother me for I felt secure by her side.

Sunday, March 11

THE CHURCH SERVICE WAS UNINSPIRING, and as an angry wind blew, Mrs. Eldridge did not tarry. Mr. Reynolds took the two of us back to the house and then returned for the men, who had remained behind to talk to the mill foreman.

It was not long after our return to the house that rain began to fall, adding to my melancholy. The water streaking down the windowpanes looked like tears, as if Julianne were weeping.

That night I lay in bed thinking, trying to marshal my evidence in a convincing manner. Julianne had knocked on the door of one of the men. Evan might be reticent for perfectly understandable reasons: he did not wish to admit his familiarity with her. Hugh might have slept through the knock. If Mr. Eldridge had his telescope pointing to the stars or to a distant house, he would not have noticed what occurred below him on the ground. Every action the men took could have been perfectly innocent. I had no way of proving otherwise.

Try as I might, I had only succeeded in building an edifice on shifting sands. Despite these opulent surroundings, Mr. and Mrs. Eldridge were no different from most people. She could be just as vituperative as a fishmonger's wife who has discovered her husband had been extending largesse to a cheap little tart; Hugh was afraid of his parents and undoubtedly would resort to bribes to hide his deficiencies from them; and Evan . . . most important of all, Evan.

I got up to sit by the window. It was an overcast night, and not a single star was visible. I recaptured the fleeting image of the man I had seen, but no matter how hard I tried, I could not know who it was. I had only seen the back of a head and shoulders, his body hidden under a heavy coat. I knew it and yet I could not give up the notion that I had missed something.

I started back for the bed.

The merest squeak came from my door. I felt rather than saw the handle being turned. Then, just as the door was about to be opened, I heard the baby cry out briefly. Very quickly the steps retreated.

I let out a sob. Neither Mrs. Eldridge nor Maggie would act that way, and no one else would come to my room at this time of night. It was the murderer. It had to be. What had he planned to do, suffocate me in my sleep? I put my ear to the door, waiting with mounting fear for him to come back. Nothing happened. I couldn't stay in this room. Couldn't wait throughout the night for his return. I took a chance. I flung open the door. The hallway was empty. I fled to the nursery.

"Maggie, Maggie," I sobbed as I shook her shoulder. "Someone tried to come into my room."

She rose up on her elbows. "You were dreaming."

"I wasn't, I wasn't."

She held me as if I were one of her children. "It's all right. In the morning you'll know it was only a bad dream."

I shook my head mutely.

"Stay with me. You'll be safe here."

"He was coming to kill me!"

"Hush."

"He's afraid of being discovered."

"Shhh."

And sometime later I quit my incoherent ramblings and fell asleep.

·~ 15

Monday, March 12

I SLEPT BADLY THE REMAINDER of the night next to Maggie in the narrow bed, so much like the one I had shared with Eugenia. I dreamt of home, then of running desperately through the night, only to stand on the precipice and hear the rushing water below, knowing that someone was about to push me. I waited in the darkness and called for help. Hands grabbed my throat, I saw red, demonic eyes, and then I was falling, falling . . .

I awoke. At first I didn't know where I was. Maggie was already up, nursing the baby in the rocking chair. I fell back against the pillow and tried with some success to calm my rioting nerves. Then I realized how bright the room looked. The sun must have been up for some time. I pushed back the covers. "I've got to get dressed. Mrs. Eldridge will be wanting me."

"Lydia, it's much too early."

I looked out the window and through the partially opened curtain saw the falling snow. I raced from the bed. The entire landscape was an endless sea of white. "How long do you think it will last?" I asked Maggie.

"Hard to say," she replied, studying the skies. "Looks as if it could be a good storm. We've been lucky so far this winter. Our luck must have run out."

"I want to go home!" I cried. "I can't stay in a house with someone who wants to kill me."

"Say nothing of that," Maggie admonished quickly.

I turned toward her. "Why? It's the truth. I've got to leave."

"You're not thinking. If it's a bad storm, you won't be able to take the train to Providence. The road may even be blocked to Putnam. This man can't be sure that you know he tried to attack you last night."

"Unless he came back and found the bed empty."

"Did you hear anyone?"

"No."

"Then he lost heart. It will be better for you to stay close to me or to Mrs. Eldridge."

"At least you believe me now."

"I'm not sure," Maggie replied. "I know all the men, and none of them seems like he would kill a person."

"Maggie," I pleaded. "I wouldn't make this up. My whole future rests with this position, and I wouldn't think of running away if I didn't believe my life was at stake."

"I know. I also know you've been worrying for days on end about your family and Julianne. Thinking about things like that, it can do things to your mind. A bad dream is still more likely. What I want you to do is to think good and hard about this and not run away because you're scared, then regret your decision afterward. You might realize that you're wrong and want to stay. On the other hand, if I were a murderer, I'd bide my time."

I paced back and forth. "What have I done?"

"You've gone looking for the truth. We all like to say that we believe in truth and justice, but we'd rather not do anything about it. Better to look the other way and pretend that nothing's wrong, otherwise we might see what our friends and neighbors—and we ourselves—are really like."

That was oh so true. Now that I had put myself in jeopardy, I was no longer enamored of justice. Julianne was so far away, a dim memory, a phantom from a half-remembered nightmare, and I wished heartily that I had left justice to God.

Maggie put the infant back in his crib. "Lydia, you can't just stand there." She buttoned her bodice. "You have to get up, have your breakfast."

"I could have it with you."

Maggie shook her head. "No, you can't. You say there's a murderer in this house. If so, he's going to be watching you. If you did something different, he would know. Then you would be in danger. He'd want to kill you real quick, before you can point a finger at him. Go downstairs or have breakfast with Mrs. Eldridge."

"I'll never be able to carry it off."

"Yes, you will. You're clever. You can do anything that you have to."

"I'll be nervous. I'll jump at every noise." I was frightening myself. What cannot be avoided must be faced with courage. Anything else would only make the situation worse. I never thought I could survive without my father, yet I had. I had had doubts about fulfilling my role as companion, and I had succeeded. I knew the man wouldn't dare attack me with a house full of people walking about. I could be cheerful and calm. I took a deep breath. "All right." With exaggerated dignity and poise, I returned to my room to dress. When my soft tap on Mrs. Eldridge's door remained unanswered, I went downstairs.

Much to my surprise, Mrs. Eldridge was at breakfast, in her dressing gown, staring out the window. "I've been up for hours," she told me happily. "I adore snow, the quiet sound of it falling, the way it lights up the world when the sun shines." She smiled as a child does beholding birthday presents. "There will be many new scenes to paint. I know it is a selfish thought, since snow will be a great inconvenience to many people, but I don't want it to stop quickly."

"It looks as if it will be a strong storm," I commented, seating myself and laying a napkin across my lap.

"It may be worse than that," Evan said as he entered. "I read that the Midwest has been wracked by severe weather. We may have the same storm."

Mrs. Eldridge raised her eyebrows. "That would be exceedingly less amusing."

I looked at Evan, wishing that with a word he could dispel my doubts about him.

Father and son came in next. They looked at each other. "Elaine, I didn't expect you to be up," Mr. Eldridge said to his wife.

"I feel invigorated," she replied, "now that I've finally managed to convey just what I've been feeling all these many months." She smiled in such a way that I knew she had gotten the upper hand.

The two men sat down. A strained smile passed for Hugh's morning greeting, and thereafter he kept his eyes on his plate. Mr. Eldridge ignored me altogether.

The morning meal was served quickly, while Mrs. Eldridge and I supplied all the conversation. She bubbled about her painting projects and whether or not we would be able to hitch a sled to the horse and travel to Bradford, under the pretext that she had to place a few orders for catalog items.

After breakfast Hugh retired to the library, Mr. Eldridge and Evan went to the office in the back of the house, and I very gladly went to Mrs. Eldridge's den to help her gather supplies to paint snow scenes. Jon Frederick spent an hour or so with us, gurgling happily. The snow, interlaced with ice, continued to fall with disturbing intensity.

Much sooner than I fancied, we were all assembled in the dining room again. I don't know what it is about a storm that sets people's teeth on edge, and why restlessness fuels discontent so quickly. No one could be still. With the exception of Mrs. Eldridge, we felt the snow weighing down on us. Mr. Eldridge barked unnecessary orders to Evan. Hugh contemplated his wine glass solemnly and between courses wandered about like a lost soul. Evan was prone to staring into space.

All this only served to increase my own apprehension. One of these men could be plotting my demise this very minute. What would happen when night came again? Had he lost heart, as Maggie thought, or would he try again? Was I to sleep another night in her room?

The wonderful almond cake served for dessert revived our spirits. Mrs. Babbage, we all agreed, had surpassed herself.

"Lydia, why don't you take a large slice of cake upstairs to Maggie," Mrs. Eldridge suggested after an uncharacteristic second serving. "I know she would enjoy it."

I nodded and went to the kitchen. The room was warm and aromatic, and as usual, everyone was bustling about.

Mrs. Babbage lifted her steely gaze from an apparently uncooperative bowl of dough. "I do hope you're not here to deliver complaints. I'm doing the best I can without fresh supplies being delivered."

"No, no," I hastily assured her. "I'm here for an extra slice of cake for Maggie. Everyone thinks the cake is the best we've ever tasted."

"Really?" Her face brightened considerably. "It's a new recipe, and I had my doubts. Would you like me to save you a piece, also?" She hadn't given up her desire to fatten me up.

I wasn't about to disappoint her. "Actually, I would."

Before she gave me the slice, I had to listen to her recount all the ingredients and ingenuity that went into making the cake.

"I don't have much of a sweet tooth," Maggie informed as she put aside her tray, "but I'll try it just the same."

"Think how happy you'll make Mrs. Babbage by eating all of it," I told her.

"You're right about that. I've never met anyone so in love with her job." She ate her cake and concurred with the prevailing opinion.

I lingered, describing the tense situation downstairs.

"Men are like that," Maggie pronounced. "You shut them up in a house, and they become crazy." She giggled. "A pity we can't teach them needlepoint and give both their hands and their minds something constructive to do."

I burst out in laughter. "Imagine Mr. Eldridge working over a dainty piece of lace with those great big hands of his." My face sobered.

"What's the matter?"

"I just thought of what might have happened while I was in bed. Those hands might have been around my throat." I stared out the window. Was the snow immuring me in my tomb? "I suppose that while we're all trapped together, no one would dare harm me. I mean, everyone would know that a member of the household had done it. There wouldn't be much of a chance to arrange a convenient accident indoors." I bit my lip. "The only other way I can think of to kill someone without much of a trace would be to put a pillow over my face. I could struggle. I'd leave scratches."

Maggie put an arm around me. "Don't start to think like that."

"I ought to. That way I can be prepared."

"Then tell Mrs. Eldridge. Then one more person would know."

"What do I say to her? That either her son or her husband tried to kill me?"

"It could have been Evan," Maggie pointed out softly.

"If she chose to believe he was the murderer, Evan would lose the job he worked so hard to get, and the real assailant might be living in the house with me."

"What about telling Mrs. Reynolds, then?" Maggie suggested.

"She dotes on Hugh, and I'm sure she is unquestioningly loyal to Mr. Eldridge. As are you."

Maggie leaned on the windowsill and looked out for a moment before turning back to me. "Yes, I suppose I am. When you're with me and I can see the look on your face, I think there is a murderer here. Once you're gone, though, I can't. You haven't convinced me that Julianne was killed. You can't tell me that one of those men, men I've known, has a dark and evil side that I've never seen."

"If there were a neat and easy solution, I would have found it, for I've pondered the problem until my mind spins. Maggie, if only I had one solid clue, one convincing piece of evidence."

"You would be dead, if you're right about everything else, and we wouldn't be having this talk."

"That's right," I mused out loud. "Nothing happened until last night. Why? He must have been aware of my activities. Having committed such a heinous crime, he would be sensitive to any events in connection with it." I thought back at how often and how carelessly I had approached the place of Julianne's demise. Any number of people could have seen me from the many windows in the house. Those who were innocent would have ignored me. The murderer wouldn't. He would watch, and each time I returned, his apprehension would grow. He would wonder. I had managed to confirm his suspicions within the last day or so. "Something I did or said frightened him. Unfortunately so much has happened in the last few days that I have no hope of discerning what it was."

"You must have some idea," Maggie persisted. "I do not believe you could have uncovered a reason to kill Julianne and not know what it is. People don't kill for trivial reasons."

I felt bereft and vulnerable. In her position, I would have many doubts. "I had best be leaving," I said. "Thank you for at least listening to me."

Outside the nursery I heard a haunting melody. Mrs. Eldridge must be playing the piano again. I went to the drawing room and found her engrossed in her music. Mr. Eldridge stood at the window, hands clasped behind his back, staring at the snow. Evan and Hugh were nowhere in sight.

"I was beginning to wonder what happened to you," Mrs. Eldridge said when she at last noticed me. "What do you think of—"

I heard the wind howl menacingly as a door opened and then slammed shut.

"That will be Hugh and Evan," Mrs. Eldridge said, rising from her seat to leave the room.

I started to follow.

"Lydia, wait a moment," Mr. Eldridge said. He walked quickly to me. "Has my wife confided in you of late?"

His eyes made me nervous. "In what way, sir?"

"I was wondering. Has she been corresponding with her brother? He does not seem to write as often as before, and it isn't like him to neglect his letters. Besides, some of the things she has said made me think he provided her with certain kinds of information."

"Mr. Veazey might be busy on account of the fire," I said. "I have gotten magazines on occasion for Mrs. Eldridge. I don't recall any particular letters." Since he was concerned that she not overhear, he listened for her approach and did not give me full attention or he might have detected the lie.

"I don't suppose it is of great consequence, and David's office *was* reduced to a shambles," he said to himself.

"Jonathan," Mrs. Eldridge said as she suddenly bustled into the room. "The weather doesn't sound good at all."

"I think the horses will be fine," Hugh said, striding very quickly to the fire. He stretched out his hands to the hot flames. "But we certainly aren't going to get out by carriage for many a day."

Evan, his face looking half frozen, came into the room. Mrs. Eldridge gave him a glass of port, which he held stiffly in his hands. "I couldn't even make it to the path. The snow and wind were too severe."

"If and when the snow stops," Mr. Eldridge said, "I'll take a look from the tower." He mumbled an oath. "I hope the roofs of the mills can bear the weight of the snow."

While Mr. Eldridge and Evan conferred on what to do about the mills should they be damaged, I asked Mrs. Eldridge why Evan tried to reach the path.

"Often enough, it doesn't become completely choked by snow because of the way storms usually pass through the valley. The other side of the river usually bears the brunt of it."

"So we're not completely trapped up here."

"We are. The men can make it through the snow, but it isn't a trip I would recommend to any woman. Her skirts would be in the way too much. Since in any case it is impossible for us to be restocked with provisions today, I had better check to see what food is on hand."

Mr. Eldridge heard her last remark. "My dear, this inconvenience will only last a day or two. We haven't been cast adrift in a lifeboat."

"Better to plan beforehand," she said airily. "Come, Lydia."

Mrs. Eldridge was enjoying herself immensely, now that she had straightforward problems with which to deal. On the way to the kitchen, she regaled me with tales of the times her family had been snowed in when she was a child and the pleasure she had had dunking David in a snowdrift when he misbehaved.

Mrs. Babbage was not happy that the storm was keeping up its intensity. She sat at the kitchen table looking decidedly morose. No, the larder wasn't empty, but the supply of milk, butter, eggs, and cream was low, and how was she ever to cook without them? Mrs. Eldridge made suggestions. Mrs. Babbage countered them.

It was almost impossible to see outside the kitchen window. I wondered about my family. Milk and eggs would be the least of their concerns. My mother and sisters would try to go to my grandparents, at least they would if they realized how bad the storm was going to be. I didn't like to think of them being stranded in the tenement. The cold would seep in the way water passed through a sieve. There wouldn't be enough wood, and this was the kind of weather in which the poor could easily freeze to death.

"Lydia?" It was Mrs. Eldridge. "You look about to cry."

"My mother, I don't know how well she can cope with a storm like this."

"I'm sure she'll be all right. It won't be so bad in the city. The storm may even lose its intensity before it strikes there."

"I hope so."

The window was rattled by an exceptionally strong gust of wind. Mrs. Eldridge shivered. "I am getting rather cold and tired and think I should rest before dinner. Go find that book you were reading to me before. That should put me to sleep in no time."

I sat at her bedside, reading loudly to be heard above the sound of the wind. After a long, weary lapse of time, she finally slept. I yawned and struggled to keep myself awake, yet I felt too uneasy to go to my own room to lie down. Since it would not do to disturb Maggie constantly when she had to attend to the baby, I decided cake and coffee in the kitchen would revive my spirits.

Mrs. Babbage was busy directing the preparation of the evening's meal, but she stopped gladly enough to prepare a little "tea" for me.

"It's a lot more pleasant in the dining room," she said, noting how I made myself comfortable at her table.

"Yes, but I'd be alone. I don't like being alone in a storm."

Mrs. Babbage almost smiled at me. "Neither do I," she confessed, "though no one else thinks the way I do." She glared pointedly at Lucy. "There is no telling what horrible things could happen when you're like this, trapped on top of a mountain."

"Good afternoon, Lydia," Mrs. Reynolds said as she entered the kitchen. She wagged a finger at her friend. "A small storm and a grown woman like you takes fright."

Mrs. Babbage crossed her arms over her bosom. "Wait till this 'small' storm is over. It will be spring before they dig us out." She nodded at her own words.

"A day or two at the most," Mrs. Reynolds said to me.

"A day or two of endless howling winds, the house groaning like some soul in hell, the well probably freezing—"

Mrs. Reynolds interrupted. "I've spoken to Maggie, and she sees no reason why we shouldn't be able to procure eggs and butter from her in-laws. We can send Ken tomorrow."

Mrs. Babbage's face immediately brightened. "That will help. I can always make soufflés at the very least. Providing he doesn't drop the eggs as he tries to get over the mounds of snow."

"The snow will cushion the fall," Mrs. Reynolds said matter-of-factly. She poured herself a cup of coffee and sat opposite me. "Mrs. Eldridge is asleep?"

I nodded.

"I don't like this sudden burst of energy from her. It isn't good. It is better to recover slowly at an even pace. Certainly it wasn't good for her to have gone into Bradford for a literary meeting." She looked at me as if I could have prevented the excursion.

"She's fine," I reassured her.

"I hope you haven't been letting her get upset," Mrs. Babbage said.

"I've done my best to spare her."

"All these terrible things that have been happening," Mrs. Babbage continued. "I wish we had gone to Boston."

"I'm just as glad to have remained this year," Mrs. Reynolds said. "All that moving back and forth gets to be hard work for me. And when the family is gone, the house isn't kept up the way it ought to be."

Mrs. Babbage huffed. "I was under the impression that Mr. Eldridge wanted to retire when Hugh was old enough to be responsible for the mills. Last winter they were planning what they would do there, and it sounded every bit as if they thought of it as a near to permanent move."

"That was before the baby, though," I said. "Isn't that why they decided to remain?"

"Oh, no," Mrs. Babbage replied, "that happened earlier. Hugh got into so much mischief in Boston they decided to remove him from bad influences. And then Mr. Eldridge rekindled his interest in riding once more, which he swore never to do again after that terrible fall he took, in the spring of eighty-six."

"No Eldridge can live long without his horses," Mrs. Reynolds observed. "He rides about the countryside in all forms of weather. It wouldn't surprise me if he went out as soon as the storm abated."

Would he be anxious for Mrs. Hamilton? I thought. Did that account for his renewed interest?

"As I recall, Julianne was quite disappointed," Mrs. Reynolds continued. "She got over it quickly enough. She even mentioned once or twice last summer that she thought she could get enough money together to go to Boston by herself."

This revelation surprised me. "I thought that had only recently become her plan."

"No, it was sometime in July or August when she became the upstairs maid," Mrs. Reynolds continued. "She had many a fancy notion about herself."

"She could hardly wait to be an upstairs maid," Mrs. Babbage said. "Julianne didn't like working in the kitchen at all. Didn't like what scrubbing pots did to her hands, and she a farmer's daughter that fed pigs and chopped wood until she was sixteen. I had to keep after her every minute to make sure she did her work properly. I must say that she became more diligent as a maid. At least she remained upstairs working for longer periods of time than she ever did here. And speaking of maids, how is Annette doing?"

"Quite well," Mrs. Reynolds said. "I find few flaws. She should be thoroughly trained by the end of the month."

As the conversation became entirely domestic, I excused myself and went back upstairs, annoyed that although the women had spoken of Julianne without my prompting, all I had found out was that whatever had given her occasion to earn extra money had come about as early as last July.

What had happened? A liaison with Evan would have been much more convenient, but working upstairs also gave her the opportunity to discover incriminating evidence about the other men. I was sure she covered up some of Hugh's drinking escapades. Did he say too much one time when not fully in possession of his faculties? It was equally possible that Mr. Eldridge had left an incriminating letter about. Or had he made the mistake of taking Mrs. Hamilton aside on that gossip-producing walk and Julianne had seen enough from one of these rooms to confirm suspicion?

No, I thought, it wasn't merely overhearing a few words or seeing too much that was responsible for her death. They would be denied easily enough, even if Julianne wished to jeopardize her position. I could vouch for how reluctant she would be to do that. If she were dismissed, she would most likely be forced to return to the farm. She had to have found something tangible.

If she had found physical evidence, where could she have hidden it? The den was unoccupied much of the time and was the most convenient. No one would ever question her presence there. What would the nature of the evidence be? A love letter from Evan, an indiscreet piece of correspondence between Mr. Eldridge and his paramour, or perhaps a letter indicating Hugh had not abandoned his dissolute ways? Whatever it was, it had to be small.

I was fairly sure that no one was upstairs, except for Maggie and Mrs. Eldridge. Most of the servants were gathered in the warm kitchen, Hugh had sequestered himself in the library, and Mr. Eldridge and Evan were in the office. This might be my only opportunity.

If I had any optimism about finding this mysterious missive, I soon abandoned it. Were one so inclined, there were almost unlimited opportunities for concealment. I sighed and set about my search; shifting through books, baskets of embroidery, and art supplies, beneath statues and behind paintings. I was on my knees, just pulling back one of the rugs when I realized it had become quite dark.

Equally suddenly, I was aware of being observed through the door I had left open so I could detect the approach of footsteps. "Who's there?" I asked, my heart in my mouth.

Evan stepped out of the shadowed hallway.

I got up. "I was just going to find something to read about art, so I can converse better with Mrs. Eldridge on the subject when I noticed a lump in the carpet." It was the best excuse I could think of. "Mrs. Eldridge might trip," I added lamely.

"I see." He went over to my sketch, which rested on the easel. "It is a very good likeness of you."

He was silent, studying the drawing as I listened to the lonely wind. "I would like to ask Mrs. Eldridge to give me the sketch—if you don't mind."

All the rooms seemed so distant from one another. I could feel my palms begin to sweat. I didn't want to stay alone in the room with him. I started to leave.

"Lydia, you don't mind, do you?" he asked again, looking at me over his shoulder.

"I have to get back to Mrs. Eldridge," I said and took but a single step. His hands were on my shoulders with lightning speed. I barely stopped myself from screaming as he spun me around.

"Lydia, I have to talk to you. It's important. Each time I try to be alone with you, we are either interrupted, or you dismiss me. Don't you realize what I'm trying to tell you, what I've been trying to tell you all along?"

I knew I was looking at him as if his words were incomprehensible. My fears stood between us. Was he guilty? All my doubts rushed to the fore. "Please let me go. I have to get back to Mrs. Eldridge."

A crease appeared between his eyebrows. "Darling, what are you so nervous about? Surely not me."

"The storm," I stammered. "Only the storm." I saw in his eyes that he didn't believe me. "I have to get back," I said forcefully. "Mrs. Eldridge is expecting me."

When I turned my back on him, it took all my strength to appear calm and walk at a reasonable speed down the corridor.

Mrs. Eldridge wasn't interested in stirring from her nice warm bed. She merely left instructions what to get her for dinner. That haven having been eliminated, I next looked to Maggie. The nursery was empty. She was probably with the servants where the fire flickered gaily and the company was jovial: better company certainly than I and my fears could provide.

The downstairs was as dark and lonely as the upper floor. I peered cautiously into each room. Then because I had no choice if I were to have any companionship, I went into the library. Far better to encounter Hugh face to face than to dread his appearing abruptly while I sat staring at the snowy landscape.

Hugh was reclining on the sofa, a half-empty glass of wine carelessly situated beside one of the legs. He smiled and corrected his posture when he saw me. "I thought you were never coming back down. What have you been doing?"

"I read a little."

"That's all I've done. I may go out and check on the horses again. Strange, isn't it, that when you can leave at will, you don't have the inclination, and once the weather becomes inclement, you feel the need to escape the confines of the house."

I sat as far away from him as possible. "Will the horses be all right?"

"Perfectly. They don't mind this weather nearly as much as humans. We're a weak lot in the scheme of things, don't you think?"

"Yes, I would say so." I could not quite hide the bitterness in my voice.

Hugh regarded me thoughtfully. "Lydia, you look very distracted." There was no sign of menace on his face, only concern.

"I'm a little tired." I shivered and stood nearer the warm fire.

"There aren't any more problems between my parents, are there? Father has been sitting about a good deal of the day saying nothing. He hasn't even touched any of his Japanese things. Which brings me to a delicate subject."

I looked at him quizzically.

"I would like to cheer him up, get his mind working in other directions before this morbidity takes permanent hold on him. Do you think you could help?"

"What could I do?"

"Ask him about family history. That's a subject dear to his heart, as you know. Or the Japanese. That would be just as good. I'd try to engage him in light conversation myself, but I never seem to do it right. Besides, he'd immediately suspect an ulterior motive."

"I doubt such simple distractions would help."

"Yes they would. Once you get him started, he won't stop talking."

"And your mother, if she comes down to dinner, how am I to stop her angry glances? I would think that they would dampen any mood."

"She's been cheerful enough all day. She enjoys having all of us trapped along with her," he said petulantly.

"It does give her a choice of company," I pointed out, my temper beginning to flare beneath the strain of the day.

"That's about all you can say about it." Something in my face prompted him to get up. He stoked the fire needlessly. "As you can see, I can never avoid expressing myself badly. Can you imagine me as a lawyer? I'd find a way to have my client hung even though he was merely guilty of accidental trespass. My parents don't seem to understand that I can't be what they want me to be. I've tried very hard. All I've managed to do is to make a complete fool of myself on a number of occasions. For the life of me, I don't know how to improve my situation other than never to say another word.

"I'm very good at writing letters, but there is a limit to how long you can take to think of a reply in the middle of a conversation. I suppose I don't know how to listen. Someone can ask at the breakfast table whether I want jam, and I'll only have heard the last part of the question and then I try to remember what else was said, and he or she will get annoyed at me for taking so long, and then I'll get mad because it seems that no one is paying any attention to me or they would know that I was deep in my own thoughts."

He looked as if his thoughts were now slipping away from me. "Would you like to be left alone?" I asked.

"No. I'd rather have company. Much company. The more the better. Only we are here and not about to go anywhere soon, so I should accept my predicament." He laughed. "I've been so unhappy of late that this morning I hinted to my father that I would like to go to school in New Haven, as Mother had once suggested. It would get me far enough away from here, and, who knows, I might even do better. Do you know what happened? Nothing. He didn't even hear me."

"He is preoccupied with his own problems."

"Lydia, that is the way it has always been."

Then why was it different for Millicent, I thought, for surely of the two oldest children she was by far the more unconventional. Had she inherited all the wit and all the ambition from their parents? I had heard that some of the wealthy never did an honest day's work in their lives and let others manage their wealth. That, however, was not the Eldridge way, and perhaps that is what made them such a long-lived family, with money and identity intact. Most clearly I could understand Mr. Eldridge's disappointment that his son could not carry on the family tradition. I speculated that in some other world it wouldn't matter which role a son or daughter had to play, that Millicent could have her ambitions and Hugh read his poetry and be a careless dreamer, and that too would be acceptable without the need of comment.

"Would it be better if you studied something else?" I ventured.

"I really can't imagine what. I'm not really good at anything Father approves of or thinks I need to know in order to run the mills." He twisted the poker in his hands until his knuckles were bloodlessly white. "I've thought of becoming a writer sometimes. He said that to be a writer I would need discipline I most certainly lacked."

"Hugh, do you have any idea what you want to do in your life, other than to travel?"

He looked sheepish. "Not really. A fine admission for someone my age, isn't it? I only know that I don't want to have anything to do with the mills or living in small towns."

"I always thought that boys were lucky because they could be anything they wanted while girls were told to stick to their sewing."

Hugh stared at the flames. "There are advantages to doing nothing more than sewing, in not having to face people's expectations to make a name for yourself in the world," he said, his voice unexpectedly serious.

He was frightened, I realized. Beneath all the talk of not knowing what to do for a career, of not wanting to worry about the mills, he was afraid of failure. I could have laughed, for I had had that fear when I entered this house, and it was so trivial now.

He continued to watch the fire as if expecting to find an answer. I saw his face grow grim. Was he thinking of death?

I looked away. What was happening to my mind, that I could convince myself that an expression on Hugh's face portended my misfortune. If only I had some proof, any proof, that would tell me whom I could trust.

Hugh tired of his reverie and to my dismay walked behind me. His hand just briefly brushed my hair. I turned to ice. He didn't make a sound other than breathing, a harsh sound to my ears. "It's so strange that you are the only person I have ever felt comfortable with. Even when I feel the walls closing in on me, when I would have thought I could tolerate not one person with me." He put one hand on the back of the sofa and leaned forward.

I got up. "It must almost be time for dinner." I thought he looked hurt and wondered if he had been about to make another personal revelation.

"Yes, it must be almost time for dinner," he said simply, and followed me out of the room. He stood at the foot of the stairs, watching me ascend, with—what, regret?—in his eyes.

Mrs. Eldridge put a quick end to any further speculation. She was waiting for me, whiling away the time by reading a magazine. "How does it look outside?"

"Better, I think, but it is most certainly a fierce storm and not quite over yet."

She glanced at her frosted window. "I daresay that it qualifies as a blizzard; however, we're safe and warm, and that is all that matters."

She got up, briefly clutching her midsection. "I should never have had any of that tonic on an empty stomach," she mumbled.

"You said you weren't going to take any more." Just in time I kept the alarm out of my voice.

"I know, but since I have been dealing most harshly with my husband, I thought I would compromise on this one small point."

I should have thrown the tonic away, claiming to have dropped it, taking the risk of having her ask what I was doing in her bureau without permission.

"Lydia, don't stand there. Help me with my dress."

I did as I was told. She seemed fine enough. What was I thinking—that she was suddenly going to keel over dead in my arms?

I should tell her of my fears. That was the only sensible solution. She would undoubtedly dismiss me for harboring such thoughts about her husband, but at least I could say I had done my duty. I tried to say the words, but I couldn't insinuate them among her constant chatter. Was I still hoping to salvage something from this horrible situation? Was I reluctant to admit defeat, that I wanted to flee like a thief in the night to an uncertain future, forever left wondering? And if I left, either because of dismissal or my own volition, would Mrs. Eldridge be fine? All I could do by leaving was to guarantee the freedom of a murderer, and how in good conscience could I permit that?

My parents had maintained that the proper course of action was always evident. But it wasn't true anymore. I didn't know my own mind, couldn't trust my own motives.

My thoughts were in such turmoil that I could hardly eat my dinner. I kept my eyes on my plate, picking at the food, ignoring Hugh's subtle hints that I should begin my conversation with his father. My heart was not in the venture. I had my battles to fight; let him learn to fight his own.

He didn't. He sank into quiet thoughtfulness and hardly ventured a word. Mr. and Mrs. Eldridge exchanged cold pleasantries. Evan drew the conversation back to business.

Slowly anger began to burn deep inside me. One of these men had ruined my only chance for success in this world, and he had the audacity and arrogance to continue as if nothing had happened, the name of Eldridge acting as a shield. Would everyone be so accepting of Julianne's death if this prominent family were not involved? I thought not. Her parents would have demanded an investigation. The good citizens of the community would have insisted on an explanation. I almost choked on dessert and as quickly as I decently could, I retired to my room.

ᴄ⌣ 16

Tuesday, March 13

I KNEW I SHOULD NOT be able to sleep well, and although
Maggie said it was quite all right for me to spend the night in
her room, I declined the offer. There was the possibility, albeit
a remote one, that I could put her in danger. I also did not think
there would be an attack on me with the storm raging about the
house. How could the murderer disguise my death? But also,
deep down, Maggie's doubts had corrupted my certainty. I
could have imagined the incidents I found so threatening. A
faceless, menacing man; was that not the stuff of dreams,
dreams that I had been having periodically since my father's
death? I had not reacted well to Julianne's death once the crisis
was over, recalling her face frozen in death, over and over
again. And I had been distrustful of this household all along.
Could the two have been combined? I just didn't know.

For hours I lay in the darkness, pondering my future. The
few weeks I had spent here had enabled me to regain some
of my former strength. Perhaps I could find employment in
a shop. Much of Providence's business district was in ruins,
according to David Veazey, so employment might have to be
secured elsewhere, Fall River possibly, or even Boston. How
ironic if I were to go to Boston. I had never had courage
before, but there comes a point when circumstance either
destroys you or makes you stronger. My bitterness and dis-
illusionment were now complete. I was tired of being a pawn,

forever expected to be meek and acquiescent, allowing people to manipulate me as they saw fit. Whatever chance I was given next, I would use it to my best advantage. I only hoped there would be another chance.

The floor creaked in the hall. Was that the murderer? My heart fluttered like a caged bird. "No," I said soundlessly to myself, "it is only your imagination or else someone on the way to the bathroom." But the steps were slow and cautious. "Keep going," I thought. "Don't linger near my door." The steps stopped, as if they belonged to a man listening intently, making sure the house slept.

Instinctively I slid beneath the bed and huddled near the wall. Should I scream? The murderer could flee, knowing he had given himself away, and be even more determined to kill me while I would be literally and figuratively left in the dark. I told myself to lie motionless, that I could still scream if I felt his hands upon me, and by my temporary silence I might learn his identity. I shoved my fingers into my mouth and tried not to breathe loudly.

Very slowly the door to my room opened. Two legs rushed soundlessly to the bed. There was a sharp exhalation of breath. The bed trembled. The covers were thrown aside. Quickly, so quickly that I almost doubted my senses, he was gone again.

Afraid to move, I remained like a statue. He was running down the hall on light feet. What was he doing? I could no longer hear him. A sob escaped my throat. I scrambled from beneath the bed and shoved a chair under the door handle. He hadn't found me and must wonder if I had hidden myself away or merely happened to be gone from my bed. I thought he would return, but he did not. I wrapped myself in the quilt and with a sharp letter opener as my weapon kept watch from the bed. A sheen of perspiration soon covered my forehead. Every sound I chanced to hear caused me to grit my teeth. I waited in agony of anticipation, almost expecting him to return to ease my painfully taut muscles and nerves. Yet he did not come.

All my strength, all my courage evaporated. The man was desperate now, and desperate men were unpredictable. He was obviously determined to kill me and do so quickly. He was willing to risk a murder directly in the snowbound household and trust that although he might live the rest of his life under a cloud of suspicion, that suspicion could never be proven.

I couldn't bear another day of agonizing fear. Only distance would insure my safety. I didn't know how, but I had to find a way to reach Providence.

In order not to give myself away by turning on the lamp, I lit my tiny candle and began to write of all I had learned since Julianne's death, doubting that I would be believed, but hoping some good would come of it. Even if Mr. Eldridge were innocent, I had no doubt that he would be furious with me for suggesting someone in his household had committed murder, and he might take drastic measures to ensure that no blot appeared on the family escutcheon. I made three copies. One letter I would keep with me, one I would leave here, and the last I would give to someone in authority, perhaps someone in Putnam, although owing to the position of the Veazey family, that might be of little use. I clutched my letters, knowing I had burned my bridges, and waited for the dismal hours of the dying night to give way to a weak and joyless dawn.

The light came slowly. The storm was ending, but its fury was far from over. Snow and ice pounded against my window. The world outside was a cruel, white expanse. I bitterly regretted not having learned how to saddle Beauregard so that I could escape without anyone knowing. I had no other alternative than to walk almost a mile to reach the Marsh house, all the while lashed by the fierce winds, blinded by the snow, my body sapped of warmth with each step. How long would it take, how long could I survive out there? Yet how long could I survive within the house? Death could come in any form, at any time. I could not remain successfully on guard for all the moments of the day, against I knew not whom.

I dressed hurriedly in my warmest clothing. I counted my money, four dollars and twenty-six cents, and wept. The plans I had had for the money I would soon receive as my month's salary, all forfeit. I had vowed when my father died that I would never dream again, never trust in the future. What a fool I had been to think the miraculous appearance of my position guaranteed a secure haven from the storms of life even for a short duration.

A woman's light footfall sounded in the hallway. Cautiously I ventured forth. Annette was carrying fresh towels for bathing. "Please give this letter to Mrs. Reynolds," I instructed. She was a strong woman and would know what to say to spare Mrs. Eldridge any unnecessary pain.

I felt Annette's puzzled eyes on me as I flew down the stairs. I opened the main door a crack. The snow was piled waist high, making it impossible to get through. I passed through the silent house as quickly as I could, hoping the back door was manageable. Halfway through the library, I heard Evan call my name.

I froze.

"What is the meaning of this?" He held up my letter.

I took a step backward. I could not summon even the feeblest of lies to ease the situation. What was the use? It was too late to hide the truth. "That-that wasn't meant for you."

"I should hope it wasn't meant for anybody. I heard you give it to Annette and fortunately stopped her from handing it to Mrs. Reynolds."

"You read it?"

"As soon as I glanced at the first sentence and saw what it was about. What wild and fantastic notions have you been entertaining?" he whispered. "You can't go running off like this, even if the weather weren't so severe. I won't let you!"

"If you read the letter carefully, you would know of my suspicions. I have no way of being certain what is correct, but somebody has been trying to kill me."

"Most inefficiently, I'm glad to say. You are far more likely to have imagined the whole thing."

"A common assumption when a woman speaks the truth and men wish not to listen. I have enough circumstantial evidence to prompt a proper investigation."

"You have nothing that isn't easily explained. I realize that events look more serious than they are because you're not in possession of all the facts. They don't indicate a murder has occurred. Hugh doesn't have the stomach to kill a fish, much less a human being."

"I'm sure he paid her money."

"Yes, to smuggle up alcohol in the morning to cure his hangovers. To hide the empty bottles. It was not the secret he thought."

"And what of Mr. Eldridge's activities?"

"Mr. Eldridge having a dalliance with Mrs. Hamilton. It's ludicrous."

"Tell that to Mrs. Eldridge," I retorted. "Why else would she be angry with that woman if she were not behaving with impropriety, and why the secret letters?"

"Oh, Mr. Eldridge is flattered by all the flirting Mrs. Hamilton directs at him, but it is no more than that and was nothing more than a minor irritation to Mrs. Eldridge. She is angry because he gave Mrs. Hamilton money and then lied about it. Mrs. Hamilton discovered to her horror that she was almost penniless when her husband died. The clandestine meetings with Mr. Eldridge were attempts to improve her finances, nothing more. She is too ashamed to tell her family of her true financial condition. David was also consulted, and in turn Mrs. Eldridge apparently wrote to him to find out how extensive the help has been and discovered it to be considerable. You see, Mr. Eldridge is a gallant gentleman who doesn't like to see a lady in distress. Why else do you think you were hired as a companion? You haven't the best of qualifications."

"That's not true!"

"David Veazey knew your father casually. When you appeared in his office, looking somewhat worse for wear, he made discreet inquiries and discovered that your father died of tuberculosis, leaving the family close to destitution."

"No." That was my secret. No one was to know why my father died. "With Mr. Eldridge's fear of illness, he wouldn't hire me."

"Tuberculosis is common enough, even among the wealthy. But if you hadn't gotten the disease living under the bad conditions in Providence, you weren't likely to suffer from it here."

My heart beat faster. "Why hire a woman from the outside?"

"For the same reason I was: a stranger with access to delicate information concerning the family is more discreet."

"The tonic, why did it have a strange effect on me when I tried it?"

"Don't you know the primary ingredient of most tonics? Alcohol. There's enough in that bottle to get a mule drunk. Since you don't drink, I imagine you experienced some interesting side effects. A number of people, including Mr. Eldridge, swear to its efficacy. He honestly thinks that if she were to take the tonic regularly, her health would steadily improve. The tonic, unlike the homeopathic medicines you are accustomed to taking, can be disagreeable to some individuals. Since they've been fighting so much of late, Mr. Eldridge believes his wife is just being obstinate. He'll abandon his faith in the tonic soon."

"And you? You and Julianne."

"I was many things to her, but never her lover. I was useful to her because I could give her a smattering of education. I gave her advice, but all on ordinary matters. In turn, she would have been willing to part with a few kisses. Anything more would have required a wedding ring. I'm not such a fool that I would entangle myself with her and her small deceits. As I said, people see through pretenses quickly enough. Years ago I decided that I was entitled to more than backbreaking labor in the mines, and I certainly deserved more than a wife who saw me only as a convenience."

"She acted as if she were jealous of me."

"Julianne was afraid you would take away what little free time I had and interfere with her tutoring. She apparently sensed what you didn't, that I was beginning to fall in love with you. Every time I tried to tell you, you ran away from me." He grabbed hold of my arms. "Lydia, don't you believe me?"

I was breathing hard. "I don't know what to think. I'll gladly admit that my reasoning has been faulty. I've never wanted to believe anyone guilty, and what you said makes sense, but someone did try to kill me." I started to tremble.

"All right," Evan said, taking me into his arms, and stroking my hair, "you've been badly frightened. That doesn't mean a murderer is in this house. I'll find out who's been scaring you."

There was a crashing sound followed by a violent howl like a savage beast.

"A window blew in upstairs. I'd better check on it." He took the stairs quickly.

"Evan, wait!" I called, running after him.

"This will only take a minute," he replied and disappeared from view.

I was climbing the stairs when I heard footfalls. "Evan?" I retreated. "Evan!" I strained my ears, hearing only the groaning of the house as the wind rattled the windows and assaulted the walls. Where was everyone? Were all the servants in the kitchen, the family all upstairs? A shiver danced up my spine. I didn't know if someone was waiting for just such a chance, and I had not convinced Evan of the justification of my suspicions. If he didn't believe me, he couldn't protect me. Hugh or Mr. Eldridge might be listening, only a few feet away. I felt terrifyingly vulnerable.

"Evan!" He wasn't answering!

In a panic, I stumbled downstairs, ran to the back of the house, escaped through the door, and out into the harsh cold. I looked first to my right and saw that the snow was two and a half feet deep, but to my horror a solid white bank rose to the eaves of the house on my left. Only the porches, cutting off the wind, had kept the snow from inundating all. I plunged into the open. The wind snatched away my hat and tugged relentlessly at my coat. Drifts, some as high as my waist, had to be breached. I fell twice. I grew fearful that I could not reach the path because of the snowbank. It wasn't easy to breathe or to see. The sun was veiled. The wind pushed constantly at my left shoulder. I was unsure of my bearings. Unknowingly I passed near the place from which Julianne had fallen, not aware of my mistake until the fence glimmered eerily in the gray light. I stumbled on, my face already numb, my hands stiff, my feet awkward.

The path, as predicted, was navigable. I almost wept. I could reach the Marshes. They were people I could understand, living uncomplicated lives. I would be safe. I forged ahead, and the barren trees closed overhead.

The wind was less severe here than in the open. The path,

however, was difficult in places, and I slid several times. I had gone not too many yards when I heard panting and looked over my shoulder to see Hugh struggling swiftly through the snow. I stopped and faced him. A veil of snow remained between us.

"How's the path?" he shouted before halting a dozen feet from me.

I stared at him. Could Hugh be so calm, so matter of fact, if he were pursuing me?

"My father saw you through the tower window and asked that I find out what you're doing out of doors." He took a step closer, halting just before I uttered a scream. "Come on, Lydia. Father is waiting for you in the tower."

What would Mr. Eldridge want with me in the tower? I didn't know whether father or son was my enemy.

"You're not stuck or frozen to the spot, are you?" He held out his hand toward me.

The way the man in the darkness had done for Julianne!

"Are you com—?"

A tremor of fear passed through me, invading every corner of my body. I was alone in the entire world with none but the trees as my solemn witnesses. Would that the endlessly falling snow could hide me from view, that I could disappear amid the downy flakes, safe until spring returned and I could emerge fresh and vibrant as the blossoms, this nightmare of a winter storm purged from my mind by melting snow.

"You can't lie to me, Lydia. Remember, I told you that."

I bolted in the same instant, running like I had never run before. My hair came loose. I didn't seem to breathe. My feet skimmed the surface of the snow. Yet I wasn't moving fast enough. He was coming closer, closer. I could hear him breathe directly behind me. Could almost feel his hand clutch my dress, yet he did not overtake me.

I faltered as the path passed the river. Trees, standing like skeletons, seemed to reach out and trap me. I was confused, no longer sure just where on the path I was. To my right lay the river with the bank buried beneath snow. A sapling caught my dress. I struggled free, tearing the cloth, in the process stepping away from the path. My shoe hit ice, I slid, scrambled to my knees, and only slid further out. All around me I could hear ominous cracking.

Half blind for want of breath, I lay panting. Now I knew why he had allowed me to run so far. There was no hope of anyone seeing my predicament. I was completely surrounded by the indifferent trees.

Swaying gently as the wind buffeted him, Hugh stood on the bank, uncertain what to do, fearing to venture after me.

I should have known it was him. The inept attempts to kill me, the way Julianne died. They were impulses, blind, stupid impulses.

"I knew from the way you've been acting that you had found out about me. You kept going back to where Julianne fell. You finally found something, didn't you? It was the button from my shirt; it tore when she clutched at it. I saw you pick it up by the hedge."

"I don't know what you mean," I sobbed. "I didn't find anything except an interesting piece of wood for Maggie to show the children."

He ignored what I said. "Have you guessed what happened? We went outside to have a private conversation where absolutely no one could overhear us." By telling me this, he was making it impossible for him to let me live. "We started to argue and wandered ever farther from the house. She wanted money to leave for Boston. I would have given it to her, but I didn't have any more to give. All she did was repeat that she needed more money. I got angry and shoved her. I forgot we were standing so close to the edge. She fell."

"You left her to die!"

"No. I'm sure I couldn't have done anything. It was just easier to leave her there. I didn't mean to hurt her; I don't want to hurt you. I've grown so fond of you. But you've discovered too much."

"I didn't." Perhaps I could dissuade him from killing me. "I was only guessing. I have no proof!" I looked around. The crown of the downed tree lay in the ice but a little way to my right. If I could crawl there, I might be able to reach the path on the other side while Hugh was forced to wade through the deep snow in the woods. I shifted my weight, and the ice creaked.

"What is proof, Lydia? It's convincing people."

"They'll think me mad!"

"I can't take the chance. I always say the wrong thing. I'd give myself away somehow. You would be so sincere. You would describe in detail how you arrived at your conclusion."

"I didn't know it was you. It could have been any of the men in the house. I couldn't even think of a good reason why you would want to harm Julianne."

His laugh was hollow. "You remember the evening before she died? I'd been drinking. Father had threatened me again. I was angry. He hadn't acted that way before Jon Frederick was born. He was beginning to think he should throw me out, make me learn to stand on my own feet. I couldn't have that. Before the baby was born, he needed me to carry on the name and take care of the mills. First Millicent becomes betrothed to a member of the most suitable family that Father could want, where there is someone who could look after his interests. Then Mother has a baby boy. She's old. She had no business having another child.

"I went upstairs. Maggie was gone, and Julianne was looking after my brother." How much bitterness he conveyed with the word *brother*! "I'm not sure what I said. Maybe that I should strangle him. I kicked the cradle, leaving a streak of bootblack." He looked at me beseechingly. "Lydia, if Julianne had told my father that, I would have been out the door instantly. I paid her what money I had. I would have stolen money to send her on her way, if I thought that would have finished the matter. I knew Julianne. She liked the baby. She was beginning to worry that I might do something while drunk. She would have told eventually. That was why I was so very angry. I couldn't control myself." He looked at me with haunted eyes.

He took a step closer. "They'll find you in the river. Her death burdened you. You couldn't stand to be without your family. You were distraught. Everyone knows that. You wandered out in the storm."

"I wrote a letter, saying that Julianne was killed."

"A letter written by a despondent and suicidal girl. No one will think otherwise. I'm an Eldridge. People look up to us, even to me. Nothing will happen to me. I'll be all right again."

"No one will believe two abrupt deaths to be accidental. They'll know you followed me."

"I'll say I didn't find you." Slowly, cautiously, he put another foot on the ice. "No one can see you. No one will hear you scream."

Tears stung my face as they fell and froze. I couldn't reach the tree without the risk of falling into the river. The only way I could move safely was toward Hugh. He was staring at me in such a way I knew he had lost his mind. No words of mine would sway him from his course, even if it might also lead to his own destruction.

"Hugh!" Evan, followed closely by Mr. Reynolds, charged down the path. Both men stopped, horrified.

I heard a groan from Hugh and thought he would swoon. He looked about wildly. He could have run down the path. He didn't. He took a further step onto the ice.

"Boy, what are you doing?" Mr. Reynolds said. "Get back onto the bank."

Evan raced to the fallen tree and climbed among the branches to reach me. He held on to an overhanging branch for support. "Give me your hand."

"I can't. I'll fall through."

"No you won't. The ice is just thick enough."

Mr. Reynolds calmly addressed Hugh. "Come on back. It isn't safe for you."

Hugh looked at the coachman steadily. "You think you can talk me into coming to you as if I were a boy and got caught climbing the trees in my best Sunday suit." He shook his head. "It won't work, I'm afraid. She'll tell you. She's like you. Righteous. So proper. She doesn't know what it is like to be driven by inner demons. To see a nightmare staring you in the face."

Evan didn't dare go further toward me. "Lydia, I didn't think you'd leave the house."

"I was so frightened," I sobbed. "I called for you."

"I couldn't hear. I thought you were safe." He held out his hand. "Trust me. The ice will support your weight."

"I can't."

"Yes you can," Evan urged. "Lydia, it's only a few inches."

It was many feet, but I didn't allow myself to think of that or the swift flow of the river beneath the ice. I looked to him. What if he was wrong?

"Lydia, you can't risk waiting. Now come to me!"

I had to take the chance. I crawled forward, my legs entangled in the skirts, feeling the ice crack beneath my hands. Mr. Reynolds kept talking as if Hugh were a skittish colt. I crawled on. Time no longer had meaning. The cold had ceased to exist. I must move, swiftly, yet not so fast as to strain the ice. The heavens spent their fury around me. I held to my course, drawing closer, fearing that just as safety could be mine, I would again be plunged into the abyss. I stopped, the groaning of the ice ominous, unable to force my limbs to obey me.

"Just crawl forward. Come to me, keep going."

"Hugh!" Mr. Reynolds implored desperately.

Behind me the ice shattered. I heard dangerous creaks, then the mass of ice below my knees gave way. I screamed from the cold as the river threatened to suck me under.

Evan grabbed my hand. My fingers were too stiff to reciprocate. He pulled as I slid into the river. He let go of the branch, and though he sank hip deep into the water, he managed to seize my forearm. With strength borne of desperation, he pulled us both to the embankment. "Oh, Lydia," he whispered, holding me tightly as I trembled in his arms. There was no need for further words. I looked into his eyes and I found all that I would need for a lifetime.

∾ *Epilogue*

August 31, 1888

THERE IS A GREAT DEAL of commotion in the house today, for we are preparing to move to Boston and are still in the midst of packing. I turn this way and that in front of the mirror in my room, making sure that my new brown traveling suit has every bow and pleat in place. I pin the hat securely to my hair. "Do you think I look suitable for Boston?" I ask Maggie, who is sitting on my bed.

"Indeed you do." Jon Frederick, as if to voice his agreement, burbles happily in Maggie's arms. "We'll miss you, Pete and me. So will the children."

Before I can express my gratitude for all Maggie has done and how much her friendship means to me, a rustle of skirts precedes Mrs. Eldridge's arrival.

"The carriage is ready," she announces. Her face still betrays the strain under which she has lived for many months, and the black dress emphasizes her pallor, but she has gained back much of her former weight. "I've always found the trip pleasant, and it shouldn't be too hot on the train. In a way it is a pity that we won't be leaving later in the year when the foliage is at its most colorful."

"Millicent has told me about some of the riding trails in Massachusetts," I say, "and how lovely they'll be in a month or two."

"Yes, that's true. They are not as wild as the ones we've been on, which makes them less challenging, but the scenery is just as picturesque and you meet more interesting people. We'll have to find you a new mount just as docile as Beauregard."

"I think I'm ready for a horse with more spirit and fewer years," I reply.

Mrs. Eldridge laughs. "Millicent and I will turn you into a horsewoman yet." She gives me a quick peck on the cheek. "I'd better not be keeping you or I shall incur Ruth's wrath for delaying your departure."

"Is Mr. Eldridge about? I should like to say good-bye to him."

"He's working in the tower, or so he claims, but I believe he is actually hiding, having been discovered most ignobly on his hands and knees gamboling after the baby." She smiles wickedly. "I shall never let him forget this. I'll give him your regards when he has the courage to show his face again."

Their relationship has returned to its natural state, and they again share the same bedroom. I must say that once Mrs. Eldridge started to regard him favorably again, his disposition improved markedly. It appears that many of their difficulties began when they could not agree on the proper course of action to take regarding Hugh. Mrs. Eldridge favored giving him complete freedom, but making him learn to stand on his own feet without assistance from the family. It was Mr. Eldridge who sought to protect Hugh from his own weaknesses with discipline and supervision.

"Lydia!" I hear Mrs. Reynolds call from the staircase.

Mrs. Eldridge puts an arm around my shoulder and escorts me out into the hallway. "Now you're sure you've not forgotten anything?"

"I'm sure. I won't have any trouble opening the house with Mrs. Reynolds. All will be in readiness when you arrive."

Maggie is standing at the head of the stairs, still holding the baby. "Jon Frederick wants to say good-bye."

"Bye-bye, baby," I coax.

He looks at me with his large blue eyes. "Ba," he says and with sudden shyness buries his head in Maggie's shoulder.

I pat his head, now thickly covered with curly blond hair. It seemed until now that I would have ample time to bid each and every person a prolonged farewell, see my room once more. All too quickly my time has evaporated. My eyes grow misty. "I'll write," I promise Maggie.

Perhaps for the last time, I hurry down these stairs to the foyer. Annette is polishing the banister. For a moment I see Julianne, beautiful and confident, performing the same duty when I first arrived.

I think of Hugh.

For days after he plunged into the river, I heard his voice in the house. I did not dare look out my window at night for fear of seeing his ghost standing on the white ground illuminated by moonlight. I recall his kind eyes and gentle manner, the way he bowed his head when rebuked, and I struggle to reconcile this image with his attempt to kill me. In those horrible minutes as we huddled in the cold beside the Sachem River, waiting for Hugh to surface—knowing he would not attempt to save himself—we created a tale, that we had gone to investigate the path, and Hugh had ventured too far. There have been moments when I think his parents suspect the truth, but neither will acknowledge it even to the other. Hugh, the Hugh they had loved and still mourn, was indeed lost. His remains lie in the mausoleum not far from Julianne's simple grave.

"Miss Hall?" My reverie is broken. "I hope you have a comfortable trip."

"Thank you, Annette." I proceed down the remaining few stairs. I stop briefly to wave to Maggie and Mrs. Eldridge. Mrs. Reynolds presses a parasol into my hand, then I step outside into the bright summer sunshine.

The grounds, lush with grass and fragrant flowers, are indeed the way I imagined them when I first arrived and so different from the threatening drifts of snow. The newspapers said that as many as four hundred people died and that the blizzard was perhaps the worst ever recorded in New England. So deep was the snow in some places that it did not melt completely until May. Even in the summer heat, a trace of cold still lingers in my soul.

Mr. Reynolds has the reins in his hands and nods when he sees me. He is about to help me into the carriage when Evan appears, carrying a small box. "I'll do that, Reynolds," he says and helps me inside the open conveyance. I smile as he takes his seat beside me.

I have seen little of Evan lately. Besides being responsible for reopening the Boston house, he has been busy training his replacement, an industrious young man by the name of Albert Smith. In a month's time, Evan will begin a new and more prestigious career assisting Samuel Lodge, Millicent's future father-in-law, in his shipping offices. "Are you coming with me to the station?" I ask.

"I'm accompanying you all the way to Boston."

Mr. Reynolds, a smile half-hidden by his moustache, slaps the reins, and the horse trots smartly down the road. The rushing air feels cool against my face, mitigating the heat. I turn my head and watch the house grow smaller. Millicent and Alex are playing tennis on the rich green lawn. They stop to wave at us, and we return the gesture. Then all are hidden by the trees.

I settle back against the seat. "I'm going to miss the house after all. Do you think the Eldridges will ever return to it?"

Evan shakes his head. "They plan to turn over the property to Millicent and Alex as soon as they marry."

"I think that will be best."

"I'm hoping Mr. Eldridge can spend most of his time at the Boston museums studying art. Perhaps in a few years, when he feels Jon Frederick can be left in the company of his sister for several months, he and Mrs. Eldridge can travel to the Orient."

"I would like to see Wales someday," I say, turning to look at his eyes. "Years from now perhaps."

He takes my hand. "I thought you always wanted to see New York."

"I still do." I laugh. "With my luck, if I went there now, I would encounter Mrs. Hamilton."

"You should sympathize with her. The poor woman has yet to find a husband, and if she does not soon, she will have to return to her sister's—and this time there will be no Mr.

Eldridge to distract her from the domesticity."

"Poor Mr. Brewster, in that case."

"I suppose she will find someone."

"Aunt Louisa did." Much to everyone's surprise she had abruptly married a widower with four children. Her departure allowed my grandparents to take in my mother and sisters. They still sew, and life remains difficult, but not as precarious as before. I help as best I can.

We approach the river.

"Mr. Reynolds," Evan says, "if you will be so kind as to slow the horse for a while."

"Right," he says. There is a sly grin on his face as he glances over his shoulder to look at us.

"Isn't time a little tight?" I ask, worried we might miss the train.

"This won't take long." Evan places a small box in my hand. "Open it."

I undo the plain package. Inside is a velvet pouch, holding a delicate diamond ring. "Evan!" I throw my arms around his neck. Though we had spoken of marriage in tentative terms, I had not expected this.

Evan disengages my arms. "Let me do this properly." He slips the ring on my finger. "From your reaction it is obvious that you accept. I wanted to surprise you when you would least expect it, and to avoid becoming the subject of those wagging gossips in Bradford. But I want everyone to know when we arrive in Boston that you are very much engaged and will a few months hence become a married woman."

"Oh, Evan, a plain gold band would have been enough. I—"

My words are smothered as Evan bends over to kiss me. Everyone in the house must have known he was to present the ring to me. Undoubtedly Mr. Eldridge is in his tower watching us this very moment. I am about to remind Evan of this, but all my thoughts melt as he holds me in his arms.